# Palmyra

# Palmyra

Susan Evans McCloud

Bookcraft
Salt Lake City, Utah

Library of Congress Catalog Card Number 99-95578
ISBN 1-57008-704-0


First Printing, 1999


Printed in the United States of America

This book is for my beloved daughter
Heather Jean
who has given me Palmyra—
and Dylan and Katie,
And so much more!

# Prologue

## Palmyra: 1820

I t was an extraordinary thing to happen in our little village; most unsettling and alarming. True, a religious revival of fierce proportions had been stirring the people for some time, and the contentions of sect against sect grew bold, even unscrupulous. But a boy—a mere fourteen-year-old boy? The Smith family had not been in Palmyra long, but they were considered respectable enough, were hardworking; landowners. What cause had a son of theirs to come out with so preposterous a story?

I remember it well. It was in the spring of 1820. I was twelve years old and my sister, Josie, fifteen. Joseph Smith's age. I could not imagine Josephine thinking or caring that deeply about anything, least of all religion. What made Joseph say he had seen a vision and was marked of God to do great things? Really—here in Palmyra, upstate New York?

This was, however, a thriving, progressive village, and most of our citizens were proud of that fact. We sat square on the path of *the* most progressive invention in the country, the Erie Canal. People were drawn here by our prosperity and the beauty of our setting. We could boast five churches, three banks, three schools (with eleven teachers), and a printing office, as well as the customary businesses—manufactories, machine shops, mills, stores, and so forth—that make up a growing community. People called Palmyra "The Queen of the Erie." I liked the sound of those words. I knew it was vain to nurture pride, but I heard Miller Reeves say to my father, "Is it pride merely to admit to the truth?"

So into the comfortable self-satisfaction of such an atmosphere Joseph Smith dropped his discomfiting announcement. How did he expect grown men to react? People who are strange always make those around them feel squeamish and ill at ease. But, perhaps because he was a mere boy, he did not anticipate that. I believe he truly expected those men who had courted his support, who had desired to act as his spiritual advisors, to rejoice with him at the rare and marvelous thing which had happened. But, of course, none of them did. What can be done with such a lad, anyway? Religion is well and good—in its place. But that sort of attention! Angels and visions? Not in modern-day Palmyra—not in a village as advanced as ours.

We girls felt sorry for Joseph. I believe in our hearts we admired him a little. By "we girls" I mean myself and my dearest friends. There were always the five of us, for as long as I can remember; we grew up that way. We were, perhaps, an unlikely group, now that I think upon it. My sister, Josephine, was the acknowledged leader, being two years older than the others and three years older than I, and by far the prettiest of all of us. However, as we all fully realized, that was the extent of her claims. Phoebe, though the plainest, was by far the best and kindest. Georgeanna was the brightest, the most clever and interesting of the lot. Theodora was a lady, refined in ways we never thought about. She was descended, after all, from the distinguished founder of Palmyra, Captain John Swift, who selected this bit of the Iroquois domain as his own in 1789. He cleared the land, assisted the new settlers who found their way here (most of them from Massachusetts), laid out the first roads, watched the establishment of schools and businesses, then got himself killed in the War of 1812. His body was brought back to Palmyra and placed in a hero's grave.

Tillie, as we called her, never let us forget this one overriding fact of her noble roots, but we did not mind. Tillie was Tillie; we took her as she was, and were glad of it. We had decided to be friends, our mothers claimed, before we were out of nappies and fairly able to crawl toward one another across the long, tickly summer grass. Kindred spirits, despite our differences—despite the fact that there were five of us, not merely two or three. We never suffered a falling out—not a real one—and we seldom quarreled. Which surely means we were meant to be friends—ordained by some force within us, and some force above us, to be part of each other's lives. We knew this with the simple, unspoken knowledge of children, and we never, through all the long years, questioned it.

So we, having our own concerns, by and large left our friend, Joseph, to his. We sensed his sin against propriety, his shame, only

2

because our elders brought it to our attention by making a fuss about it, thus stirring our guileless curiosity. If anyone had asked me, I might have told them that Joseph was a gentle boy who was kind to girls and to animals, and he had the loveliest smile. I might have told them that he did not seem weird in a freakish or disgusting way, that he was not lazy nor dishonest, boastful nor proud.

All this I might have told them, if I had been encouraged to think about it. I do remember one summer night when I had gone to bed early and I lay stretched out in the evening coolness. I could still hear the song sparrows from their nests in the thickets along my father's greening wheat fields. I smiled at their merry trill, remembering the phrase of their song, which my mother had taught me: "Maid, maid, maid, put-your-tea, kettle, kettle, kettle." I remember being happy and closing my eyes in my happiness to offer a prayer of thanks unto God. He came into my mind then, this Joseph, and what I had heard of the vision he claimed had come to him. I let my mind try to fit around the idea, try to picture the spring grove, calm and still, and damp with the dews of morning. I could picture the young boy kneeling there. I could picture light and glory streaming through the newly leafed arms of the trees. I could imagine the flow of God's love. I remember thinking, *It could have happened, just as Joseph Smith said it did. He could be telling the truth, after all.*

3

# Chapter 1

### Palmyra: Spring 1827

I t is about time, Esther! You're always the last one here. And look, you still have dirt on your hands."

It was, as usual, Josephine who scolded me. But then, she was right. I *was* always the late one. I had been loath to leave the new seedlings I had been planting, and some particles of black fragrant soil still clung to my hands.

I bent over and wiped them along the soft grass. "Someone has to be last," I replied.

"Last, but not *late*, Esther. You do not have to be late."

"I am sorry, Josie." Unable to help myself, I smiled at her. She looked so fresh and pretty in her new summer frock. She had talked Mother into it last month, when the late March gales still blew their way into April.

"I am marriageable age," she reminded Mother. "I cannot hope to catch a beau in an outmoded gown."

*You could catch a beau clad in an old gunny sack,* I thought. *You already have six or seven.* But I had not said a word. Mother would give in to her. Mother always gave in to her. She too liked pretty clothes. There was a conspiracy of sorts between them; unstated, but nevertheless unassailable. Perhaps the natural harmony of two beautiful women who understood each other's needs. I did not know. I had my own pursuits and desires; I cared not overmuch about theirs.

"What is it this time?" Phoebe asked. "Have you something to tell us?"

"Isn't a perfect day like this reason enough to get together?" Georgie winked at me as she pulled up clumps of long, slender grass with her fists and dropped the sweet stuff into her lap.

"As a matter of fact . . ." Josie drew her words out, enjoying the attention. "I have made up my mind . . ."

We all leaned forward a bit, on cue, anticipating.

"I intend to become engaged before summer is over and to be married by Christmas. I have always wanted a Christmas wedding with sleigh bells and high-laced boots on my feet and thick fur wraps 'round my shoulders." She hugged her thin arms to her body, immersed in her own delicious imaginings. A scampering breeze lifted her yellow curls and blew them about her head until they looked like a shimmering halo.

"Who is the lucky boy?"

Josephine paused. She let dignity settle over her like a fine silken shawl. "I have not made up my mind."

"Have any proposed yet?" Georgie's black eyes were dancing.

"Henry has—for the third time."

"Henry doesn't count. He has been proposing to you at least once a year since you were seven." Theodora spoke with poise and authority as she bent over the teapot and began to freshen our cups.

Josie laughed. "It does not matter who proposes and who doesn't," she informed us. "*I* shall decide."

We had no doubts that she would. She had never waited for circumstance, for the whims or wishes of others to deter her or to dictate their terms. She knew what she wanted and went after it. It was only that she always wanted so much!

"A wedding will be lovely," Phoebe sighed.

I felt a little catch at my heart. I knew Phoebe wanted Simon Turner to ask her to marry him. She had been in love with him for as long as I could remember. And he returned her affections, at least in part. But there was Emily, too. Emily's family had been in Palmyra only three years, but I think Simon fell in love with her the first time he set eyes on her small, delicate, elfin-like face. They say such things can happen. I do not believe he meant to be unfaithful, or even unkind to Phoebe, but what can one do? He was torn; it was easy to see the anguish of his dilemma. But my heart went out to my friend. She had not half the beauty nor charm of her rival. But she had a full-blown woman's heart, with enough tenderness and devotion, I was certain, to make any man happy and proud. But life does not work as it "should," nice and tidily, and *Beauty*, I had often noticed, can lead nine men out of ten around by the nose and very well have her own way.

"What about an autumn date?" Theodora was suggesting. "Would autumn not be better than winter? Such a bitter cold can blow off the lakes in the winter—"

"And such an ocean of sticky mud can clog the streets in the autumn!" Josephine countered. "No, I do not wish to be plastered with leaves and mud, thank you. Christmas! Christmas it shall be!"

She was so unquestioningly sure of herself! It irritated me a little; it always had. If Josie's disposition had been somewhat sweeter . . . but then, it was no good wishing. She was as proud as a peacock and as spoiled as a princess, and that was that. When we were all children we had worshiped her beauty and her boldness. Now that time had closed up the age gap and we were all young women together, we saw her with different eyes. But we knew she loved us—it was knowing so surely that she loved us that made it easier to put up with her now!

"Too bad young Joseph Smith just got married," Tillie said out of nowhere. "He is a bright, handsome lad."

Josephine laughed. "He is altogether too strange for me, thank you."

The suggestion was meant to be largely a joke. But I recalled to myself the several times Joseph had worked for my father and how polite and kind he had been. *Surely he would make a good husband,* I thought. *There is something in his eyes when he looks at you that holds you, that draws you—that makes you feel warm, even safe, inside.* There was still talk about him—angels and visitations—but I paid it no mind. It is the nature of some people to look after everyone's affairs but their own. I had little interest in what did not concern me. And I had much to concern me right now.

This scatter-brain marriage scheme of Josie's came at an awkward time. Our mother had passed the seventh month of her pregnancy and would soon approach her confinement; this, in itself, was a miracle. Josephine had been her first child, I her second. Then there had followed a series of years when she had suffered from the loss of a full half dozen children to as many different causes and ailments: two little sons dying at the same time from scarlet fever; an infant daughter from influenza; two others living only hours after their birth; and four-year-old Thomas, whom I remembered, drowning in the canal. A dismal catechism. But things looked hopeful now, truly hopeful. And

Mother was being patient and taking such care! If this child was born safe and well, a marriage would not prove a hurdle; I could take over much of the work of it, and we could rejoice all together. But if otherwise—tragedy and the emotional chaos that would follow! I shut the picture out of my mind. *One day at a time,* I reminded myself. *Do not court trouble. Let tomorrow take care of itself.*

Our conversation at length shifted from weddings to half a dozen other topics; we five could talk about nothing and anything for hours on end. It was good just to be together, just to feel spring at last gentling the earth. Our lives were ahead of us. And in the thin new air our dreams hovered, like so many angel shapes, their wings brushing our hair, their voices humming hope almost audible in our ears.

I was the last to arrive and also the first to leave. I had a few dozen plants to set out still, and someone had to get supper started. Georgeanna was a schoolteacher, so her evenings and weekends were her own. Phoebe did fine handwork for the fanciest dress shop in town. Theodora and Josephine were not employed in the business of producing a living for themselves. Tillie's father was a banker and made sufficient money to keep his family in style. Josie, to be fair, helped with the household chores and, from time to time, with the farm work; but she was too fastidious and high-strung to be of much use in the real, dogged, slug-it-out kind of work. It was in the kitchen that she came into her own. But even there she needed time and first-rate ingredients to make her culinary magic shine. I knew she would follow in an hour or so and stir up something to tempt Mother's appetite. I was content to get back to my garden, to work out of doors until the frosty fingers of the evening shadows crept over the darkening earth and drove me inside.

I hummed under my breath as I walked away, and kissed my fingers to my pretty friends, dotting the green lawn with their soft colorful gowns, gracing it more surely than flowers. *I am happy simply to be here, in this place,* I thought. *I am glad just to be alive as this fair spring comes in.*

Phoebe made May Day frocks for all five of us. She is a wizard with a needle. Mine was the soft blue of a robin's egg with bound leaves of almost chartreuse green festooning the shoulders and a broad sash that matched the green of the leaves. I was pleased; the shades went well with my coloring—my green eyes and the strawberry blonde of my hair. Josie wore rose, as muted and faded as old brocade, with her lemon bright curls tumbling over the braided roses tucked at her shoulders. Phoebe wore white, but her gown boasted very full gigot sleeves which tapered down to her tiny wrists. Tillie too wore white, but with an abundance of lace; lace was her passion and trademark. Georgie had chosen a jaunty fabric with bunches of forget-me-nots tied up in a colorful string scattered throughout the cloth. And, in keeping with the smartest fashion, each of our gowns was belled out by an abundance of undergarments, and we definitely swished as we walked.

Phoebe was a dear: because of her, when we gathered with the other young people in the wide, tree-shaded lot behind the Presbyterian chapel at the corner of Main and Church Streets, we clearly outshone every other girl there. *"Belle of the ball!"* Josie whispered, excitement coloring her white cheeks with an attractive blush. I did not care about that. But I will admit I *felt pretty,* as though the gentle May morn had been born for my pleasure and mine alone.

"Here we come a-Maying in the clear, fair morn . . ." We were singing all the lovely ditties we had sung since childhood. For a moment I closed my eyes. How easy it was to go back, to see all five of us in pigtails and pinafores: me with ink stains on my fingers because I was always scribbling something; Josephine with the ends of her hair caked with ink, because the boys were always teasing her; Georgie with her quite beautiful nose stuck in a book; Phoebe carrying—

"Esther!"

I jumped, startled, as a firm hand shook me.

"Come back, will you, Esther? They're choosing partners." Eugene bent half over in an exaggerated bow. "Will you, m'lady?"

I blushed—I always blush, and have discovered no way of stopping it!—and gave him my hand.

He pulled me into the circle that was forming. I noticed, with a sinking heart, that Simon was dancing with Emily, and Phoebe stood

9

by the side. The music started, and the intricate pattern claimed my attention: circle left, circle right, two balance steps forward, four running steps backward. Dancing has never been easy for me. But I still felt beautiful, and my heart thrilled when we reached the part where the boys walk forward, kneel on one knee, and unfasten the ribbons—the long rainbow-bright ribbons which have been floating like butterflies—then return bearing one for themselves and one for their partner. I curtsied low, with as much grace as I could muster, and felt my cheeks grow warm at the expression in Eugene's eyes when he raised me up and looked at me.

As the intricate weaving began—clockwise, under the boy's ribbon, with eight skips—I saw that Phoebe did have a partner, though not *the partner* her heart cried for. I had forgotten to look for which lad Josephine had deigned to bestow her favors upon as she began her campaign of entrapment, but the very thought made me smile.

"Thank you for being with me," Eugene murmured, closing his fingers with ardent pressure over mine. "In this whole array of beautiful women, Esther, you are the fairest."

I cast my eyes down. I did not know what to do, what to say, when he behaved like this. I possessed no coquettish skills like my sister and could not return him a quick, clever rejoinder. Yet his words were sincerely spoken; what good would coquetry do? I found myself merely pressing his warm hand in return and feeling the hot blood flow to my cheeks.

10

> I've been rambling all this night,
> And some time of this day,
> And now returning back again,
> I brought you a branch of May . . .
> Awake, awake, O pretty, pretty maid,
> From out your drowsy dream,
> And step into your dairy here,
> And fetch me a bowl of cream.

As we sang the words a meadowlark rose from the fringes of our grassy meadow, mere feet away, his lilting trill a harmonious accompaniment to our melody.

If not a bowl of your sweet cream,
A cup to bring you cheer,
For God knows when we'll meet again
To be maying another year . . .

A sudden chill shivered over me. *Is this what growing up means?* I wondered. Never before had those closing words held special meaning for me. Now, as I glanced around at the bright faces of the lads and girls I had known since childhood, I wondered where the next year would find us—and the next, and the next—as life pulled us in dozens of different directions and shaped and molded our futures anew.

When the cavorting circle broke up at last it was to flock to the long tables which literally sagged with their burden of food. This day we ate dainties which would not be offered again for another year: candied violets, cookies flavored with rose water, strawberry cordial, mint syllabus, rhubarb tarts, elder flower pudding, iced honey cakes, and red currant ice cream.

I stayed beside Eugene and tried not to worry about the others; they had not dubbed me "Mother Hen" when I was only seven for nothing! But it was curiosity that drove me to cast my eyes every now and again in my sister's direction. Her admirers, as usual, were hovering around, like obedient knights in a queen's court. I knew there were three or four who could be dismissed without thought, who were not really "in the running," as the saying goes: patient, faithful Henry, Timothy Ikins, Ralph Jensen . . . and probably James Sadler, though James would make a good husband, especially to one as high-strung as Josie. But, alas, he was not handsome nor dashing enough. Robert Sumsion, whose looks could melt the heart of any girl who happened to turn her eyes upon him, was like a bright, pretty toy Josephine played with—something to delight her fancy, but not serious marriage material, for he had no family connections, no promising trade, and only fair to middling prospects. The poor boy did not realize that.

The coldness with which Josie regarded these flesh-and-blood men was something I had not stomach enough to dwell upon. Instead, I slipped my arm through Eugene's and counted myself lucky to have

11

his attentions. I had been fond of Eugene for quite a long time. Odd that he was the brother of Emily, my dearest friend's rival. Yet he shared her same sweet disposition and had inherited the same trim, compact figure, Dresden china features, and arresting blue eyes.

"He is too short," Josephine had criticized from the beginning. "He looks like a boy, though he's a year older than I am."

"Yes, and he will always look fresh and young like a boy. When he is forty and fifty—even sixty."

She had dismissed me with a wave of her hand. "Suit yourself, Esther. You have always had your own tastes . . ." Indicating quite clearly *inferior tastes, especially to mine.*

I looked over to see Theodora's brothers approaching, waving their arms to attract my attention. "We've got news!" Peter cried.

"You're hired on!" I guessed. "The canal company accepted you two skinny half-pints. Must be through your father's influence," I teased.

Randolph beamed. They were used to me. "Told you she'd guess, Pete."

"I'm happy for both of you! When do you start work?" I cried.

"Day after tomorrow. The spring rush is already in full swing and they need extra hands."

I nodded. "Pay attention when they train you, and follow the safety rules. And be polite to the women—always. That will not go unnoticed."

Peter inclined his head in playful acquiescence. "Anything you say, ma'am. We will follow your instructions to the letter."

"You could do worse!" I countered. I was most fond of both these boys. Randolph was fifteen and Peter fourteen. I would not have let my own sons associate with the rough canal men at such a tender age. But Lawrence Swift held a stubborn belief in a work ethic that overwhelmed all other considerations. He may have been born to wealth and influence, but he had extended his advantages by his labors, both of mind and of hand.

I watched them frolic off to tell the next person, then turned to Eugene. "Do you think Simon will ask Emily to marry him?"

My question took him a bit by surprise.

"Do you know if he has broached the subject with her?"

"She would not tell me, Esther! Especially because of you."

I sighed. "I am fond of Emily," I told him truthfully, "and would be more so if my loyalty to Phoebe did not get in the way."

"Emily cannot help the situation! She has done nothing petty or underhanded—"

"I know that!" I placed my other hand on his arm, my eyes entreating him. " 'Tis merely one of the terrible misfortunes of life, Eugene, that one person's happiness will spell misery and bitter disappointment for another." I leaned my head against his cheek and could feel his sun-warmed flesh through the thin veil of my hair. "You understand."

"Yes, but if Emily marries Simon, you five will ostracize and abandon them both, and in a village this size that will be no small thing."

Ostracize and exclude, perhaps. But abandon was a strong word for Eugene to choose. I peered at my companion closely. "Is Emily really concerned about such a thing happening?"

"Of course she is! Would not you be, in her shoes?"

His question pierced through me. What mischief, what heady truth potion had the May Day air carried that it should affect me in this way? I chaffed at the irritating burden of my own concern over Emily's happiness. Her well-being, if she married Simon, did not rest with me.

13

"There you go, furrowing your brow in that way again," Eugene said, watching me. "I want you to take my words to heart, but I do not want you to fret yourself over them."

" 'Tis one and the same."

"With you it is, more than with any other." He was scolding me gently, but I could see pride in his eyes. It pleased him to know that my temperament was different from Josie's. He was one of the few never taken in by her beauty and flirtatious ways.

"Come, Esther," he said, "I must get you a plate before all the choice morsels are picked over."

I walked along, enjoying the touch of him, aware that his presence delighted and warmed me and enhanced every other pleasurable sensation I was feeling on this gentle spring day.

## Chapter 2

### Palmyra: Spring 1827

We could not find Tillie when it came time to go home.

"She's gone off with Joel Hancock," Georgie informed us.

*That is encouraging,* I thought to myself. I knew she cared for Joel more than she admitted. I also knew he did not meet with her father's approval, did not begin to measure up to the "requirements for a future mate" that her father had set. *Can she hold out against him? I wondered, when the time comes?*

Theodora lived in the largest house in Palmyra—such a house! Too elegant for the rest of us, it stood on its commodious corner lot like a glittering gem set amid cheap, dull store-bought jewelry. *An advertisement,* she called it, *of all my father is and all he imagines himself to be.*

We walked past her house without stopping, then deposited Georgeanna at the corner of Main and Jackson and Phoebe remained with us to where Church turns into Canandaigua and her father has both his house and his saddlery shop. I was surprised that Josephine had chosen to accompany me rather than selecting one of her admirers as escort. We had nearly a mile farther to go along Canandaigua Road in order to reach the long stretch of our father's farm.

At first we walked in silence; Josie concerned with her thoughts, I with the sights and sounds of the countryside through which we passed. Still, my preoccupation was the less; I was the first to spy Doctor Ensworth's buggy pulled up in front of the house, his sleek bay horse standing patiently, with the reins thrown in a hasty half loop over the post.

I felt my heart catch in my chest. "Josephine!" I clutched at her arm.

"Heaven preserve us!" she muttered. "It can be only one thing."

So it was. As we entered the dim, cool kitchen the doctor was walking from the back bedroom, our parents' bedroom, toward us. He squinted against the wedge of light the opened door directed at him. When he recognized our shapes he grunted in satisfaction.

" 'Bout time you two showed up." He growled the words, but I could hear the relief in them. "Esther, your mother's took to hemorrhaging again. I suppose you know what that means."

I nodded.

"She is to stay in that bed till the baby comes, if it takes another three months!"

I nodded once more and noticed, out of the corner of my eye, that Josie had removed her lace shawl and mittens and was filling the kettle with water.

"Would you like some tea, Doctor?" she asked.

"Very much," he replied, "but I've got no time for it. Now, listen carefully to my instructions, the both of you. I'll not explain them again."

He launched into a list of things Mother could and could not eat, various herb teas we should ply her with—"And rub her legs to stimulate circulation. That rosemary and lavender liniment you made last summer—you got any left, Esther?"

"Yes. We'll keep good watch," I assured him.

"You must. We can't have a tragedy this time."

I swallowed, my throat tight.

"Mother is not the most pleasant or accommodating of patients," Josie reminded him.

"That has nothing to do with it, missy," he barked back at her. "You do as I say. And don't leave three-quarters of the work in your sister's hands, either."

He walked heavily to the door, shuffling as though the effort to lift his booted feet would be too much for him. "Been up all night with a birth," he mumbled. "Other side of town."

"It didn't go well?"

I did not need him to confirm my words. But he lifted one thick eyebrow, where the gray hairs were already curling round the black ones. "Lost both mother and child," he said. My immediate concern darkened my features.

"Anyone we know?" Josephine asked.

"Canal family. Skinny little wisp of a girl who shouldn't 'a been having a child in the first place. Complications . . ." A shudder passed

15

through his compact, thick-set body. I put my hand on his arm.

"Have that tea, Doctor," I urged. "It will only take a few minutes and prove well worth it."

With a sigh he consented and lowered his tired body into a chair.

"Is Father in there?" I asked, nodding toward the bedroom while I stirred honey into his cup, where the leaves of the lemon balm were beginning to diffuse their fragrance. In ancient times this tea was drunk for its ability to comfort the heart and drive away melancholy and sadness. I knew it would soothe and revive the doctor.

"Your mother is resting," he informed me. "I believe your father has already slipped back to the fields."

*Poor Father,* I thought. Distress renders him awkward and tongue-tied, though not unwilling to help. He would work his fingers to the bone for Mother, and for the rest of us. But he had no notion of how to administer comfort on a sit-down, intimate level. Indeed, it was difficult for him ever to simply sit still.

When Doctor Ensworth was ready I walked with him out to where the tired horse and the faded buggy waited. "Is the danger great?" I asked. "Is there any chance she might—"

"There is a fair chance, Esther," he assured me, clutching my hand and patting it in his fatherly manner. "But only if Rachel exercises restraint and wisdom." He paused, his left foot on the running board, undecided.

"Tell me," I urged. "I should like to know anything that might help or make a difference."

"I hesitate mentioning it, since I am not certain," he began, hoisting himself heavily up onto the lumpy seat stretched over the sagging springs. "But I believe there is a chance we might be dealing with twins here."

I felt my chest contract in fear, and also excitement.

"It isn't size; your mother scarcely gains an ounce when she carries her babies. But it seems I have determined more than one heartbeat, in varying positions." He shrugged.

"That could be—"

"Yes, let us hope I am mistaken, my dear." He nodded to me as he clucked his tongue to the faithful beast, who lifted his head in response.

16

I watched them move off in a small cloud of dust that clung in my nostrils as it sifted back to the earth like fine flour. I rubbed my eyes with my fists, the way a child would, and realized that I felt tired, though the day had scarcely begun. I did not look forward to dealing with Mother over the next weeks, not at all. I wondered if Josephine would participate, and dampen her ardor for her own enterprises, even a little, in the name of mercy and cooperation.

I walked back into the house. Before the door closed behind me I heard Mother call out. Her voice sounded tired and more frightened than fractious. I glanced at Josephine, then headed back to Mother's room.

My mother is a private sort of person, one who keeps her emotions, even her thoughts, to herself. I looked at her now, lying white and pale against the pillow, and it seemed there were new creases lining her forehead and feathering out from her eyes. I smiled at her.

"It will be all right," I assured her. "I shall take good care of you. We'll pull through this thing together."

"I am afraid to hope."

Her voice was so small, so thin and girlish, that it wrung my heart. "You *must* hope, Mother. Hope is our strongest ally!"

"I have never had your kind of strength, Esther," she replied. "Josephine and I. You are like your father, and I don't understand . . . I . . ."

Her voice was faltering, and I could hear tears, like water running cold over stones. A chill fear pounded against my temples.

"It doesn't matter, Mother! Be yourself. Believe in your own way."

She lifted one thin hand, then let it flutter back onto the coverlet like the broken wing of a butterfly, frail and defenseless. "I am so tired, Esther."

I dropped down onto my knees and drew up that cold hand. "It's all right, Mother. Sleep. Do not worry. I shall take care of things here."

She smiled wanly. I was distressed anew as I saw tears fill her eyes. *This is unlike her!* I felt a sense of panic rise, like a hot flush, to my face. *She covers emotion with a bright, brittle shell, the way Josie does. I have never seen her break down this way.*

17

I stroked the thin hand. "I'll see you through this," I soothed. "Things will be all right, Mother, I promise."

I sat beside the bed a long time, until I was certain her sleep was deep and unbroken. Then I went slowly from the room, avoiding the boards I knew would crack and creak. There was a dull ache in my lower back, and my feet felt heavy. I looked around, but could see Josephine nowhere. *Where could she have gone?* She would certainly not be at work in the garden. Had she carried a pail of food or a cool glass of buttermilk out to Father?

I let myself out through the kitchen door and walked a few yards to where the rise at the back of the house gave me a clear view of the fields and woods in all directions. Shading my eyes, I could see Father's figure driving the horse-drawn plow in the distance. He was alone. No other shape, human or beast, was in sight.

I sighed and felt the discouragement shudder through me. There was some washing up to do and a pile of clothes all sprinkled and ready for ironing. By then the dough would be risen enough to form into loaves. And it would be time to begin boiling potatoes and frying chicken for supper. Work. Work enough at hand to drive thought away. But not a sense of despondency. That could settle, thick and choking as the dust the doctor's carriage wheels had churned up in the dry lane, and cling, a dull layer to dampen the soul.

Two hours later Josephine breezed through the door, giggling, bright-eyed, smelling of gaiety and sunshine. I looked up from the table I was scouring, not attempting to soften my expression.

"Oh, do not be vexed, Esther! I knew you would be." She flung herself into Mother's rocker and began it moving with the toe of her small pointed boot. "I didn't *mean* to go off and leave you."

"Well, that makes it all right then—"

"Mr. Hall came by, asking for Father. And we got to talking. I had never before realized how good-looking he is, Esther. His eyes are so blue—"

"And his carriage so fine."

"You knew he had a new carriage?" Josephine's eyes, as golden brown as the skin of a doe in midsummer, blinked back at me. "That is just it, Esther. He said, 'Since your father is not here and I have time on my hands, it would be a pity to waste it. Would you honor me, Miss Parke, with your presence for half an hour? You would be the first woman to step inside my new buggy.'"

"So you went alone with him? And time simply got away from you."

"His manner is so polite and deferring; there was nothing improper, Esther."

"I did not imply that there was."

I set down my brush and bucket and took a seat facing her. "He is nearly ten years your senior," I reminded her.

"Eleven, actually. But he has never been married before."

"So he is in the running?"

"Oh yes!" Josie leaned back and sighed in satisfaction. "He is a gentleman, fine to look upon, good company. And he has property! Did you know the gristmill is his—not to speak of the house and—"

"Did he show you his house?"

"We merely drove up to it. I did not go inside with him."

I leaned back, prepared to admit defeat, as I always did. *Could anything bring her to her senses?* I wondered. "Well, perhaps he is a better candidate than the younger lads. He can be depended upon to understand and behave decorously."

"Whatever are you talking about?"

"I am talking about the fact that a lively courtship and marriage are not in the best of tastes now."

"Just because Mother is ill again?" The tone in Josie's voice made me shrink inside. "She is having a baby, Esther. There is nothing uncommon or extraordinary about it."

"Yes, there is, and you know it." I felt myself losing patience, the way one loses hold on a heavy bucket, feeling it slip through your fingers and watching the white milk splatter all over. "Josephine, please. This baby is due in less than two months' time."

"Two months' time! We will be well into the summer by then, Esther. I must have my courtship and then a proper period of engagement before a wedding can take place."

"And a funeral? A funeral requires no such preparations, does it?"

Her face blanched a little, but she replied evenly. "You exaggerate,

19

Esther. You know you always do. You are trying to frighten me into doing what you want."

"Doctor Ensworth confessed that he thinks Mother may be carrying twins. He fears complications."

Josephine sighed again. "Well, what am I to do?" Her lower lip came out in the pout that had characterized her since she was a child.

"Help by not harrowing her mind with further worries and burdens."

She considered. I could almost see her mind working, while her foot tapped a little pattern against the floor. "You may be wrong, sister. Weddings are not worries, but occasions for happiness. Why, if I were to make a particularly good match . . ."

I turned from her, to conceal the distaste I was feeling.

"It might be just the thing, Esther, to take her mind away from her troubles—divert it into pleasant imaginings!" She was pleased with herself for having thought of this. "I'll go in to her now."

"You'll do no such thing. She is sleeping soundly and should not be disturbed."

"Really, Esther. Anyone would think you were the older, the way you boss me around."

*Yes, they would, wouldn't they?* I thought. But I did not reply to her. I could not trust what I might say. Truth is, I *felt* older. To all intents and purposes I was the more mature, the more responsible of the two of us. It seemed I always had been. And Josephine liked it that way. Even now, it gave her an excuse to fancy herself slighted, to be justified in how she was feeling and what she was deciding to do.

"I'll change into my work dress and be out to help you in a few minutes," she said.

I could hear her humming as she walked back to the room we shared. *Is it a gift to be oblivious to life the way Josie is?* I wondered. *To possess a protective shield that prevents anything from going far enough to sting, to wound, to stir up the deep waters?*

I wished I could answer that question to my satisfaction. But at that moment I did not know how.

# Chapter 3

### Palmyra: June 1827

I finished the planting in time and my garden thrived, the sweet-smelling herbs especially. Georgie left us to spend a few weeks at her aunt's house in Albany. Mother drank teas of rosemary and chamomile for digestion, woodruff for her nervous headaches, ragwort for the swelling in her legs and feet, primrose for pain in her joints, and nettle to stimulate her sluggish circulation. I placed cornflower compacts on her eyes and tempted her appetite with the first tart strawberries, the first tender lettuces and peas. I enjoy this kind of nurturing. Mother responded nicely and tried her best to cooperate, though that which Josephine claims is true enough: both of them love to be pampered and served. Father went forward with the planting and cultivating of his fields, and my sister went forward with her unique matrimonial plans.

There was obviously some truth to her claim; Mother *was* enjoying planning and conjecturing about what sort of a wedding her eldest daughter would have. Late afternoons she would sit in her rocker, with a comforter over her knees, Josie curled on the settle beside her, face glowing, words tripping over each other. Once she said, "What will I wear, Josephine? Will I be able to fit into a decent frock?" I wondered then if she was steeling herself for disappointment, rejecting that faith I had pressed upon her, knowing only that the pain of loss following hope would be too sharp to bear. Indeed, if the planning, and what stood behind the planning, caused her distress and uncertainty, she kept that to herself.

Alexander Hall, despite the mature, solid nature of his appeal, did not monopolize the romantic field yet. Josie would have her fun. She would string all her old beaus behind her for as long as they would take it, especially now when she knew she stood on the verge of truly committing and settling down. I watched from a distance, content with my plants and my poetry and the patience of growing seasons, which all real gardeners know.

June came clothed in yellow daffodils and forsythia, with violets like stars in her hair. Ten days later a gale blew inland from the coast, as cold and blustery as April, spitting brittle rain between spells of harsh pale sunlight. And on this day of gray brooding skies and foreboding, Mother's babies bestirred themselves and attempted an entry into what appeared to be a disinterested, inhospitable world.

Father was in the fields, of course, Josie gathering eggs, myself at work in my gardens, when Mother stumbled to the door and cried out as loudly as she was able. My ear, tuned to quiet things, heard the faint, echoing strain, and my flesh turned cold. I called for Josie and ran with long strides toward the kitchen door, which stood open and empty now. I heard no sound from within.

With a sensation of dread I entered, my eyes darting about for sight of her. From behind me Josie cried out and pointed. Mother was crumpled on the floor like a rag doll—lying so still! her face white as a sheet.

"Go for Father!" I hissed. "Run as fast as you can, Josie." *Should I attempt to move her at all?* I crouched low, rocking back and forth, undecided. "Mother." I touched her forehead. It was clammy and cold. "Mother!" I shook her raised shoulder gently. She did not move at all.

I rose and paced the small, confining room, because I could not hold still. Then at once I realized that I must go for the doctor. Father and Josie were coming across the fields. If I rode Tansy bareback I could be halfway to the village by the time they arrived!

I raced to the barn, my fingers trembling as I pulled a halter over the mare's nose and urged her forward. Action! How blessed a thing it is when the mind is pulled outside of itself by a concern that is an agony, helplessness, and fear.

It was an experience I have not felt like remembering or recounting, even in the daily journal I keep. I was chilled to the bone by the time I arrived back at the house, riding behind Doctor Ensworth. I felt chilled to the bone all day. Chilled at heart, perhaps, more than anything. Somehow the skilled doctor saved the first and larger of the twin boys, though the smaller, shriveled and skinny as a newborn sparrow, seemed to have little chance. Somehow, perhaps by the sheer force of his own will and determination, Doctor Ensworth roused my mother back into life. She was weak from the loss of blood and had sunk into a trance-like state. He stayed with her for the better part of that day, bent over the bed, stirring the dim embers of her essence with his breath, as it were, keeping the pale flame from blinking out.

The vigil continued throughout the night and the next day, and the next, and the day following that. Neighbors brought in food. Someone milked the cow and saw to the livestock. Someone took care of the feeding of the hens and Josephine's dogs; someone gathered the eggs. Someone watered and weeded my gardens and Father's fields. I realized later that Josephine actually organized the relief force; she could not bear the dim, stale stillness of the sickroom. The presence of people was a reassurance to her, as also was the mind-saving relief and necessity of something to do.

My father would not leave the house. He sat beside Mother's head, stroking her hair, talking old nonsense to her. I sat at her feet. On that first day, while the rain beat like skeleton knuckles rapping at the window panes, I huddled in a corner, all cold drafts and shadows, and held the small, nameless infant as he breathed out his short life in my arms.

I have seen animals, from mewing kittens to gangly calves, struggle for life—watched them shudder and convulse in the throes of defeat, and accepted the mystery as a sad fact of mortal existence. I have seen old beasts and old people die. I had stood beside the lifeless bodies of my brothers and sisters when death, in the form of disease or accident, had, with a swift, indifferent hand, snuffed out their tender, high-burning flames. I had never before held to my own heart such a new, frail pulse of life—no more than a sigh, a breathing of the eternities, with that glory still clinging to him, still bright and fathomless behind his pale, dim eyes.

I sang to him, I whispered words I do not remember into his tiny pearled ears. I could feel his patience. I could feel his love, along with the myriad nameless things looking out from his eyes.

All that day he remained, and into the night. I would let no one else touch him. Phoebe's mother found a wet nurse for the other twin, who was crying lustily now—reaching out for life with his two little fists curled tight.

I held the child nestled in my arms, each breath more weak, more frail than the last. I would not allow even Doctor Ensworth to take him from me. He stood above us and shook his head. "They came too early, Esther. Twins have a habit of doing that. This little fellow's lungs, and I suppose other vital organs, have not developed fully enough to support life."

*Support life!* The flesh had failed this spirit—fine and strong and capable—thus refusing him place here, forcing him to go back—*to go where?*

My mind reeled with questions—the need to *know* like a keen hunger in me, gnawing away at my bones. I sent my agonized cry out into the ether, beyond the walls of the room, beyond the pathetic, finite limits of man's understanding. I received no reply, save the wisdom and love that could not form itself into palpable expression, which I saw in the small dying eyes.

I knew when the end came. I sensed it before it happened. The immensity of it gathered around me, and suddenly I felt nothing but light. *Light.* And a sense of joy, like the very joy of the heavens about which bright angels sing. My whole being lifted, and sorrow mingled with a happiness I could not describe. At the very last, when the weight in my arms seemed to lighten, when the breath in the diminutive body seemed scarcely discernible, a strange thing occurred. The child's tiny hand, lying against mine, moved and groped, and clasped over my finger—warm and firm. And I felt such a love sent forth in that touch, such a love surging through me, that I knew beyond doubt my dear spirit was saying good-bye—saying all the things that could never be spoken between us, leaving me with this gift.

I did not realize I was crying until Doctor Ensworth crouched down beside me on his thick, stiffened legs. When I looked at him, I think he saw the wonder in my eyes, and his own filled with tears.

"Let me take him, Esther, and have the women take care of the body."

"No. I want to do it. Tell me what I should do."

He was patient. I followed his instructions with sure hands, each ministration a service I was happy to render. I still felt the child's spirit near. For hours I was encased in that love, for the rest of that long day—which began for me before the pale dawn seeped into the sky. *Hallowed.* That was the word that came to me. This infant's birth and death had hallowed my existence, left me changed, left me more than he had found me.

"What name shall I put on the records?" Doctor Ensworth asked me.

I answered without thinking. "His name shall be Nathaniel, which means 'gift of the Lord.' " Nathaniel had also been one of my great-grandfather's names. It seemed fitting. And worthy of the small wayfarer, wherever he might be now.

I did not want to put this child in the ground before my mother could even look upon him. Yet no choice was given us, and Doctor Ensworth thought it might actually be better that way.

The weather was unrelenting, as though our whole tragedy must be enacted before summer would again show her face. We walked, a small group of us, chilled and silent, to the hill above Church Street, which is the oldest burial ground in Palmyra. The coffin we lowered into the deep hole was so small; I had forgotten how thin, deflated, and empty my Nathaniel's abandoned body would be. The Presbyterian minister, Jonathan Porter, conducted a short ceremony at the site of the grave. My father and I attended his church, which sits on one of the corners of Church and Main Streets, flanked by the Methodist, Baptist, and Episcopalian places of worship—one sitting square on each corner in quiet defiance of each other. Mother and Josephine had never been churchgoers. In truth, Father and I enjoyed being alone together on quiet Sabbath mornings. It was a nice way to begin a new week.

"Nathaniel Parke, son of Jonah and Rachel Parke," read the rounded stone Mr. Jackway had carved. I paid for the carving myself and knew the kind man had stayed up most of the night before in order to finish it. "Born June 11th—Died June 12th." The dismal dates haunted me. I asked Mr. Jackway to carve: "Purity requireth no testing. The spirit has gone home." Home to God. I knew that was what the words meant. But they were no more than words to me.

We sang "Abide with Me" and "Rock of Ages." The words trembled in my throat.

25

While I draw this fleeting breath,
When mine eyes shall close in death,
When I rise to worlds unknown
And behold thee on thy throne . . .

I could not picture a heaven, nor a God within it! No image would come to my mind. Those infant eyes, large and calm as the heavens, spoke of what they had known—what seemed dark and mocking, entirely impenetrable to me.

While the others filed off I stayed behind to say my own last good-byes. Prolonging the moment, I walked around a bit to see what neighbors fate had afforded my brother; what souls, laid here long ago and lately, he rested beside.

Three or four were unknown to me; then I noticed Gideon Durfee, one of the first founders of the village, and the names Hopkins, Harris, and Osborne, representing other early families. It was then that I saw, not far distant, the grave of Alvin, eldest brother of the Smith clan, who had died tragically nearly four years ago. I remembered the time and the general sadness at his loss; he had been a most promising youth. Twenty-five years old. I wondered what he had thought of his younger brother and the strange experiences he claimed.

At length I knelt beside the freshly disturbed earth, drinking in the damp fragrance of soil, which I find pleasant, and alluring even in its own way. "I am sorry you did not live to draw the scent of black soil into your nostrils, Nathaniel, to feel the sun on your face. To see flowers and hear birds sing." I spoke in a low voice, out loud. "I am sorry you did not live to laugh, to know what love is—to kiss a girl, and make plans for a home of your own."

My voice choked and I could not say more. I buried my face in my hands and cried openly for the first time since that delicate life had expired in my arms.

We buried Nathaniel on Thursday. Early Friday morning Mother opened her eyes.

At first they did not seem to focus. Indeed, as comprehension came slowly, I felt a shrinking, as new plants shrink before an intense sun as it begins to wither them. Doctor Ensworth had strongly advised us not to tell her of the death of the child.

"She has one live, healthy baby to put her arms around, to nurture. That will be the best tonic to help her get well."

"And who decides the best moment to inform her of the loss of the other?" I asked.

"Let natural circumstances determine that," was his answer. "Perhaps you will sense the right moment."

"Perhaps we will not," I replied.

"Do not worry overmuch, Esther," he soothed. "You take too much upon your own shoulders. When your mother is stronger she will be able to bear the grief more easily than she could now."

So we sent for the wet nurse, Maggie Wells, to bring the child over. My father had not yet named his son. "That is Rachel's province," he replied whenever anyone asked him.

"Your child is well and safe," I said to my mother. "It is over. While you slept Maggie Wells has cared for him. Right now, as we speak, she is bringing him here."

Her eyes widened, and for a moment her face looked as youthful and vulnerable as a girl's. "A son!" She breathed the words like a prayer of thanksgiving. My father's eyes shone.

When I lowered the plump, squirming child into the curve of her arm she laughed softly, as though someone had told her a lovely secret she could not quite believe. For a long while she gazed at him, then reached out one thin hand and touched his cheek. I felt tears well behind my eyes, burn in my throat, and coughed nervously to clear them.

"He looks like you, Jonah."

"He is as fair as any of your daughters," my father replied.

I backed out on tiptoe and left the two—rather, the three—of them together. For the first time I felt a loosening of the terrible constriction around my heart, enough to realize what a tenseness of apprehension and sorrow I had been laboring through.

I hummed under my breath. *I will stir up some lemon jelly for her,* I thought. *It is one of her favorites and will sit mild on her stomach after she has gone these long days without food.*

I do not know how much time passed before my father came out into the kitchen. I do not know if things would have been different had I been in the room, been with them when my mother announced the name she had selected for her son, for this miracle child which had emerged from her fear and her pain.

My father was tight-lipped when he told me, his eyes veiled over with worry. "She wishes to call him Nathaniel." He almost hissed the words out, as though he did not quite believe them himself.

Might I have blurted the truth to her, unable to stop myself, in that horrifying moment when the word left her lips?

"No, Father, no! Have you suggested another?"

"Two or three. Urged them on her, despite my boast of leaving the whole thing in her hands."

I sat down, my legs feeling too weak to support me. "Whatever shall we do, Father? I had no idea!—I never dreamed—"

He placed his hand on my arm. I could feel the lean, sinewy strength of it. " 'Tis not your fault, Esther. Do not vex yourself so."

I called to Josephine, who was working the new butter in the pantry. "Heaven preserve us," she said when Father told her. "There's no way out of it now. Frying pan or the fire, that is all the choice we have, Esther."

I knew she spoke true. But what would be *best*—best for Mother? Tell her now, before she began to think of her son in terms of the name of a dead child, whose existence she was not even aware of? Or would that push her back into the darkness again? Wait, wait only until the following morning, let her build up even a little strength?

Father was as distraught as I. "Go in to her, Josie," I begged. "Sit with her, divert her. Talk of anything but the name! Father, go to your work for a couple of hours. I shall set the jelly to cooking and try to think what to do." I shuddered at the very words I was speaking. "Come in early for dinner," I told him. "We three shall counsel together and make our decision then."

He nodded, his forehead creased with concern, and went off, grateful I believe to have someone else take over, lift the hot coal out of his tender hands. I went about my work with a vengeance, struggling to make my stunned mind concentrate on the tricky problem at hand. *Why,* I agonized, *do such things have to happen? What kind of omen is this?*

Then I chastised myself mentally for being so superstitious. If I could somehow turn it all to *advantage,* make my mother feel good about it! I fussed and stewed through the morning. In truth, I had not thought to pray. Perhaps my training in that area had been deficient; indeed, I knew that it had. My thoughts turned only inward, expecting to find the perfect solution within my own mind. It was a chance thing, really, that made my thoughts turn to Nathaniel—the Nathaniel I'd known.

A little bird came to light on the ledge of the wide stone window frame and pranced his way into the kitchen, pretty as you please. He did not seem frightened, but rather attracted to the warm yellow color of my cooling jelly, and perhaps to the aroma as well. When I spoke to him he cocked his head and looked back at me, his eyes bright as buttons. I believe he was a finch of some kind. He chirruped something back at me, and with a sudden rise and fluttering of feathers, he lifted and flew toward me, landing on my wrist and twisting his head again in that quizzical manner.

"Have you been somebody's pet, love?" I cooed, delighted, scarcely daring to breathe lest I frighten him off.

I swear if he had been able he would have sat there and talked to me. I nearly reached out to touch him, so familiar he seemed. Then, with nothing to startle or divert him, he lifted suddenly off and returned to the ledge, where he hovered and fluttered a moment before removing his presence from me, leaving the room somehow empty because he had gone.

*Removing his presence.* I felt the little bird to be some kind of messenger—to turn my thoughts, if nothing more; to lift my sights higher than my own sense of inadequacy and frustration.

I put down the dish towel, walked back to my bedroom, and fell down on my knees. It was not the most eloquent of prayers I uttered, nor the longest, but it *was* sincere. By the time Father arrived I knew what I must do. When I told him he nodded assent.

Mother's room was cool and dim because the windows were shaded, yet it still felt stuffy inside. *Tomorrow,* I thought, *I will let in some fresh air and sunshine, and bring out the mop to chase some of this stale dust away.*

29

She was lying awake, drowsy, perhaps half dreaming. When she saw me her eyes softened and she sighed contentedly.

"I should like to feed him myself," she confessed, "but I am grateful that Maggie is willing."

"Yes," I agreed. "But in good time it will come to that. He will be a constant drain on you soon enough." We both smiled.

"Mother . . ." I sat down on the bed beside her and reached for her hand. "I have something wonderful to tell you. Another miracle, really. Something I want to share with you—but it will not be easy for me."

She was all attention. Her eyes narrowed as she examined my face.

"I had an experience, a more sacred and wonderful experience than I could ever imagine. I had it while you were sleeping, unconscious, your spirit hovering near yet away from us. I had a spirit experience, too."

"Esther." She breathed the word. "What are you trying to tell me?"

"I am trying to tell you about your son Nathaniel Parke, Mother. I am trying to tell you about the child I was privileged for a few short hours to know and love."

I went on. I did not relate facts and details; I poured out my heart. I tried to make her see what I had seen, feel what I had felt. All the tender yearnings and sufferings of that day and night came back to me, formed themselves into a gentle shadow of the reality, like a memory imbued with substance and life. As I spoke she relaxed, yet at the same time she seemed to grow stronger. I like to think that Mother, too, felt Nathaniel's presence there with us the way that I did.

When I had finished speaking a silence fell between us, but the silence was good. She began to cry softly. I put my arms around her and pulled her head to my shoulder. There was acquiescence in her tears and an acceptance that I knew would make things all right.

After a little while she asked for her handkerchief and blew her nose. "Jonathan is a good name," she mused. "I have always been fond of it."

"A strong name. It means 'given of God,' " I said.

"Then Jonathan it shall be."

She took a lock of the baby's fine, wispy hair and curled it around her finger. Jonathan slept on, breathing evenly. "He is very lovely," I said.

We sat together for a long time, until we heard Maggie's voice in the kitchen with Josie. They came into the room together, chatting in a normal, cheerful manner that drew us in.

"What have you decided to call him, Rachel?" Maggie's rose face was filled with curiosity.

"Jonathan."

"Be that a family name?"

Mother laughed a little. "It is now," she said.

"And a fair, strong one," Maggie pronounced. "Looks like a Jonathan, don't he?"

I glanced over at Josephine. She arched an eyebrow as if to say, "How did you accomplish that?" I rose and smoothed my skirts out. "I'll dish up some lemon jelly for both of you," I said, "and a cup of iced ginger tea to go with it. You just sit here and talk."

I moved toward the door. "Come, Josie, and help me." As I walked into the kitchen I realized how light I felt. The terrible burden had lifted. I could breathe again. I wanted to laugh; I wanted to dance. And summer was wafting her gentle wings through the air, chasing the dank shadows out of her fragrant, flowered domain.

I found myself glancing heavenward before I turned to my duties with a grateful heart bubbling over, and a lilt to my step.

# Chapter Four

## Palmyra: August 1827

I was actually the first to notice the stranger when he came into town. It was that day when I returned alone after burying Nathaniel. The canal is not far from the graveyard. But I remember thinking it strange that a gentleman, so finely attired, should be walking on his own into town. He had carried a rather remarkable walking stick of which I took note. It boasted the head of what looked like an old Egyptian goddess—gold-leafed, surely, for it fairly glittered despite the shortage of sun. He twirled it in his hand as he walked, seeming entirely at ease with himself. I remember that he was tall and carried himself well. He had a fine head of hair beneath his tall hat, and it curled around his temples in a becoming fashion. I did not see his eyes. Perhaps if I had seen his eyes, I would have known better.

Summer wooed and lulled us, blessed our growing things with her warm breath, and with gratitude we accepted the pattern of long, pleasant, drawn-out days. Mother improved slowly, but her progress was steady. We saw much of Maggie those first weeks, bringing little Jonathan and fetching him back again. Mother's milk never came in. After a time we began to supplement his diet with goat's milk, and he seemed to like that well enough. Indeed, he was an agreeable little soul from the very start. Our kitchen is sunny, and Mother's old rocker curves comfortably against the back. She spent most of her hours there, part of the hum and bustle of things going on around her, seemingly content to come along slowly and easily.

At times *I* was not! I do not mind work; indeed, many forms of it I relish. But summer's demands are many and never ending, and, like as not, when I turned round to find Josephine, in want of a little assistance, I would discover she had flitted away. *Not to be bothered.* That was her attitude her last summer with us. Alexander Hall was courting her in earnest now, and she delighted in his attentions. Once or twice, in frustration, I appealed to Mother, but she seemed in a daze, oblivious.

"Your day will come, Esther," she would sigh, in almost honeyed tones, and I knew she was remembering her own youthful days. "Josephine has allowed herself to play the field too long. It is right that she look seriously for a husband now, before she becomes too old and finds men looking another way."

*As if that day would ever come!* I steamed inwardly. Besides, it was not "right" that she be even more lazy and self-centered than usual. She is a better cook than I and she knows it. Yet most of the meals fell to me. My gardens alone, heaven knows, were enough to consume me. Piling all else on top of it, I had not a minute to breathe.

But Jonathan's presence was a veritable balm to all that, easing the sharpest headache, the dull throbs in the small of my back, the exhaustion of hours spent out in the sun. I marveled then and shall always marvel at the power infants and children have to draw people out of themselves and, in no way in particular, lift and refresh the spirit with the unspoken awareness that nothing else matters save what they embody of innocent beauty and love.

The first day I allowed myself to go out and about following Mother's recovery, I met with a sight that sincerely astounded me. I saw Tillie—our Tillie—promenading with the stranger who had walked into town from the boats. He cut a fine figure still, and she looked her best. Theodora may happen to be less pretty than some girls—her nose is a bit long, her skin sallow, and her hair thin and flyaway—but she makes up the difference by *trying*. She takes great pains with herself and enhances her good points, and is never sour or petty, as many girls are. Bolstered by her *position* in life as coming from *the* best family, she has learned the wisdom of capitalizing on her assets and brushing all else aside. But the stranger! I must learn something of it. I made bold to cross the street, that I might encounter them.

Tillie's eyes lit with pleasure when she spied me. "Oh, Esther, how well met! Come meet my new friend."

I turned my gaze upon the gentleman, who eyed me appraisingly.

33

Presenting me first, as was proper, Tillie introduced her companion as Mr. Gerard Whittier, from the city; which, of course, meant New York.

He bowed low over my hand in a most proper manner. "What has brought you to our little village?" I asked.

"Banking. He has banking interests here, Esther." And I wondered at the proud tone in Tillie's voice.

"And you are acquainted with Theodora's father?" I pressed.

Tillie made a face at me, but the gentleman replied. "Mr. Swift has been very kind to me, assisting my efforts to establish myself and extend my business involvements here."

Then I knew. Lawrence Swift, that miser, was grooming this haughty stranger for a future son-in-law. Had he already told Tillie that?

We spent a few minutes in small talk before I excused myself and walked on down the street, resisting the strong temptation to glance behind me. Oh, Tillie. He was not fit for her! From the very first I knew that. Even though he had not yet met my gaze square in the eye.

Georgeanna returned from Albany, and as though she were only waiting for her mistress's arrival, her cat, Iris, gave birth to six kittens, each one a separate, delightful combination of color and design.

We all came running like so many schoolgirls, pressing round the new creatures, exclaiming over this one and that. I could not help thinking, as the old cat lay contentedly washing her new offspring, how easy her maternity had been compared to my mother's. Here Nature was fully in charge and did her work well. And, if any of the kittens had happened to die, Iris would not have mourned them, but would have got on with the business of living and taking care of the rest. All so simple, because the complex human element was missing.

*He is at peace with God now, free from the cares of this mortal life.* I thought of Nathaniel and shivered. No pretty pictures came to me, no sense of resignation or peace.

Each of us laid claim on our favorite kitten, and Georgie laughed at us. "You will change your minds half a dozen times," she predicted, "before they are ready to leave the nest."

We knew she was right. Through the years Josie and I had adopted at least a dozen of Georgie's kittens, and some had met rather ignoble fates. Only two were left, good mousers both of them, and they lived in the barn.

"Perhaps a little house cat would be nice for Mother," I mused.

"A fitting replacement for Josephine," Phoebe suggested. "How is the campaign coming, anyway?"

"Nicely, as planned." Josie preened a bit, because all eyes were on her.

"Still a winter wedding?"

"Indeed."

"And you've made your choice?"

She hesitated.

"I believe she has contrived that her choice has chosen her and is satisfactorily smitten," I offered. "Now she must choose again, to accept the man who has chosen her and is waiting with baited breath."

Everyone appreciated my humor, but Josephine did not recognize the barbs hidden here and there in my words. She fancied herself clever; she always had. As long as she felt in control, things would go forward as planned.

"Tillie may beat you to it," Georgie grinned, "and you shall have to be content with a close second, Josephine."

Josie arched her back much like a vexed cat would. "Whatever do you mean, Georgeanna?"

Theodora's face colored uncomfortably, and she looked down at the ground.

"What is this, Tillie?" I asked in a low voice. "Has it to do with Gerard Whittier?"

She nodded, but would not raise her eyes.

"Leave her alone," I ventured. " 'Tis a choice her father has made for her. Perhaps it will not come to pass."

"Oh, it shall 'come to pass,' all right, as you put it, dear Esther. I have nothing to say in the matter."

"Well, tell us, what is he like?" Josephine was all ears, her interest piqued more than she desired to admit. Had quiet Tillie landed a bigger fish than the one she was dangling on her line?

"He is a gentleman from New York," I ventured again. "Tall, well formed, with the polished air of the city about him, and I would say handsome features—wouldn't you, Theodora?"

My heart went out to her; I had to assist her somehow.

"Yes, he is that," she agreed cautiously.

"And in banking," Georgie interjected.

Now Josephine really perked up. "Then he shall be able to take care of you properly."

"That is what Father believes."

"Do you like him well enough, Tillie?" sweet Phoebe asked, concerned, perhaps thinking on her own disappointments.

"We have met but three times, I scarcely know him. But he appears to be . . . a gentleman sincerely."

"Well! Fancy this happening!" I smiled, seeing Josie could scarcely contain herself.

"Father is pushing for a betrothal, and so is Gerard." Tillie spoke the words softly, waiting to see our reaction.

"So suddenly! What of Joel, Tillie?"

I scowled at Josie for asking.

Tillie shrugged her thin shoulders. "What of Joel—we are fond of each other, but it has not gone beyond that."

"If the choice were in *your* hands . . ." Georgie leaned forward, waiting.

Tillie raised her eyes slowly. "I know the things Father cares about are important, and I try to respect that." She hesitated. We were like sisters, the circle of faces she looked upon. We had always shared our most intimate thoughts with each other. "Yes, if it *were* up to me, I should—I should prefer wedding Joel and living more simply. If . . ." She let her hands flutter, like faltering birds, to her lap. Lovely hands—slender with long, tapered fingers—Theodora's one point of pride.

"Sweetness!" Georgie cried, smitten with Tillie's unhappiness, as I was. "Could your father not be persuaded?"

"Has he ever been, Georgie, in any matter you remember?"

We fell into a glum silence, the lot of us, each thinking her own dreary thoughts.

"Well, I shall not make it a *race,*" Josephine announced, perhaps purposefully diverting attention. "I mean to have my courtship in full measure first, with time to stitch and fuss and prepare the dainties I want for my marriage bed."

This brought a host of reactions, as she knew it would, and we began babbling like girls again. I watched Tillie rouse herself and join in with the others. But I could not help wondering what unspoken longings and fears sat like a cold hand on her heart.

For the next few days Josephine stewed, as I knew she would.

"I always intended to be first," she pouted. "And it is only right I should be."

"You are forgetting that Theodora does not *wish* this, Josie. It is none of her doing. If her father marries her off to this stranger you must support her with your love and excitement. It would be cruel to do otherwise."

For once Mother took my side of the matter. "Your sister is right. You can afford to be generous, Josie, seeing as how you have been given in all things your own free choice."

"Then Alexander Hall it shall be!" she muttered. I could see her determination harden. "He is older and established. None of the young boys could keep me in style."

I left her to her wiles, pleased that Father's wheat fields were heavy with grain, that my herbs and vegetables were thriving—all things growing at good pace, Jonathan among them. A bit of color was even returning to Mother's cheeks.

*Each day is a blessing,* I remember thinking. *Each day that passes kindly and pleasantly, free of mishap.*

The following morning I was aroused by Josephine shaking me into wakefulness; this was certainly rare!

"Esther! There has been a fire in the Presbyterian church! All the men are being roused to fight it."

I rubbed my eyes. *Was it morning?* The square of sky outside my window looked cinder gray.

"Father is taking the wagon in. I thought we could ride along with him. Hurry now, or he'll leave us."

I sat upright. I could hear the muffled ringing of the alarm bell, eerie and lonely-sounding in the still night. "What time is it?"

"Nearly dawn. Hurry, Esther!"

Once we were settled on the wagon seat and jostling along the potted roads toward the village, I began regretting letting Josie talk me into going along. I would much rather have been in my bed cuddled under the blue and white coverlet Mother had woven for me when I was a child. But I think Father was glad of our company. And, if a fire, there might very well be injuries and need for women's help.

I was surprised to see so many wagons and horses drawn up to the churchyard. Was there so much cause for alarm? I felt my stomach muscles tighten as I took the hand Father extended and climbed down from the seat.

People everywhere, but I could not see where the fire was; there was no sign of a flame.

"I think it's all over," Father surmised. "People are coming back, you see."

He was right. The faces I looked into were tired, many streaked with soot. Some wore expressions of relief, but many were tense with anger.

"What is it?" I cried, seeing Tillie's father and tugging at his sleeve. "Was someone badly injured?"

He answered me eagerly, almost pouncing on my question. "Several of the lads were burned, none badly. The fire was started a' purpose, you know—Joe Smith up to his mischief again."

I felt myself withdraw from the coldness in his voice. "Who said it was Joseph?" I demanded, surprising myself. "Has that been proved?"

He stared at me as if I had just taken leave of my senses. "It was him, all right. That . . ."

He clipped off a string of colorful expletives that left me shivering. I backed away from him, feeling an answering anger rise in my throat like bile.

"I believe that you, and any others who accuse him, are mistaken." My voice was bold, even strident. "He is married now, you know. And he and his wife were not even in town last night."

Mr. Swift whirled back to face me. "You have that on good authority, missy?"

"On the best. And I will give proof of it, sir, if it comes to that."

I was bluffing! My head was ringing with the audacity of it! " 'Tis no small thing to falsely accuse another," I added, lifting my head a bit. "I would discourage the others if I were you, sir."

He turned from me, disgust in his face, even in the lines of his body, as he walked back to his friends. I was trembling so hard that I had to grab hold of the fence post to steady myself.

"What is it, Esther?" my father asked, coming up beside me. "You look white as a ghost."

"I have grown weak suddenly, Father. Might I wait in the wagon?"

"Of course, girl. I shall help you."

"No, I'll be all right." I took a few steps to prove it. "And, Father, if you hear talk of Joseph Smith being responsible for this, will you— well—attempt to discourage it?"

He peered at me for a moment, then nodded his head. I knew I could trust him. I made my way back to the wagon and crawled up to the seat, drawing deep breaths in order to slow my heartbeat and calm myself. But the air still tasted of smoke, and there was a settling of cinders smudging the dew-wet ground.

After a little spell I noticed three young men walking toward me, one of them limping badly. As they drew closer I recognized that the one with the limp was James Sadler, one of Josie's old beaus.

"Where's your sister?" he asked, gazing up at me.

"You have been hurt," I replied.

Just then, as luck would have it, Josephine made her appearance— on the arm of a quite smug and contented Alexander Hall. I saw the younger man wince.

"James here has been burned badly, fighting the fire," I said, hoping to move her to sympathy.

My sister glanced up, arched an eyebrow, and took on the manner of a scolding school mistress. "You boys ought to be more careful—or else leave such serious work to older men."

I wish I had not seen James's face. He was perhaps the best of her beaus and would make any girl a good husband. I dropped my own eyes in shame.

After the crestfallen trio shuffled off and Mr. Hall had torn himself reluctantly away, I lit into her. "Josie, how could you? Have you no decency, no compassion at all?"

39

She blinked back. "Whatever are you talking about, Esther?"

"You know what I am talking about! Your behavior a few moments ago—your treatment of James!"

"Oh, Esther! He's just a boy, my dear." She scurried up to sit beside me, her eyes ashine. "Alexander has just asked if he might speak to me alone tomorrow. He will come after Sabbath services, for he wishes an audience with Father as well."

I remained purposefully unimpressed and unmoved.

"Esther, you know what this means!"

"It means that Mr. Hall intends to propose to you. Do you intend to accept?"

"Of course I do, silly girl."

"Then heaven help him," I muttered under my breath.

I sat hunched and miserable until Father at last emerged from among the dim shapes and drove us, sleepy and heavy-eyed, home. I cared not that my sister was vexed with me. I was disgusted with her.

"Half an hour," I said to my father, "just a little catnap before I start breakfast."

He smiled and nodded. Halfway up the stairs I turned back. "Did the talk about Joseph die down?"

"Enough to avert trouble, I think," he replied.

*Thank heaven for that, at least.* I had accomplished some good that morning, though not half of what I would have liked to. *People will run their lives amok, with precious little anyone can do to stop it,* I thought as I pulled the cool covers up over my head. But I did not like being ashamed of my sister. *Will she ever grow up and take real responsibility for her own life?* was the last conscious thought I had before sleep settled over me and kindly blotted all thought and sensation out.

# Chapter 5

*Palmyra: Early September 1827*

As my mother's health improved, her obsession with Jonathan increased, whereas I would have expected it to work just the other way round. She was protective of the child to the point where Josephine and I could barely endure it. She wished never to let him out of her sight, trusting no one. Could he sit on a blanket at the edge of the gardens with me while I harvested the ripe squash and tomatoes? Certainly not. A bee might sting him, or flies annoy. Could Josie mind him while she sewed on her trousseau? What if she forgot to keep her eye on him and he rolled over and—*what?* harmed himself somehow, lying on his tummy? It was sadly pathetic to watch her. No, thank you. She would keep the child by her side. She could scour the pans, churn butter, and bake bread while she looked out for his safety and comfort. Any task that would take her attention off the infant for any length of time more than minutes was allocated to me. I did not mind much. But I worried about the future—the days when Jonathan would be crawling, then walking and wanting to fend for himself, explore his new world a bit. Would she grow worse? Would her attentions smother him—would her fears fester into an appalling obsession? I dearly hoped not.

In truth, I had other, weightier matters that concerned me. Scarcely had August shook out her flowery skirts and departed than Theodora came calling one morning, bright and early, hoping to catch me, I knew, before my gardens drew my attention.

"Will you drive with me, Esther?" she asked. "For only a few minutes."

"Of course," I replied, wiping my hands along my apron, then untying it from about my waist.

"Where is Josephine?" Tillie whispered.

"In the back room cutting dress patterns," I said, just as quietly.

"Must you announce your going—off with me?"

I realized, with those words, that her voice was tense, her manner nervous. "No, they'll assume I'm out in the garden and not worry, not for a while at least."

"Good." She tugged at my hand. "Come, quickly."

She was driving her mother's town carriage; a most rare occurrence. I climbed up beside her, even as the wheels began turning and she clucked to the horse. She said nothing, and I ventured no questions, until we had cleared our farm and topped the ridge to where the road turns into a cool copse of birch and hemlock through which a thin stream meanders and sings. She steered the wagon in as far as it would go and dropped the reins so the mare could graze. I heard grackles scolding from the high branches and saw a cardinal, like a streak of flame, dart across our path.

"Gerard has spoken to my father, without even approaching me first. They two have agreed. I am affianced to him—the marriage date is set, Esther! For six weeks from now!"

I am so quick to anger! I felt indignation sweep through me with all the aggravation of finely ground sand, like sharp bits of glass, pelting one's face and arms in a windstorm. "My dearest! Have you no appeal? What of your mother?"

She shook her head. "They are both angry with Peter, you see. He has left his position on the canal and run home, complaining that the work is too hard for him."

"It most probably is, Tillie. He is young for such rough company, anyhow."

"Yes, *I* agree, but they do not! And they need something to lash out at. You know how it works. Thus they are aligned together in this matter of my marriage." She put her cold little hand on my arm and grasped it tightly. "Esther, I am not ready for marriage yet!"

"Not to this man, in particular."

She hesitated, but I would not mince words now. "Come, dear, with me of all people you can speak honestly. There is no danger here. Only comfort, and the courage to endure. This is what we must provide for each other, now that Life is staking her claims on us."

With a shudder she moved toward me and buried her head in my shoulder. "What shall I do, Esther? I am frightened! Sometimes there is an expression in Gerard's eyes when he looks at me that is appraising and cold. Perhaps my fears are unfounded . . . but we are not like enough in many ways I feel are important."

*And he is to have in his safekeeping this precious soul!* I seethed inwardly. "Can you get it postponed, even for a while?"

"He is as eager as my parents are! I do not think they will listen to me."

We sat in silence. I stroked her hair, soft, like the fine filaments of spun cotton. I could hear the thin sounds of the water moving over its stony bed. I could hear the chatter of sparrow and jay overhead. I fancied I could almost hear the painful throbbing of Tillie's heart.

"Will he take you away?" I ventured at last, having to ask it.

She sat up, wide-eyed with consternation. "I have not even thought about that! I came to you directly—not having anywhere else to turn."

"You shall always have me," I assured her stoutly. "I'll watch out for you, Tillie. There is no man alive who can prevent me from doing that."

She smiled weakly. No further words were needed between us. After a little while she drew up the reins and turned the mare round. I could feel her reluctance. The weight of it was as odious as if it had been my own.

We parted at the foot of the narrow lane leading up to our house, and she drove on. I stood a long time looking after her, wondering about life, feeling the confinement of a woman's role, a woman's relative lack of personal determination, more keenly than I had ever before in my life.

*There must not be many men such as my father,* I concluded, *who offer the same freedom and respect to a woman as they claim for themselves. Why is this? Why?* I could not answer the question, not at the moment. I turned and walked up to the house, with a weariness upon my spirit more draining than any exhaustion of muscle and flesh.

When Tillie's announcement was made public, Josephine could not hide her displeasure.

"Do you think she has done this to spite me?" she asked.

I grabbed at her arm and turned her to face me. "Do not ever say that—not to myself, not to anyone—ever again!"

Josephine froze. She could *feel* the resolve that blazed in my eyes, that made my voice shake. "From this moment forward you ought to think of what you can do *for* Tillie, not anything different, not anything less."

She answered nothing; and when Josephine answers nothing, that is a victory of sorts. But my heart was nonetheless heavy within me as I went out to my chores.

I saw Peter again before I saw his sister, so I hailed him as he walked past the dry goods store. "How goes it, my man?" I asked. "Has your father forgiven you yet?"

He hung his head, truly ashamed for his weakness. I came up closer and said gently, "Now, Peter, really, I have heard stories of how bad conditions on the canal are. Surely you found them all to be so."

I was saying, *Tell me about it,* and I was glad he took up the invitation.

"The work *is* hard," he began, "we hoggees being at the bottom of the order, driving the mules and horses. And the wages is low, 'specially when you consider we work in six-hour shifts and get no time to ourselves."

"How is that?" I asked, taking a seat beneath a shady oak and motioning him down beside me.

"Why, we're expected to feed the animals and take care of their wants during off hours, as well as mend harnesses—that be no small task!—and cook our own food."

I nodded and handed him a biscuit from my parcel. He took a hefty bite before continuing. "There was never enough food, Esther, and never enough time to sleep. I felt dead on my feet most of the time. Why, we slept in the stables with the horses when we did get a wink!" I saw the expression on his face tighten and alter. "But that wasn't the worst of it."

"What was the worst of it?" I sat for a few moments in silence, waiting, while Peter struggled with something inside himself.

"If some poor hoggee like myself—some frightened, skinny little orphan boy with his bones stickin' out of his clothes—couldn't control them big mules when they got tangled or frightened, he'd get beaten awful by the captain, 'specially if one of the animals died."

I shuddered. "Have you told these things to your father?"

"Naw." He looked down again and finished his biscuit in a single bite.

I handed him another. "What about Randolph?"

"He don't mind the drinkin' and fightin' the way I do. I can't sleep for the sound and the smell of it." He glanced up again, his blue eyes as open and innocent as a summer sky. "Some of them fellows is big and mean, Esther, and they do awful things."

I shuddered again and reached out to put my hand on his shoulder. "You did the manly thing, Peter," I said firmly. "I'm proud of you."

Those words gave him pause. He blinked, uncomprehending.

"A real man avoids that which is low and crass—especially that which is evil. And, nine cases in ten, he pays the price of ridicule and misunderstanding for his stance and his principles." I could see comprehension creep into his gaze. "It is not merely your father and your youth, you know. It will ever be thus, Peter, even when you are grown. True courage is shown when a man embraces that which is just and noble and holds his place—no matter what other men think of him or do to him."

The blue eyes smiled, as soft and unsullied as a kitten's. "You know what to say, Esther, to make a fellow feel better—you always did."

"Truth is truth. If I can recognize some little bit of it, then I am grateful," I said. A slow grin spread over his relaxing features. "Stick to your guns, Peter. Do not let *anyone* distress or discourage you. In the end you will make your father truly proud of you—and be able to hold your head up as well."

I walked to the corner of the family lot with him. Before we parted I placed my hand on his shoulder again and made his eyes meet mine. "I have a favor to ask *you,* Peter."

He nodded, sober and willing.

"Be kind as can be to Theodora just now. She needs kindness more than you know. And . . ." I hesitated. "Watch out for her. If she needs me—even if you only sense it—will you come for me, day or night, no matter what?"

45

He nodded, his eyes wide.

"Give me your word on it."

"My word, Esther. My solemn word that I will do as you say."

I hugged him then, unable to help myself. "God bless you, sweet Peter," I murmured, then hurried off in a flurry, disconcerted, confused by what I had said to him. *God bless you.* Why had I used that phrase? I had not *felt* that sentiment much, not spoken it freely—not, I realized suddenly, until Nathaniel died.

*But that makes no sense!* I reasoned with myself. *My faith has but faltered and questioned since that day.* But I saw, too, that my heart had been more tender, more *aware,* for want of a better word, than it ever had been.

*More vulnerable to suffering,* I thought, rather bitterly. *More able to recognize and feel it, even in others.* I was not pleased about that. If this meant growth and maturity, I wished for a moment, with all my soul, that I was merely a girl again, skipping off to school with my friends, thinking only of the needs and delights of the moment, pleasured by simple things, unaware of the underlying layer of tragedy, perfidy, and heartache that lay so close beneath the calm surface upon which childhood treads.

*I could have scratched it away with my fingernails,* I thought, *and revealed the black decay and disease of it—there, beneath the sweet grass and the blossoming flowers.* That was a grim thought, indeed. I lowered my head and hurried onward. Work was my most sure diversion from painful thinking—and there was surely enough of it waiting at home for me.

Josephine and I settled upon a gray kitten, fluffy and green eyed, with mottlings of rusty red streaking the tips of her long fur; she was handsome, indeed. From the first moment we brought the little beast home, Jonathan was enamored of her. A toy that could move and make sounds, brush against his soft cheek to tickle him, jump and pounce and play in the ways he understood.

Mother was skeptical. "Kittens can do damage without meaning to. What if she scratched at his eyes?"

"We'll keep her basket in our room nights," I suggested, knowing it was futile to argue the point with her.

46

"It is not nights I'm concerned about," she rejoined. "I can't keep an eye on that kitten all day."

"She sleeps by the stove for hours," Josephine soothed. "When she's awake I shall keep her with me and only allow her to play with the baby when I am around."

"Kittens grow. And cats are even less to be trusted. She ought to be put out in the barn."

We said nothing. The more we labored a point, we were learning, the more stubbornly she adhered to her unreasonable premises and conclusions. And the little lad took such delight in his pet.

When we were alone together, Josephine turned concerned eyes at me. "It will be worse when I'm gone," she said. "Mother will give you *no* peace."

"We'll deal with that when it comes," I said, a bit surprised by her comment.

"Which will be sooner than we realized."

There was a musing behind her words. Was Josephine entertaining second thoughts? Or just realizing a bit of what it would mean to go from home and forever leave the world of her childhood behind? It struck me then how seldom she let me inside that pretty head of hers, how seldom she spoke of *thoughts and feelings,* rather than opinions, desires, and needs.

It seemed we made an unspoken pact that morning to be united— gently and firmly, but nevertheless united—against our mother whenever necessity required it.

*Against.* There were sad implications in that word which I did not like to think about.

47

# Chapter 6

*Palmyra: Early October 1827*

I saw little of my father. He was always busy in field or barn, I in garden or house. There was a day a few weeks after the kittens episode when he entered the kitchen midmorning, greatly agitated, his countenance dark.

"What is it, Father?" I asked, sitting him down gently and placing a cup of tea in his hand—hoping desperately it was not some new horror about Mother he was to uncover for me.

"I was in one of the public houses this morning, Esther, reading the newspaper from New York, and I overheard Willard Chase and a bunch of his friends talking—nay, boasting together."

"Concerning what?"

I sat down, leaning my chin on my elbows, sensing I would want to hear what my father was going to say.

"Concerning their efforts to discover Joe Smith's gold Bible."

"Do not call him 'Joe,' Father; he has always gone by 'Joseph.' "

"You are right. When these men spit the name *Joe Smith* out of their mouths, venom as thick as saliva, my blood runs cold."

"What is it, this gold Bible? I've not heard mention of it."

"You do not frequent the taverns and public houses." My father grinned and slurped his tea noisily. "I'm not certain, Esther. I believe he claims to have found some ancient record in a hill near here and means to translate and publish it. So *he* says. Folk claim it is a hoax he means to get up for profit."

I raised a skeptical eyebrow. "Sounds unlikely, doesn't it?" His eyes were still clouded, so I added, "Do you believe they are up to some mischief?"

"I do, indeed. They had a conjurer with them, some character who lives a good distance from here, and I don't much like the look of him, if truth be known."

"And what is his purpose here?"

"To discover where Joseph has hidden his treasure. Some think it is just that—a cache of some sort, worth money; not old records at all."

"I see. How did this story first get circulated?" I topped his cup and put out a plate of bread and butter.

"A friend of the Smiths', Martin Harris, told one or two others. Then it spread like wildfire; it seems folk remember still young Joseph's claim of a vision some time back."

"That was six or seven years ago, when we were no more than children!"

"Well . . ." Father shrugged his broad shoulders and stuffed half a slice of bread into his mouth, enjoying the unexpected repast his visit to the house had supplied.

"What were they saying? What do they intend?"

"They intend to go after him and get whatever it is he's hiding. I heard the stranger bawl out, 'I am not afraid of anybody—we will have them plates in spite of Joe Smith or all the devils in hell.' "

I felt a shiver pass over me. "Unsavory character," I muttered. "Do you think they would do him harm?"

"I've no doubt of it, Esther." Father pushed his chair back and took one last draft from his cup.

"Surely there is something you can do to prevent them?"

He shook his head. "What could I do, daughter? Men aren't thinking reasonable when they get actin' like that."

"Go to the sheriff, the constable. Demand that someone aid and protect him!"

"On the strength of a few words I overheard? Do you believe they would pay me mind, child?"

No, I was certain they wouldn't!

" 'Tis a shame, though. It makes my blood rise, why folk can't just leave each other alone. Joseph's done work for me many a time, hasn't he, Esther, and we've never had cause to complain. Indeed, I always preferred him to most of the young men hereabouts. He is the hardest of workers and seems to exert a calming influence upon the others."

I, too, remembered that. "Indeed, it was always so," I agreed.

Father left to return to his work, but I paced the room in frustration. Injustice has always alighted my anger like a match set to kindling! I liked Joseph Smith. I always had. And his was a good family, kindly and neighborly in their ways. I did not understand such goings-on! Thus provoked, I felt an uneasy sensation through the rest of the day.

Late in the afternoon, while the baby slept, Mother and Josephine drove into town. Though I held my tongue, I wished I could ask them to keep their ears open about the Joseph Smith matter. But I dared not trust either one of them. Besides, they were intent on an entirely different sort of errand—the procural of a good set of pots and pans with which Josie could set up housekeeping. Calvin Speer, who ran the mercantile, owed Father for the loan of his mule and harrower and had agreed to a trade.

"Good luck," I cried after them, relieved, if truth were told, to have the house to myself for a spell. I would take an hour, just one precious hour, to catch up on my journal entries and to read a bit further in Walter Scott's *Marmion,* which I had not touched for days.

I had no sooner settled in the parlor, with my books, pen, and ink spread before me, when I heard a knock at the door. The front door—which was used only when guests came. *Who in the world could it be?*

I turned the latch with reluctance, but was unprepared for the figure I saw standing uncomfortably before me, twirling his hat in his hands and not quite meeting my eyes when I invited him in.

"Mr. Hall," I said, "Josephine has driven to town with my mother, just this half hour ago. I fear they will not be back for some time." He stood unmoving. "Is anything the matter? Is there something I can do for you?"

"Forgive me, Esther," he began. "I saw your mother and sister in town, and I fear I acted on impulse."

"You came out to speak to me alone, then?" I have never been one to beat around the bush in important matters. I indicated a chair and sat down myself to encourage him. "Pray proceed, Mr.—"

"Alexander—we are soon to be brother and sister. You may call me Alexander."

"I will, sir, when that time comes."

He coughed into his hand. "The very subject and reason for my coming here."

"The wedding?"

"Yes."

"You are having second thoughts?"

His face colored like a schoolgirl's. "Heaven forbid! Rather the other way around. You see, I am no longer a lad, Esther, but a man who has been this long while alone and companionless. I have tried to be patient with Josephine and give her her head—in this as in all things."

I knew at once where he was going. Why is it so many men have such painful difficulty expressing themselves, save perhaps in matters of business, which is not the same kind of speaking at all?

"You are concerned about the date for which the wedding is set?" I encouraged.

"Yes! You see, every November, before bad weather sets in, I travel to New York on a buying trip—business mainly, but there's always time and money left over for a bit of pleasure!" His skin was flushed still, but I pretended not to notice.

"I see." In truth, I did see. "And it would seem both natural and desirable to have the marriage take place before this date, so that your new wife could travel with you. What a pleasure that would be—a sort of extended honeymoon."

"Yes, I knew you would understand the matter, Esther."

"What does Josephine say?" He hesitated, licked his dry lips. "Come, sir, I have lived with her these many years. You do not need to defer before me."

"She is so set on her own way. She envisions Christmas balls and festivities, herself wearing furs and fine gowns, and everyone there to see her. 'A wedding will go by half-noticed,' she claims, 'if you stick it right in the middle of the harvesting season.'" He sighed. "Perhaps she is right."

"Perhaps."

"She says we can go just as well in December—but it is not that easy, miss. The roads are sometimes impassable by that time, and I have a group of merchants, from various cities throughout the state, who meet at the same places and the same times, year after year. You see, we provide bargains and discounts for one another, purchase and trade, and make projections for the new year."

*Poor man. He shall not find it easy to change his ways,* I thought.

"That does not describe a honeymoon trip," I said gently. "It appears best to me that you continue with your old plan, as usual, and travel to the city yourself." A crestfallen expression was already creeping into his eyes. "A new bride would only distract you—think of it. Perhaps even make things . . . awkward in front of your friends."

He was beginning to take my meaning. "Yes, of course. I . . . did not think of that," he mumbled.

"You were looking forward to the prospect of companionship, of being with your pretty wife. That is understandable."

Alexander Hall swallowed and nodded. "Yes, I confess it." He stood and retrieved his hat from the table where he had placed it. "Perhaps you have the better, the wiser solution, Esther, after all."

"I fear that I do. You know Josephine." I longed to add: *If you don't, you should. And if you do, do you fancy yourself man enough to handle her?* Instead I said only, "There are good things in place in your life that you should not summarily abandon or alter, just because you will be married."

He considered this, holding his hand out in thanks to me. *Gentle soul,* I thought, *she has dazzled you. Pray your sight remains colored in her favor.*

He left as he had come; awkwardly, apologetically. I settled down to my book again—but found it much harder to concentrate than before.

I could not sleep that night. I found myself tossing and turning, distracted by the wind in the low eaves, vexed by the play of light and shadow drawing their shifting patterns across the painted planks of the floor. Was it the conversation I had earlier with Alexander Hall that was upsetting me? Josephine and Mother had come from town well pleased with their purchases, eager about the approaching marriage. Then I remembered Joseph Smith and what my father had told me.

I slipped out of bed and walked to the window. The moonlight was pale, little more than a fairy glow diffusing dimly through the densely leafed trees. I was at home in the world of nature, yet gazing out at the scene I felt myself a mute and ignorant outcast from a world more vast and remote than I could imagine, much less comprehend.

*Sojourners . . . wayfarers on earth.* The words came to me like lines of the poetry I am so fond of reading. "Trailing clouds of glory," Wordsworth had written. I felt no glory. Only a loneliness, a terrible isolation of spirit. I crawled back into my bed, and tried to warm myself into the slumber that eluded me.

Less than four weeks until Tillie's wedding. I turned my thoughts from my sister, who must wait her turn now. Theodora's mother was determined the occasion should be the most dazzling Palmyra had ever known, but Tillie remained listless, only as interested as propriety demanded. Oh, she could dissemble with the best, hold her head high and fool the disinterested masses. I speak of her spirit, her heart—that sacred core of her being to which few of us were privy.

Mrs. Swift had provided Phoebe, our consummate seamstress, with an array of most gorgeous fabrics with which to fashion a trousseau fit for a princess. We licked our lips and caressed the shimmering stretches of linen, watered silk, and heavy lace, a bit envious. By "we" I mean largely Phoebe, Georgeanna, and myself. Josephine delicately removed herself from the temptation of admiration. She had taken my words enough to heart that she resisted criticism and comparison—but what else is lack of interest? And in this case, as my sister well knew, comparison would leave her holding the shabbier end of the stick, and she would have nothing of that.

There was an afternoon, early in October, when I left Phoebe's after spending the major part of the day sequestered in the airless sewing room, my legs cramped with sitting, my fingers cramped with attempting the small finishing stitches that did not come easy to me. I felt the need to walk, stretch my muscles a little, before driving home in the light wagon Father had lent me.

I directed Tansy to the old cemetery and left her by a patch of sweet clover while I climbed the steep, leaf-blown slope to the top. *How long it has been,* I realized, *since I last visited Nathaniel's grave!* I felt an eagerness to be there, to perhaps commune with his spirit, at least seek the peace of those quiet surroundings that seemed like a salve to the soul.

I walked without haste, enjoying the taste of the autumn air and the not unwelcome warmth of the sun on my hair and my uplifted face. At first I noticed no one, as I dropped down on my knees beside the small plot and, with ungloved fingers, brushed the debris away.

There was nothing to intrude, to break the spell of peaceful serenity which enfolded me. When I did hear a sound, I looked up, unalarmed, and felt an unexpected sense of pleasure when I recognized the man who stood over me.

"Your . . ." His eyes were on the dates carved into the small stone.

"My infant brother," I answered, as I rose and extended my hand to him. "Esther Parke. We knew each other in school, though only a little. You are Joseph Smith, are you not?"

With a slight bow he acknowledged it. I had not seen him this close, I realized, since he had become a man grown. He was tall. His warm fingers gripped firmly. His features were strongly drawn, his complexion light, his hair, also lightly shaded, growing thick and luxuriant. There was an expression about his face that made it appear more than affable—*benevolent* was the word that came to my mind. And his blue eyes seemed to penetrate to my heart, so that I found myself suppressing an impulse to confide—right this minute, out of nowhere—all the fears and heartaches of my life to his gentle listening.

I pulled my thoughts back, knowing I must say something. "You are living here with your new wife, I hear."

"Emma and I are about to remove, actually, to Harmony, Pennsylvania, where her family is."

"Oh?"

"I have some work I must accomplish, and hope to be able to succeed with it there." He smiled; a sad smile, I thought, but there seemed a buoyant light in the expression, strange as that may sound.

"Your brother is buried a few feet from here, and you have come to take your leave of him," I guessed.

The smile deepened, but so did the sadness. "Yes. In many ways Alvin was the best of us, and I still miss his kindness and counsel."

I understood. We both turned our faces toward the low spot where the noble young man slept. There seemed no need for conversation between us; I felt an ease in his presence that astounded me.

"Is it a difficult work that awaits you?" I said, wondering at myself for asking the question.

"Indeed, it is that. Challenging beyond what my capacities seem to be—but glorious beyond expression!"

His words, like his look, seemed to enter some inner chamber of my soul and find lodging there. I found myself saying, "I am sorry you have been hounded by crude, greedy men." The expression in his eyes made me falter a little. "My father heard . . . told me something of the matter . . . ," I stumbled.

He nodded solemnly, but that light still danced behind the blue eyes.

"Have you sustained harm from these villains?" I was suddenly curious concerning what happened that night a few weeks ago.

"Not enough to take note of. I was pursued while walking alone through the woods, assaulted several times, but I was always able to fight off my attackers successfully."

"It is a shame," I sighed.

"I have worked for your father several times in the past years," Joseph said, as though just recalling the fact. I nodded in response. "He is a good and just man."

The words of praise pleased me. "He speaks highly of you, as well. Even I remember what a conscientious worker you were."

"It is gratifying to be remembered and regarded with honor," he replied, bowing over my hand, preparing to take leave of me.

"I wish you the best of success in your new ventures," I said with enthusiasm.

"Thank you, Esther. You, too, will realize the desires of your heart and fulfill a good work in your lifetime."

The blue eyes held mine for an instant before the man turned away. I stood a long time after he had left, as though the spell of his presence still lingered, like the benediction of those singular last words he had spoken to me. I marveled at this, at the light and purity of his spirit that I had felt so strongly—and could neither gainsay nor understand.

55

*Chapter 7*

*Palmyra: December 1827*

I am not one who becomes excited over weddings. Indeed, I look upon them as little more than formal necessities, forced upon us by society, necessary in order to get on with the real business of life. I enjoy seeing men and women dressed in their best and looking fine as much as the next person—but I am not enchanted, nor in any way taken in, by the show. Besides, at weddings everything that is real and meaningful is smothered by a layer of excitement and lavish pretense. I prefer the idea of a few choice friends and a small country church, music, and flowers amid sincere, heartfelt congratulations—and the bride not so exhausted and distracted that she cannot even identify what she herself is feeling, much less respond to the feelings of others!

There. I have said my piece—perhaps all the more emphatically because of the two very difficult weddings I went through.

Theodora's marriage *did* take place, much as her father and mother ordained, planned, and executed it. She remained a gentle, pliable participant throughout. I do not know if the beauty and excitement got through to her. Her skin was as pale as new snow, her graceful hands still as white stones in her lap or dropped down at her sides. She smiled; she accepted congratulations with a graciousness that did justice to her spirit and to her excellent upbringing. She wore the glow brides are supposed to have access to; accompanying it: a tiara of jewels in her hair from which her veil floated, diamond-shaped ear drops, a gown exquisitely crafted of the finest tulle over a white satin slip, the skirt ornamented with two rows of festoons, edged with three narrow pipings of cherry-colored satin, arranged so that the roses in the festoon were attached to the broad white satin rouleau at the bottom of the dress, creating a most stunning effect. A bouquet of hand-crafted roses and hyacinths was placed at the termination of each festoon in the upper row, and the sash at Tillie's waist was of broad cherry-colored satin, falling in exquisite folds.

I could go on and on, but to what purpose? She did look more beautiful than she ever had, or perhaps ever will. But that should be able to be said of all brides. Gerard Whittier, resplendent himself, seemed proud enough of her, perhaps genuinely pleased with the young lady who walked at his arm, so that at least appearances were well served.

I had been granted a few moments alone with Tillie the evening before.

"We are to go to Canada for a brief honeymoon," she told me. "Gerard says it is most lovely there."

"So I have always heard."

She smiled nervously. "I shall make the best of it I can, Esther, and try sincerely to love him."

"I know you will, dear."

"And we *are* returning here, you know. Father has given me that assurance. We are to spend six months or so in the city. By then old Mr. Andrews will have retired, and Gerard will step into his vacated position—and I can come home."

"In time for May Day!" I exulted, attempting to encourage her, but then recalling a bit glumly my heavy thoughts on that morning when I had contemplated all the places the coming year might take us.

Latisha, who is only two years younger than Theodora, entered the room then and interrupted our *tête-à-tête*. There was no way I could protest without making a fuss, but there were so many questions I had not yet asked. In the end, as I was leaving and bent to kiss my friend's cheek in farewell, I whispered into her ear, "You must promise to write, Tillie. And give me addresses, if you have them, of places where you will be stopping." She nodded and laid her cheek against mine. "Real letters now, promise! If you are really in need of me, I want no brave theatricals."

"Oh, Esther!" she cried. "How can I bear to be parted from you!"

I held her head to my shoulder and cradled her, as I might cradle a child. Latisha looked on, not attempting to hide her incredulity.

"I am certain *I* shall not react in such a manner when the time comes for me to be wed."

"I am certain you will not," I agreed, equably. "But you know what a tender heart your sister has, and we have been dear friends since our earliest childhood."

Latisha held her pretty nose up in the air, not deigning an answer. She had always been a bit jealous of the closeness we shared, and who could blame her? She was but a few years younger and might well have been included in our group, save for the elusive fact that such unions, I am convinced, form themselves—upon some natural lines that we cannot always even define, much least modify. She did, after all, have friends of her own. But they shared nothing as sweet and extraordinary as what we had known.

I took my leave, feeling my own loss nearly as keenly as I felt hers. I attended the ceremony the next day and the lavish festivities that followed, and watched this handsome, haughty stranger wisk our Tillie away from us to a life that would be no longer a part of our own.

Throughout the evening Josephine chatted gaily, imagining, I am sure, her own approaching enthronement as bride and wife. Phoebe and Georgie and I found a quiet spot near the back of the gardens where we could sit together and mourn for a few moments in peace.

It would have been bad luck to express our concern for Theodora in so many words, but *feeling it* further united us.

"No tears," Georgeanna said brightly when she saw our eyes fill and swim. "Our love must be strong, not weakened by doubts. We send Tillie out upon the current of our love—like a magic carpet to take her forth and uphold her."

How wise Georgie could be!

I half rose from the stone bench, suggesting we return, when my eye caught a movement, and the movement solidified into two solid figures I could recognize—dancing through the shimmering twilight together: Simon Turner and Emily Thorn. *Why is sorrow ever present, no matter the occasion, no matter the efforts of joy to dispel it?* I thought bitterly.

Perhaps Georgie had seen them, too. She turned to Phoebe with a question that kept us occupied for another ten minutes or more. When at last we rejoined the others, Emily was drinking punch with her mother and several other ladies, and Simon was nowhere to be found.

Josephine had things precisely as she wanted, precisely as she had planned. A December wedding, heading off the holiday season with the magnificence she had desired. Ten times prettier than Tillie, she was the picture of elegant, breathtaking beauty; a perfect bride. Alexander Hall was beside himself. His eyes softened and melted whenever he looked at her, and I recalled with a pang that Gerard Whittier had not once looked at Tillie that way. We had thought Theodora would be able to return for the wedding, but a sudden storm crippled the city, while out here the sun shone upon a sparkling wonderland of iced trees and snowy fields. But the streets were passable, and the spirit of the coming holiday was like a spice, crackling the very air with anticipation.

I was happy for my sister. I was nearly as happy for my mother, who looked ten years younger in her new gown, for which no expense had been spared, and with her hair piled atop her head in one of the latest fashions and her pleasure softening the harsh lines the years had etched in her face. My father was gallant with her, and Josie most gracious, so that both of them shone like fair lights that night. I was glad of it. I was glad to sit back, an observer by choice.

But what infectious madness do weddings engender? Not one but several old ladies took up seats beside me and, without asking, offered their sage advice.

"It is time for you, my pretty. The men will not wait forever while you make up your mind."

*Where has this come from?* I wondered the first time.

"You have your older sister wed now, Esther. It is time to look to yourself. So many nice boys would be willing if you will but give them the chance."

"You can follow soon enough yourself, dear, if you wish. I should like to see you happily wed, lass, and settled down. You will make a better wife than half the girls in the village."

A wise nod of the head. A scolding finger, kindly wagged. A gray head bent close to pronounce its gentle warning. I nodded graciously to each of them, though I was seething inside. And I was entertaining such a mood when Eugene Thorn stood before me and asked if he might pull up his chair beside mine.

I acquiesced—anything to rid myself of this gaggle of annoying, though well-intentioned, counselors! I knew how Eugene felt about me, but I had not expected the wedding spirit to overcome him as well!

"Esther," he began after a few minutes, lifting up my hand and holding it loosely in both of his. "You look truly lovely tonight."

*Beauty from within,* I thought. But his eyes were shining, so I held my peace.

"You have always believed Josephine to be prettier than you are," he scolded. "It distresses me, Esther, that you cannot perceive your own beauty, how much more powerful and alluring it is than hers!"

I bent over the punch cup he had placed on the low table before us and sniffed it, and he laughed despite himself, shattering the intensity his words had created.

"Really, Esther," he persisted, stroking my hand, leaning close to me. "Do not put me off this way. Do not make it so hard for me to speak of matters that—that are close to my heart."

I stared back, astonished. Whatever could he wish to talk about—here?

Perhaps he sensed my reluctance. We sat in the ballroom of the *Queen of the Erie* hotel, which had cost the new, beaming husband a pretty penny. It was too cold to go outside. Nevertheless there was a lovely promenade of sorts opening into four small, cozy reception rooms. "Will you walk with me, Esther?"

I could not refuse him. We crossed the length of the room, nodding and speaking to friend and acquaintance on either side.

"This will not do," Eugene fumed.

"It will do well enough," I replied gently. "What is it you want?"

He would not answer. He steered me, instead, along the wide hall until we came to the first room. "In here," he said, "where we can breathe for a moment alone."

I sighed. I had been fond of Eugene for as long as I could remember. He has a gentle heart and a good mind, and I had found that he could be trusted. And he did look handsome that night! I enjoyed the touch of his hand on my arm as he encouraged me in the right direction. I had always liked the sense of his nearness. When I was a young girl I sometimes used to dream about—

"Esther." There was such a yearning in his voice that I looked up and smiled. "Forgive me if all this"—he waved his arm vaguely—"has increased my desire for you. I have loved you for so long, Esther."

*And you have loved me so well.* I felt the warm color rise to my cheeks, unable to prevent it.

"I want you to be mine. I know I can make you happy—or at least I shall spend my whole life in trying."

The earnest face bent over mine suddenly took on an expression so boyish, so vulnerable, that my heart raced. His dark eyes were very close to mine, his mouth so near that I could see the pulse beating in his throat, feel his breath—

I let him kiss me. I was nearly twenty years old and had my own hungers to deal with. Perhaps I believe every girl should celebrate weddings with a kiss of her own. I closed my eyes, and I felt his touch like a warm fire spread over my flesh.

"I love you, Esther . . . my beautiful Esther . . ." He spoke the words against my lips, against my cheek, against my neck, where his mouth pressed and seared.

I pulled gently away from him. "Eugene, please." I faced his gaze squarely.

"Marry me, Esther," he said.

I hesitated, then shook my head gently. "In good time," I murmured, "in good time, Eugene. There is enough of marriages just now."

"None more hopeful of happiness and harmony than ours," he protested.

"Which is exactly why we can wait."

"You make no sense, Esther."

"Reason never makes sense when spoken to passion," I told him. Then I tried to explain. "First and foremost, I cannot even think about leaving Mother yet, before she has even accustomed herself to the loss of one daughter."

"Your mother will never give you up easily, especially now."

I knew what "especially now" meant. It was a reference to Jonathan and her unnatural protectiveness in regard to him, her general neglect in regard to all else.

"This is true," I conceded. "But I could not be cruel enough to leave her unprepared, Eugene."

He knew already that he had lost. He sighed and turned his face away from me, attempting to hide the bitterness that twitched along his muscles, defining the fine lines of jawbone and cheek.

I took that dear face in both my hands and turned him back to me, distressed at the pain I was causing him. "I love you, too," I cried suddenly. "I believe I have loved you for years."

He glowed from the inside out. He caught up my hands and pressed them both to his lips. "I believed you loved me," he breathed. "But hearing you speak the words makes all the difference." I could feel the pulsing of his joy through his fingertips. I smiled, a bit tremulously.

I wished to do nothing to spoil it. So I met his warm lips again—astounded at myself, at the eagerness with which everything within me responded to his caress.

The weather held for Josephine's wedding, and then broke forth with a fury. She and Alexander were stranded in New York City; dismal prospect. But Josie made it into an adventure and turned her husband's fussing concerns into delight and wonder; she has a natural talent for that. *I hope she loves him a little,* I found myself thinking. *I hope she comes back really loving him.*

Correspondence from Tillie had been skimpy over the months, to say the least. Was it fortuitous or a stroke of ill luck that, because Josie was so long in the city, she found out where Theodora was living and paid her a surprise visit, hoping to delight her old friend? She is canny, Josie is, and saw at once through the brave facade of things. When she arrived home this was the first thing she told me, giving it precedence over the recital of her own amusing and amazing experiences.

"Does Tillie live in a grand house? No, she does not," she stated emphatically, curling her long legs up beneath her and settling into the corner of the sofa with as much ease as a cat. "Does she have money? Enough. The remnants of what might once have been legitimate, even impressive. The Whittiers command a certain respect in the city, all right. I looked into that."

"How clever of you." I resented her matter-of-fact, almost gloating manner. But, of course, she brushed this mere annoyance aside.

"It is a *brother-in-law*, Esther, who manages the bank Gerard boasted of running. Imagine that! He *is* in banking, all right. A junior partner of some sort, bound to his relatives because of his own intemperance and high living."

"Do not tell me this," I pleaded, covering my eyes with my hand.

"So, you see," she continued, ignoring me, "he has lied to the lot of them. *I* believe his family sent him to Palmyra to marry well, in hopes it would settle him down a bit. He could not look for a bride from among their own society, for everyone there knows of his ways."

I felt sick to my stomach and a little light-headed. *My poor brave Tillie. No wonder she has not written much to me. She knows how easily I read between the lines.*

"Do not tell the others—do not tell anyone else!" I entreated.

"Really, Esther." My request did not please Josephine. "Are you not making a little much of this? He'll come back to Palmyra and make a finer living than most still. And Tillie will be a grand lady here."

I stared back at my sister. Then, unable to help myself, I blurted. "*Grand lady!* Married to a man who has deceived her—a weak man, unworthy of her trust and affection. You are married yourself, Josie—how would that sit with you?"

She fidgeted a bit.

"Why do you choose to be blind and unfeeling?" I continued. "Have you learned no compassion yet?"

Josephine sighed and unwound herself. "I am sorry this brings you such pain, Esther. I should have known."

"Does he treat her ill?" I had to ask it! "Have you seen him treat her ill, Josie?"

"He behaved like the perfect gentleman when I was around."

"He knows his manners, at least," I thought aloud, "and observes them. But what of when they are alone?"

"She can avoid having overmuch to do with him, you know. In such a marriage, that is not difficult."

"As long as she keeps out of his way!"

"She has money to spend, Esther. He would not dare deny her that. And there is so much to do in the city!"

"Especially when one is lonely and unhappy, removed from friends and family."

63

"How dramatic you are! I had forgotten." Josephine spoke the words with unconcealed distaste.

"Do you promise me?"

"Promise you what?"

"You know very well, Josephine! It is most important Theodora must at least have a good reputation to hide behind."

"Oh, all right. You are so tedious, Esther." Josephine stretched herself full length and yawned. She was really quite beautiful, with a shapely form to be envied. And she had taken on a contented air, like a cat who has just licked to the last drop a full bowl of cream.

*At last she is being pampered as she has always desired,* I thought. *Perhaps she has made the right choice after all.*

Mother was delighted to have Josephine home again. She had Father harness Tansy to the light wagon nearly every day and insisted we drive over to Josie's house, to take tea, to examine her new acquisitions, to waste time in the most inane conversations.

I accompanied her the first three mornings, then begged off upon the valid excuse that I had work to do that could not forever be neglected. She took Jonathan with her, of course. She liked having me to drive, so that she could hold him on her lap securely. But Father contrived a way to tie him to the seat with strips of old sheeting that would hold him upright and safely secure. The lad was approaching a year. He was large and long-legged for his age, especially in view of his rather puny beginnings. This pleased and encouraged us all. He remained a sweet-tempered child, despite the affections smothered upon him. I was even more grateful for that.

We girls, minus Tillie, had met a mere three days following Josephine's return, that we might hear of all her adventures. We drank gallons of tea and sat in Georgie's sunny parlor for hours. I was a bit nervous the entire while, but she kept her promise and spoke not a word concerning the horrors she had uncovered. *How long will this last?* I could not help wondering. *One day she will give in to her impulses, with the excuse that she had simply slipped without thinking, that she had meant no harm at all.*

I made it a point to send a letter off to Tillie weekly, as regular as clockwork. After a while she began to reply, sharing with me tidbits and snatches of what she was doing from day to day. Every now and again she would write, "Gerard and I went to the theatre," or "Gerard and I took tea at his sister's." I know she wanted me to see him as part of her life, to believe all was well. I wanted that, too. But I was unable to provide what was not there to see.

Josephine purred through her days, her contentment spreading to encompass Mother. I had no objections to that. It had the effect of calming her a little and thus making our lives more pleasant. I saw Eugene on Sundays when Father and I went to meeting. Sometimes he drove me home in his smart buggy behind his matched team. Sometimes he stayed for supper, and sat into the evening with me, listening to the poems and snatches of stories I chose to read to him. Every so often dances were hosted in the town hall, and he would call for me, and we would spend the entire evening together. At such times the intimate feeling that had been with us since Josie's marriage would wrap its warm tentacles round us. We would attempt to bask in it and ignore it, both at once; we would struggle to be content. In this manner the weeks became months, and the months went by.

# Chapter 8

## Palmyra: Early April 1828

**T**illie is home! I saw them coming from the canal in her father's carriage. And, Esther, there were two wagons behind them filled to the gills with their things!"

In my pleasure over her news I laughed at Josephine's silliness. "How soon do you think she will call on us?"

"Why don't we call upon her?"

Her words burst my bright bubble. "We must give her time to settle first, Josie." Already my thoughts, grown suddenly uneasy, shifted back and forth, trying to guess at facts I did not know yet. "Do you suppose they will stay with her folks for a while?"

"I've no doubt of it. That house can accommodate more than two families without them running into one another for days on end!"

Josephine was happy still. She had fallen into a routine with her new husband which pleased them both. He worked long hours overseeing the work in both his mills and all the details that go with operating a large, growing business. She had her days free to do very much as she pleased, for Alexander maintained the services of the woman who had done housekeeping for him when he lived alone. Josephine could sleep late, go shopping, daydream away her hours—and her salvation was that she knew how to cook! The old adage "The way to a man's heart is through his stomach," has much truth in it. She kept him well fed, with mouth-watering dishes, and her companionship through the long evenings was enjoyable, making him feel vital and young, I would suppose.

I was much surprised the day following Tillie's arrival to see her mother's fine carriage coming up our long drive. I ran out to meet her, unable to suppress my excitement.

"So soon?" I cried. "I had not dared hope for this."

"Mother sent me," she confessed. "They will let me do nothing to help."

How thin and pale she looked, her almond-shaped eyes too big in her face, the length of her nose accentuated by this unnatural gauntness. I knew at once.

"You are with child! How soon—when is the baby expected? Come inside and tell all."

I insisted on settling her in mother's rocker with a nice cup of tea, however, before I would let her begin.

"It happened almost at once, Esther, I fear," she confided. "And I do not want to be a mother—so soon."

I understood. I entertained insecurities of my own concerning that role; not aggravated, as hers were, by a husband I could not trust.

"You are here now, sweetness," I assured her, "and we shall all pamper and care for you, and make it all right." I watched as tears filled her eyes. "Is it more, Tillie?" I asked gently. But she shook her head and lifted her cup to her lips.

*Not yet,* I thought. *She is not ready to confide in me yet. Stating a sad truth outright to another person makes it all the more perilous. Then where is there to hide?*

67

Ills never come singly, but in twos or threes. So it happened with us. The same week Theodora returned to Palmyra, Phoebe appeared at my door. I thought she had come to collect some fabric remnants I had said I would give her to use in making clothes for Tillie's layette. But it was not that at all.

"Sit down and cut yourself a piece of this ginger cake," I said, "while I gather them together for you."

She put her hand on my arm. "I had a visit from Simon last evening."

I stopped and sat down beside her. I could see the veins, thin and purple, beneath her high, broad forehead; with Phoebe a sure sign of distress. *A visit from Simon,* spoken like a death knell. "He is marrying Emily, isn't he?"

"He came to tell me himself, so that I might not be unkindly surprised by someone else blurting the news of it to me."

"That was generous of him." I tried to keep the biting edge from my words.

"I have long expected it." Softly spoken. "In some ways, it is even a relief—just having the thing done and settled, you know."

*To be sure. But you have never loved anyone besides Simon,* I thought to myself. *And I doubt if you ever will.*

"Life goes on." She sighed and reached for the gingerbread, then let her hands fall back in her lap. Even her long, glossy ringlets seemed to droop with the general air of despondency.

"Oh, Phoebe. Why must it be like this? Why must life hold more disappointments than it does pleasures?"

"Esther, you know that is not true. You—of all people—seem to know how to look for the good and find it."

I shook my head. "Not really."

"You feel others' sufferings too deeply—and believe that it is, somehow, up to you to cure all of them."

We smiled at each other then, and I went in search of the fabric, and at length sent her on her way. But a helpless feeling, the keenness of her deep disappointment, accompanied me like a clinging, mocking shadow which I could not dislodge or send scampering away.

The third trouble showed itself soon after.

On Sunday morning, following the service, Eugene asked if he might drive me home. There was something subdued about his manner, and he remained quiet even after we had left the busy streets of the village behind.

"What is it, Eugene?"

"Nothing much, except that you have come off victor and shall have your way after all."

"You are talking in riddles. Pull off up ahead into that little copse of plane trees where we can talk."

He did so, silent still. I could see the muscles in his lean jaw working.

"Something has happened. Please tell me."

"My father has need of me."

A strange, disconnected beginning. "Your father has always had need of you, since you were a boy of nine or ten."

It was true. Eugene's father was a blacksmith, and Eugene his eldest son. He had run a modest establishment, with only himself to work it, until his son became old enough to train in the trade and be of some assistance to the father. Eugene was adept with riveter, sledge and anvil, but he had little heart for it. What he liked most—and what recommended him most to me!—was the written word, the smell of ink, and the clattering sound of the printing press hard at work. He had already served the better part of an apprenticeship in the local printing press, done reporting, and turned in copy for our daily newspaper. Modest beginnings; but most beginnings are modest. He entertained, as all creative minds do, extremely high hopes. Now, unwittingly, his father and I had combined to squelch and oppress those hopes and ambitions that were dearest to him.

"Well, now an opportunity has presented itself for him to buy out old man Simpson and step into an outfit worth having, with tools and equipment—*and customers*—he's only dreamed about."

I responded slowly, my own thoughts turning. "I am happy for him, Eugene, as I am sure you are, too."

"I didn't expect the news to distress you, Esther, the way it does me."

69

If his voice had been angry or edged with sarcasm I might have reacted differently. As it was, I flung my arms round his neck. "I deserve such a rebuke from you," I cried, pressing my lips to his cheek. "You have been patient with me and full of kindness and tenderness. My heart truly aches for you!"

He half grinned. "Too late. My luck, of course." But he had relaxed a little, and my touch had soothed his feelings and fears.

"Has he the money necessary to lay out for a purchase?"

"Every cent he's scrimped and saved over the past twenty years will barely do it. But that means he cannot pay labor until he gets on his feet again, until profits begin to come in."

"How long, do you think?"

"*He* thinks six months to a year. I said I'd give him the six months, then six more to work for us—which means a spring wedding, Esther."

"What I have always wanted."

"Aye, spring, with your precious gardens all planted and starting to bloom."

"May," I breathed.

"May it shall be. But—I must have your word on it, Esther."

*This day—this very moment?* I wondered. I looked into his eyes. The green lights in them were burning, and I knew my answer was yes.

"What are you saying—exactly?" I demurred, wanting a bit more.

"I am saying I love you with all the energy and devotion of my soul, Esther." He put his hands over both of mine where they lay in my lap. "I want you to belong to me—and I want to belong to you. I want to be together for as long as the good Lord will grant us." He stopped. His deep-set eyes, penetrating mine, softened. "Will you marry me, Esther?"

"Yes. With all of my heart, Eugene. I will be proud to become your wife."

He enfolded me in his arms with such exquisite tenderness that I felt like a piece of fine Dresden he was afraid he might break. The reverence of that touch made this one of the most wonderful moments of my life. I leaned against him, feeling the lean strength of his body, and I reached up a finger to touch his hair where it curled at his neck.

We remained thus a long time. It seemed all eternity had stopped for us—held its breath at the wonderment of our joy.

I remember thinking, as we covered the remaining distance to my father's homestead, *How filled with surprises life is! What appeared as a difficulty, a setback, a denial, is really a spur to action, to the fulfillment of hopes and promises worth working and waiting for.*

By mutual consent, we told no one of our engagement. It was enough that we each knew—and held the hallowed certainty in our hearts.

Plans for the May Day festivities were eclipsed by the frenzied planning for Simon and Emily's wedding, of which we girls were determined to be a part. Eugene's words still echoed in the back of my mind: *If Emily marries Simon, you five will ostracize and abandon them both.* I wanted nothing of that sort to take place. There is enough sorrow in this world of ours, heaven knows. I did not wish to live with such a weight of unhappy guilt on my head.

Phoebe understood. We had her tacit support. But I did not let myself think overmuch about the terrible cost her gallant heart paid. A six-week engagement! I believe they both were so nervous about it, they just wanted to get the deed done. So we four padded our heartache with good intentions and lent our efforts in support of the cause.

I should say, we three. Phoebe was, understandably, excused. But, by and large, so was Tillie. She had not the strength at present to do much of anything. Many an afternoon her mother, or one of her father's employees, would drive her here in the carriage, and I would set the rocker out under the shade near to where I was working, preparing the soil to receive my first seedlings, and we would talk. Oh, we neither revealed nor uncovered anything earth-shattering. We merely let the sun seep into us, as healing as the unspoken affection that united our hearts.

At such times, what can one person do for another, save hold forth the sacred offering of love? If I had probed and learned of my friend's deepest secrets—uncovered her fears and revealed them—what good would that do? Only love has power to strengthen or alter—I was beginning to understand and believe this as I never had done before.

71

May Day came, however, three weeks before the wedding. But the magic was not there as it had been the year before. A fine drizzle of rain subdued the ardor of the celebration, shortening the frolicking of limp-frocked women and their ardent companions. Even the food had to be served inside the cramped, steamy church house rather than out-of-doors.

*Happiness can never be repeated or replicated the way we want it to be,* I realized. We five girls, shimmering with youthful hopes only one brief year ago, had perhaps made a pretty picture. But the components had changed. The image would never again be simple and picture-perfect.

*Life offers compensations,* I told myself. *The real thing is better than the shallow illusion.* So I told myself over and over again.

I forget at times that Georgie is what is commonly called "a sleeper." There is much more to her than the pleasant, congenial surface that meets the eye. How many times had she said during the past weeks, "I am not in a hurry to find a husband. I have my teaching to challenge me and my cats to comfort me; I am content."

Yet here she was, I noticed, on the arm of a young man—leaning close to speak something into his ear, laughing at his witticisms, vibrant in a manner I had never seen in our Georgie before.

The young man, whom she introduced as Nathan Hopkins, was the new teacher who had been hired and brought in to replace old Isaac Rogers, who must, by all means, hold the record for the most elderly teacher in the entire state of New York.

"Remember, I told you," Georgie prompted. "The school board had agreed to let Isaac finish this term, but his eyesight kept getting worse. He could not read the words the children wrote in their composition books—could not see enough to do the necessary writing or correcting of assignments himself."

"That is too bad." I recalled now that she *had* told me about it.

"Yes, he was a true teacher, and served well. The children will miss him for a long time to come, and that is how it should be." She patted the arm linked through hers, entirely at ease. "But we, and they, have been fortunate in his replacement."

"Mr. Hopkins came highly recommended, I remember."

"Yes, and beyond recommendations, he is a good man. And sincerely interested in his students' welfare."

Nathan Hopkins was not as comfortable with this interchange as was his companion, but he smiled amiably. He was a large-framed man; nothing slender or scanty about him. There was a kindness and openness to his features I liked. Indeed, I would almost call him handsome, with his round smooth cheeks, his round brown eyes—even his head was round with its crown of brown hair. He spoke in the same manner; his words were softly rounded and pleasing to the ear, not sharply clipped or sloppily muttered.

So, Georgeanna was drawn to him. If he was what he appeared to be, I could understand why. At times I envy her ability to take life as it comes, make the best of things, and move on. She does not torture herself with trying to understand, the way I do. Nor does she foolishly attempt to change what cannot be changed. Such practical wisdom I lack. If it had not been for the peace of my gardens and my books, I would have been a sorry jangle of nerves and frustration!

❧

As things turned out, we girls, in deference, stayed a bit on the periphery of this particular wedding. Emily felt ill at ease when we were around, and I understood that. How could she rejoice openly and freely with our presence, our composed faces, a constant reminder of the awkwardness of her joy? Enough to let her know that we supported and did not resent her. Enough for the future to build upon.

Simon was just as bad. He could not look any of us in the face. Quiet, gentle Simon, with his narrow boyish features, with the somewhat perplexed, somewhat watchful expression he always wore on his face! He had done nothing disgraceful. And it was true: sooner or later he *had* to make a choice that was incapable of making both women happy, or, for that matter, of making him entirely happy. I believed he would always cherish deep feelings for our Phoebe; though this was not to say he would not make a very good and faithful husband to Emily. Of that I had no doubt.

Though not lavish, by any means, the modest wedding seemed to capture a beauty and dignity that touched my heart deeply. I was closer to the event than the other girls, because Eugene is Emily's brother, and I was there on his arm—there with his eyes saying every time I looked up at him, *Very soon now our turn will come. And there will be no wedding like our wedding, Esther, no love like ours!*

I found myself inclined to agree with him! I found myself longing for him, in every sense of the word: reluctant to be removed from his presence; feeling flat and peevish and at loose ends when our responsibilities drew us in separate directions, shattering the harmony which seemed to exist only when we were together, moving and thinking as one.

73

## Chapter 9

*Palmyra: July 1828*

Josephine waited until the wedding was over to tell her news; I am sure she did not wish the simple little event to eclipse her in any way.

"I, too, am with child," she announced, her creamy cheeks glowing.

"You are keeping right up with Tillie," Georgeanna teased; then, seeing her face, ran to hug her. "I am pleased for you, Josie! When do you anticipate the new arrival?"

My sister appeared studied for a moment. " 'Tis difficult to say yet. Perhaps January—perhaps a little earlier, to celebrate Christmas and our wedding anniversary and the birth of our first child all at once."

*How she does love celebrations,* I thought—*and herself the center of the festivities!*

Her generally sedate and somewhat taciturn husband received the news with an anticipation that was irresistible. This was an experience I do not believe he had truly expected. He had remained unmarried for such a long time that he had put thoughts of fatherhood away from him, as a state obtainable for others but not for himself. Oh, how he did try to conceal his almost child-like pleasure at this wonder which had been laid at his feet! Watching him, one had to smile in response to his pleasure.

Of course, Josephine glowed—as though she had done something incredibly unique and clever already, which, perhaps, in a way she had. Conception—birth—the coming forth of new life is, indeed, a miracle. Perhaps it was merely the way she seemed to take personal credit for it that was a bit galling to me.

Excitement in the air. Change. Constant change. I suppose that is what life is: a constant sifting, readjusting, redefining; nothing ever static and predictable.

Except, perhaps, Nature. Here the same flowers grow each year from the same seeds: the nurturing cycle, the ripening, the bearing, the reaping—these, thank heaven, remain timeless and true.

The long, sultry summer is upon us. I enjoy it. I am content in the little things, in the slow, languid hours, in the quiet places where bees hum and the lazy cat stretches herself in the sun. I know that here there is little change. I know that I avoid change whenever I can. My little brother has changed. He patters barefoot among the rows of my gardens, careful to avoid stepping upon the growing plants. He examines the caterpillars and potato bugs that roll up like tiny gray pebbles against the palm of his hand. He is a sweet child. Sometimes I look into his eyes and think of the other one sleeping on the hill above the city and wonder what he would have been like—what the two of them would have been like together. Does Jonathan, in some manner he cannot yet define, miss the brother he never knew? The bond between twins is a very real thing. Is there some part, however small, missing in this perfect little boy digging in the dirt at my feet?

Solemn thoughts. Jonathan holds up a bit of bright-colored glass for me to examine. There is wonder in his eyes, like a glow shining outward. It is the same wonder I feel, but cannot express as openly or innocently. This is certainly one of the reasons why children are so essential to the balance and well-being of life.

I was there to see for myself. Tillie and I had been to visit the milliner, and she had asked me to drive home with her to examine some baby things one of her neighbors had sent over. We were in a fine mood, in keeping with the fair, gentle morning which was unfolding around us. Was it happenstance only that we decided to walk round the grounds to pick grapes from the sagging vines that grew along her father's back fence? Was it chance only that took us there at the moment Randolph stumbled out of his mother's toolshed, clothes rumpled, face mottled, and breath soured with the effects of too much cheap whiskey?

When I saw Tillie's face I made her sit on one of the long, cushioned benches scattered throughout the grounds, and ran to confront the lad myself, before he could slink away.

"What nonsense have you been up to?" I demanded.

Randolph sucked at his bottom lip and said nothing.

"You spent the night in there?" I indicated the shed with a movement of my head, and he nodded. I knew boys well enough to skip over the obvious. "Was there more than a drunken brawl involved—is that why you could not return to your quarters?"

I had looked into his eyes. I saw fear there, as well as dull misery. He stared back at me now; answer enough. "Was anyone hurt?" I pressed. "Are you in danger?"

Randolph swallowed painfully. "Some was hurt, I do fear, Esther. Though it was none of my doing. They were after us from the start."

Tillie was leaning forward, attempting to hear us, catching only a word or two. I led him a few yards away to where the shading arms of an old apple tree served to partly obscure us. I did not want him to bolt and run.

"What friends were you with? Who was after you, and for what reason?" Silence and a shuffling. "Randolph, speak to me. Have you not always been able to trust me?"

With a sort of shudder passing over his face and along his thin frame the boy acquiesced. "I've a bunkmate and a couple of other chums. They sell cheap corn liquor and make a bit of a profit on the side. But it's thrown them in with a rough lot."

"I am not surprised."

"Well, it's a rough life for the most of them, Esther. Boys with no homes to go back to. Some with no folks at all. They have to make it on their own, one way or another."

"And what about you? That is *their* excuse. What reason have you for such stupidity?"

"You don't understand!"

"Do not choose to misunderstand me and be offended," I retorted. "*You know better!* And you have better awaiting you, Randolph. Don't let the canal harden you like the others."

"The canal was my father's idea in the first place. You know how he prides himself—and we must all fit the pattern of the hardworking Swifts, who can handle anything and roll up their sleeves with the best and the worst of men."

"I know this, indeed," I replied.

"I have to survive, Esther." Randolph moved to lean against the cool roughness of the tree.

"You look miserable," I told him. "How much sleep did you get last night?"

He shook his head and ran his hand through his tousled hair. "Don't know. Don't care. I have to hightail it and get back now, Esther, if I don't want a tanning."

"Why don't you give it up, as your brother did?" I suggested.

The beginnings of a grin played at the corners of his mouth. "I like it too well."

"You like the roughness and the danger?"

"Maybe. I like the adventure. I like answering to anybody rather than *him*." He indicated with a black look the house that loomed a short distance off.

"Be very sure of that," I said, speaking the words slowly, with emphasis, and placing my hands on his arms. "Be certain sure, Randolph. For you may get exactly what you are now after, my dear boy—and no more."

For the space of a heartbeat he met my eyes, then slipped from under my fingers and, with a few deft movements of hand and foot, vaulted the fence and called out from the other side.

"Do not betray me, now, Esther. You promised!"

With a sigh I waved at his departing figure, then turned back to face Tillie, sitting white-faced and silent. "I do not believe he even noticed you here," I began, seeing the disappointment that darkened her eyes.

"He is in trouble, isn't he?"

"I believe he is," I confessed reluctantly. " 'Tis almost unavoidable considering the conditions and the company! Can you not speak to your father and get the boy out of there?"

I regretted the words as soon as they were out of my mouth. Her mouth tightened into a painful little line and she shook her head.

"Talk to my father! That would never have been possible, but so much less so now that he is"—her eyes widened as her mind searched for the right words—"displeased with us."

"*Us?* Perhaps your husband, Tillie. But—"

She shook her head again. "There is no difference in his mind."

"The baby. Is your father not pleased at the thought of a grand-child?" I was groping, as well as attempting to divert her.

Her sad mouth lifted in a brave little smile. "More than he wants to admit—I hope. Once he gets us settled in a house of our own, and the image back in place as it should be—successful son-in-law, and all that—"

"Gerard is not all your father hoped he was?" I offered tentatively.

"You might say that." The thin smile again.

"But there is surely a legitimate place for him here? He can be of use to your father?"

"I believe and sincerely hope so." Theodora sighed. Her sweet al-mond eyes trembled with the emotion she was suppressing. "Father despises deception of any sort. There is now a coolness and a caution between the two men."

"Just what you need." I tried to make light of it. There was no re-sponse from her. "Well, surely men have their place in one's life," I con-tinued recklessly, "but they are not the *whole* of it."

"They need *not* be . . ." Tillie sat up a little straighter and re-garded me intently. "But it will be that way with you. When you marry Eugene you will give him your whole heart, Esther. For you it could be no other way."

I sputtered, taken aback by her blunt perception.

"I wish . . . oh, well!" She shook her head as though to clear it of all thought, all feeling. "We cannot always determine our fate."

"But we can determine to be happy, despite it!" I cried, placing my arms round her and pulling her up to her feet. "And we have this to look forward to, don't we?" I placed my hand on the swell of her stom-ach. She smiled back; a true smile, freely given. "Let us go in and see those tiny treasures now."

She led the way. I felt a bit of a hypocrite, spurring my dear friend on to gaiety and a courageous acceptance, when I was still miserable in my own heart, still trying to forget the pinched face and glazed eyes of the lad who had run so eagerly back into a world that was flexing its claws in its eagerness to tear and harm and weaken him—run pell-mell, with no one to stop or protect him at all.

78

*No rest for the wicked!* Georgie came to tell me the news, and I did not believe her.

"It cannot be true," I said bluntly. "Her parents would never permit it."

"Her parents have no idea!" Georgie laughed.

*Tillie's sister, Latisha, keeping company with a canal man!* "Does Tillie know?" I asked. "Does anyone—who could do anything?"

"I have no idea. Nathan Hopkins heard two of the women teachers talking about it—Ellen Thompson was always a favorite with the young girls. Perhaps Latisha confided in her."

"The girl has always been headstrong," I stewed, "and after observing what marriage has done to her sister, perhaps more determined than ever to decide her own fate—while, truth is, she is merely doing to herself what her father did to Theodora!"

"Do not fume so," Georgie said soothingly. "We know nothing of the man in question. Perhaps he has much to recommend him."

"Oh, Georgie," I wailed. "You shall make an excellent mother with your patience and wisdom. I run off like a house afire every time something sparks my emotions!"

She smiled indulgently. "That is what we all love about you, Esther! You really and truly *care.*" She planted a kiss on my cheek. "Say nothing to Tillie or Josephine just yet."

"Of course not."

She was halfway down the walk before I hurried after her. "Georgie," I cried. "School is not in session now. How is it you were in the company of Nathan Hopkins?"

She turned her head and tossed me a bright smile. "He has been seeking *my company* of late."

"With no objections, I gather?"

*How pretty Georgie is when her black eyes are sparkling!* "Absolutely no objections at all!"

This has been a profitable summer for my father. His wheat is producing abundantly. He purchased a new mule for himself and lumber to frame in a room at the back of the house for my mother, with windows looking southeast so that the sun will slant warmly on winter afternoons—a room where she can spin and set up a loom without our constantly tripping over it.

I find this most thoughtful of him. I believe Mother does, too, though she will not express such emotions in my presence. But now he goes farther than that. He has asked her to travel with him on one of the boats to the city—view the ocean and tall buildings for herself, eat in a few fancy restaurants, stay in a nice rooming house. I am amazed at this kind of generous proposal coming from my father. I am even more amazed by my mother's response: she has flatly turned him down.

"I could not think of leaving Jonathan for so long," she tells us. "What would he do without me?"

"Be just fine," I assure her, biting my temper.

"What would I do without him?" *This is the crux of the matter, after all.*

"Try not to worry," I tell her. "I am fully capable of taking care of the child. Think of it, Mother. Father has promised you new frocks and bonnets in the very latest fashions." She is as vain of her person as Josephine is, and shares the same weakness for fine clothes.

"Theodora's sister-in-law lives in the heart of New York, remember. She has offered to send anything we ask for. She is very accommodating."

"Mother, *please!*"

She lifted her great child-like eyes to mine, moist with fear. But my father had already turned and walked quietly from the room.

"He doesn't understand. None of you do!"

I turned from her, too, not wanting her to see the look that came over my face.

That was two weeks ago. My father did not pick up the boat tickets he had the agent set aside for him. He has not mentioned the outlandish notion again. When I drove to Tillie's the day before yesterday I offered to take Jonathan along with me. Mother declined.

"There is plenty enough for him to do here," she said, "without letting him get under your feet."

Even Josephine cannot cajole him away from Mother.

"I shall soon have a child of my own," she consoles. "Surely Mother will let Jonathan come then, to play, to help me care for the baby."

I nod, but I do not hold my breath. I have noticed that my father finds more and more projects to do of an evening after the dinner meal is eaten—things that keep him in the barn or about the yard until the late summer darkness at last nudges him inside. By then my mother has usually gone to bed and the house is silent. He either tiptoes back to join her, without the aid of a candle, or dozes by the fire long after I have kissed him on the forehead and gone to my own room.

81

## Chapter 10

*Palmyra: August 1828*

I encountered Latisha's "gentleman in question," not by accident, but because she had the audacity to bring him round on purpose to meet me! I believe she enjoyed my discomfort as I struggled with how to react to him, how to behave.

Brazen! Latisha was barely seventeen and thought she knew enough about everything; and that ignorance was her worst enemy. She is, really, not much prettier than her sister, but she has more spirit than Theodora and a willfulness of which we girls—who used to mind her when she was still in nappies—had long been aware.

Jonah Sinclair. That was a fine name, fit enough for a gentleman. The man who owned it did not look anywhere near that part. He was short and ordinary-looking, with so much hair growing on his head and face that he gave the appearance of being bushy and unkempt; in truth, he was not particularly clean. He must have been at least twenty-six or twenty-seven to Latisha's seventeen, perhaps more; perhaps he carried his age well, as many men do. What was more, he worked as a towpath walker along the canal, and told me so with no more compunction than if he had said he was a cutthroat and highwayman.

Yet Latisha corrected my thinking—which she could read on my face most clearly—by the explanation she gave.

"The men who walk the path are usually the skilled and trained ones, the same who dug the channel and made it work in the first place, and Jonah is one of these. He knows more than anyone else, so he checks the locks and aqueducts for the least sign of cracks or erosion. Anything important, or really life-threatening, is referred to Jonah and the other walkers."

"A domain of ten miles, every inch of it mine," Jonah beamed at me. "Day or night, it's up to me to keep everything safe and shipshape."

We three were in the parlor when this conversation took place. I excused myself on the pretense of fetching some tea. In reality, I needed a few moments alone to compose myself. I was ashamed. Of both my thoughts and my behavior. As I listened to these two simple people it had struck me how much Latisha wanted my approval, wanted me to like her beau, to be happy with her. *Why do I have to be smug and hold myself distant from them?* I asked myself. *In truth, that makes me no better than her father, in his bleak, judging ways.*

When I returned I brought the tray, laden with the teapot, the best china, and bowls of peach cobbler, which I had baked that morning, swimming in cream. I was ready to listen now and make up for my earlier coldness. During the remainder of the time they were here we spoke of nothing unpleasant—certainly not of the consequences of stepping so far out of her social class by keeping company with such a man. If she was brazen, she was also much more innocent than I had imagined. I think she truly believed that all would work out well for her in the end because she wanted it so.

The second week of August, Georgeanna announced that she was marrying her Nathan Hopkins. When we did little more than stare in amazement she giggled like a girl.

"I know what I want," she explained in her simple way, "and Nathan is it. We want to be settled before the new school term begins. There is no good reason to wait."

Georgie's father owns the hardware store. He is solidly successful, solidly respected. Georgie is the oldest of the children and the only daughter. Her father would see to it that she had as fine a wedding as anyone and a decent send-off into life.

Judith Sexton, Georgie's mother, is even more practical than her daughter, so there would be nothing fancy or frivolous here. I noticed in all our discussions that Georgie did not ask Phoebe to sew a wedding gown for her. I knew, of course, why she declined. Phoebe has been bent over stiff with thread and needle for several months, crafting other people's happiness into things of tangible beauty that they could touch and take delight in. More and more of us, a constant stream, turning to her, cooing over her lovely creations—heedless of *her state*—as she is forced to observe joy and fulfillment from a distance, smelling the fragrance of it, but never having any of the luscious stuff, like sweet flowers, piled into her empty, aching arms.

Josie would say I exaggerate. But I saw Phoebe's eyes when she thought no one was looking. I saw the haunting loneliness there. And a longing that drew my heart out from me.

So. Our plans all went forth: Tillie's approaching confinement, Josie's blossoming pregnancy, Latisha's wedding (if she had her way about it), and now Georgie's wedding too. I did not speak of any of this to Eugene when I saw him. He would only remind me glumly that there was still no room for the two of us to fit our plans in. His father was doing well, thanks to Eugene's help. And, with so much work to occupy his hours, the days passed quickly—more quickly for him than for me. I turned my hand too often to things that required little mental attention, and that left me with too much time to think. And, in all my thinking and puzzling and protesting, this longing inside me continued to grow. I wanted to be *with* Eugene! I wanted the life together, which we had planned so carefully, to take root and begin. I felt I was wasting precious time—and to what purpose? I knew where my happiness lay, but I was saying, "No thank you. I shall stay where I am for a while." Georgie knew better. She did not concern herself with style or social expectation. She seized with gratitude and delight the gifts life brought to her. While I sat alone in my garden to wonder and brood.

Simon came one morning to ask for herbs for Emily. Before he got the words out, I, of course, guessed why.

"A child due already?" I attempted to smile. This was happy news, surely. I prepared my little cheesecloth bags of clove, chamomile, chervile and lemon balm, and a little marjoram for good measure, then tied them up with thin twine. "This should do for a while. I'll drop over myself in a few days and see how she does."

"Emily would like that. I believe she is just a little . . . frightened."

He spoke the word with a tone of apology. "I can understand that," I assured him, thinking of my own mother—thinking offhand of a dozen others whose health, as well as comfort, was endangered by this condition so natural to women. "Tell her to try not to worry. Worry will not help one bit."

*Kind, gentle Simon,* I thought, as I watched him mount his horse and I waved my hand to him. *You have neglected them both shamefully!* I scolded myself and determined right then to follow my promise up by a visit within the fortnight.

It is the most lovely morning of the month, pale and cool, with a promise of fall in the air, and the little brown thrushes are competing with the bright wheeling bluebirds to sing their praise to the day.

Alexander appears at the door; not Josephine, but Alexander, with a pinched face. He says, in an unnatural, rasping tone, "We have lost the baby, Esther. Josie's in bed, and safe, Doc Ensworth says, but the baby . . ." His voice cracks and he buries his head in my shoulder.

I stroke his hair, and think of my sister lying in this man's arms, loving him. "I am sorry, so sorry," I croon, "but there can be others."

"I do not want others!"

"I know . . . I know."

After a few moments he lifts his head and pulls me to my feet. "Will you come with me, Esther?"

"Of course. Let me get a few things together." As I pack my satchel I wonder about Mother, who happens to be churning butter, Jonathan helping her. I glance up at Alexander. He knows what I am thinking. "Would you like me to tell her, or—"

"Please, Esther, will you? I'll wait in here."

I want to shout at him. It is not my job to do this, and I tremble at the very idea. But he is at the moment simply incapable; one good look at him tells me that. I resent having to be the one. I try to march out, firm and resolute. Mother looks up when she sees me, and senses something.

"Is that Alexander's horse tied out front?" She wipes her hands along her apron. "Is there some kind of trouble, Esther?"

"Josephine has lost the baby, Mother. He wants me to go with him at once."

She says nothing. She sinks back to the low stool, as if suddenly deflated; no breath, no substance left to her. I put my hand on her shoulder. "Try not to worry, dear. I shall take good care of her, and be back as soon as I can."

"I should be the one to go." She stands up, though not very steadily.

"You have Jonathan to look after, and I am the one skilled in nursing." Unspoken between us is the memory of *her* ordeal—her loss, her hovering between death and life. I move and press my lips against her cheek, which feels soft and cool to my touch.

Tansy is saddled and waiting for me. This man and I move out together. Less than a year ago he was little more than a stranger to me. Now our very souls are woven together by shared love and shared pain.

"Stop fussing, Esther! You are making my head ache."

Josephine's eyes were puffy and red-rimmed, but she would not cry before me.

"I was not so far along, after all. Better it happen now than later." She sighed and sank back against the pillows. Her curls looked like damp, shining tendrils of corn silk. "I shall have my figure back in time for the harvest dance."

"Josie, stop it." I sat down beside her and took up her hand. "Do not pretend with me. Or with your husband, for that matter. He is taking this very hard."

"He is, is he?" Her full mouth began to pout a little. "As if this business has anything much to do with him! He just wants a son."

"And you? You just want a daughter to dress up like a princess— a daughter as pretty as yourself, to make all the other girls jealous."

Because I spoke the words kindly, Josie smiled with me. "There will be other times, won't there?"

"Of course."

"And I am young yet."

"You are very young yet."

"But Alex isn't." She knitted her white brow in a consternation I felt was more assumed than sincere.

"What are you thinking?" I asked.

"I am thinking that he keeps telling me he wants as many children as I will give him."

"Really?" It pleases me to know that. "You are certainly young and healthy enough to satisfy that request, dear."

"But I do not want an old, doting husband who dies with my children half-raised."

"Alexander is not so ancient that you need concern yourself!" I laughed. But her face was screwed up still. "We shall see. Must I wait a good while before trying again?"

"I believe the doctor would say so."

"I do not want to be too far behind. I do not want *you* to be a mother before me, as well as everyone else."

I let the remark go. Josephine is Josephine. There was nothing I could do about it. But I did voice one warning. "Be kind to Mother when you see her. This is very hard for her."

"Harder on everyone than on me, you would have me believe!"

"You know what I mean, Josie."

She was silent, which, for her, was acquiescence. "I shall go boil up some water for tea now. And make you some of those mint and cucumber sandwiches you fancy."

I took a plate in to her, and another two hours later. While she rested I looked at what work there was to do, but between them she and Alexander kept a tight house. I made a pitcher of lemonade and watered the row of house plants she had along the south window, then picked up the mending basket and began on the toe of a sock. I found myself dozing, and let my eyes close, the stockings sitting untouched in my lap.

My mother arrived just as Josephine called out for me, and I awoke with a start. "Go ahead, go in to her," I urged. "I shall be right here if you need me."

Idleness is not easy for me. I could hear the soft murmur of their voices, a good sign, from the next room. I decided to pour glasses of lemonade as a refreshment. The plate I was preparing was not quite ready when I heard a knock at the door. I was surprised to see Tillie's face peering back at me.

"I stopped by your house and your father told me you were here. Is Josie all right?"

I nodded. "But I am glad you are here." I held the door for her to enter, truly pleased and relieved to see her.

"I am so sorry this had to happen," Tillie sighed, her voice betraying a struggle against the specter of insecurity and chance Josie's miscarriage pressed home to her—especially with her own ordeal pending. "Well, I thought you might like some help, or at least some company. Besides, I have news."

I ushered her to Josie's amply cushioned rocker and put one of the glasses of sugared lemonade into her hand, and advised her not to make her presence known for the time being. "You will press home Josephine's own loss too painfully," I reminded her. After we discussed the state of the patient in the next room for a few appropriate moments, she leaned close. "I can wait no longer to tell you!" she hissed. "Jonah Sinclair has approached my father, requesting Latisha's hand."

I was as amazed as she wanted me to be! We exclaimed together. I guessed at the horrors that might have befallen the imprudent Mr. Sinclair. But Tillie shook her head, the wonder of it still unsettling her.

"Not a bit of it!" she assured me. "Just as Father stood and began clearing his throat for the onslaught, Latisha herself entered the room. She walked right up to him and said, 'If you do not let me marry Jonah I shall run away with him, Father, and, his work being what it is, the disgrace of it would spread all over the state.'

" 'You wish to be a laborer's wife?' my father growled, his face turning a dull purple."

"Oh, Tillie," I breathe, "what I would give to have been there to see this! What did she answer him?"

" 'He is as good a man as any, and better than the son-in-law you now have! Besides, I love him.' " Here Tillie stopped and smiled bravely. " 'He has the means to take care of me, so you need not concern yourself on that count.'

" 'And when you come crawling back again, wanting new frocks and fancy things like your sister—wanting more than milk and potatoes?' he barked.

" 'You may throw me out, if that ever happens, Father. But I do not intend that it shall.' "

I put my hand up to my mouth. "Aren't you proud of her, Tillie? Perhaps someone should have tried standing up to the old man long ago!"

As soon as the words were out I realized the mistake of them, and the blood drained from my face. But Theodora took my hand up in her elegant slim one. "It's all right, Esther. We *have* tried before, you know, both the boys and myself, but he was like flint to us."

"It is partly the timing, I suspect. And mayhap he has learned something over the past little while."

Tillie shook her head solemnly. "It is the threat more than anything, Esther, and the presence of the man there to hear it—who, if he did not marry his daughter, would spread the shame of the story abroad."

I nodded, realizing she had the truth of it, but overcome by amazement still. "What do you think of this Jonah fellow?"

She shrugged her thin shoulders. "I have set eyes on him only twice. He does not *seem* to be a person Latisha would be attracted to."

I agreed. "But there may be more to him than meets our casual, critical eye." I was thinking of my own rather awkward experience.

"You are sounding like Georgie now!" she fondly accused.

"Do they intend to marry soon?" I asked.

"Soon enough that I shall still be looking like this when she sweeps out in her bridal gown!" Tillie lamented. "But I suppose it cannot be helped."

"You have the blush of motherhood," I told her honestly. "And there is no greater beauty. Try not to mind all the rest."

We talked a bit longer, while I listened with one ear to the sounds coming from the adjoining room. I was relieved when she rose to leave; I did not relish an encounter or any sort of a scene just now.

We walked to the buggy together, and I was surprised to see Peter dozing on the driver's bench. "Why did you not come inside and say hello to me, young man?" I chided him, and held my cheek up for a kiss.

"Orders from headquarters!" He stole a glance at his sister, then grinned shamefacedly. "She wanted you all to herself."

"Whatever is this, Peter?" I reached out and touched the large ugly bruise that had discolored his left cheek and puffed out the skin under his eye.

"Bit of an accident," he replied offhandedly.

"Watch yourself, lad. You don't want to scare the girls away." I made light of the matter. But, in truth, I was thinking of his brother

89

and drunken brawls and men with large fists, some even with knives. I was so lost in my imaginings that I jumped when Alexander came up beside me and waved to the departing visitors.

"I overheard you ask young Peter about his swollen face, Esther. I can tell you how he came by it."

I shrunk, instinctively, from his statement, though I forced my eyes to meet his.

"He's an errand boy for his father's bank, you know."

I nodded, thinking, *Gerard Whittier runs that bank now.* I believe Alexander read my thoughts, because a sadness came into his eyes as he continued.

"Tillie's husband's the culprit, I fear. He drives the boy something fearful."

"You mean—Gerard struck him?" I gasped.

"Saw it with my own eyes, though the man's cruel ways are not a secret."

My knees turned to water and I had to sit down or simply crumple.

"I'm sorry, Esther. 'Tis indeed a bad business. But I thought it better coming from me than—"

"Yes. Yes, thank you." I put my hand on his arm and leaned gratefully for a moment before returning inside.

Mother was still with Josie. I sat in the rocker and waited impatiently, because my prickly mind was in a rage again and would give me no peace! *It is this awful man's child who should have aborted!* I fumed, unable to stop the shameful thought from coming. *He will be a mean, demanding father, and my poor Tillie an anxious, overly protective mother! While this gentle man here*—I let my eyes rest on the sparse, tidy figure of Alexander, who sat patiently beside me. *He will be a wise father and raise his sons to be good, noble creatures. Does it make sense that he be denied while men like Gerard Whittier strut about in their pompousness and pride!*

I felt tears in my eyes. They were more than tears of frustration. They were tears of protest at the pain people can cause one another simply by living their lives.

# Chapter 11

## Palmyra: October 1828

Tillie's father had his revenge, of a sort. The wedding he orchestrated was far from lavish, the guests he invited were few, and the dowry he settled upon Latisha much reduced from its original proportions. None of the groom's friends were allowed access to the festivities.

"I will turn them all out on their ear," Mr. Swift promised, and Latisha did not force the point.

Indeed, she cared little for his machinations. After all, she had won the day. She was the young, vivacious bride, parading on the arm of the man she wanted. Theodora took it with excellent grace—big, miserable, and unhappy as she was—while her sister fairly glowed.

I had a chance to observe Gerard Whittier at close quarters and was surprised by his affable manners. As the afternoon progressed I even found myself thinking, *Perhaps people, myself included, have judged him wrong.* I forgot for a few moments the smooth, persuasive power of the hypocrite. My unrelenting diligence, however, paid off at length, for I caught him in an unguarded moment scolding Peter roundly for some previous offense of his. The boy's face went white. He took a few steps backward, but Gerard grabbed him by the collar, for they were in a somewhat sheltered cove set into the gardens. But just then I stepped up.

"Let the lad go," I said, keeping my voice as pleasant as if I were saying, "Excellent sandwiches, aren't they?" But my eyes met his squarely as he glanced up in amazement. "Peter is as good a boy as they come," I continued. "Everyone in Palmyra thinks so. And many people of note, sir, whose influence you ought to regard, have observed the harsh treatment he receives at your hands."

The man arched a cool eyebrow and began to speak in defense of himself, but I brushed him aside. "No pretense, please. I shall not play games with you; it is a waste of your time. But I give you fair warning to take care in the future, for more eyes are upon you than you should like to know, and an accounting may be required, if you do not mend your ways."

I took Peter by the hand and drew him away with me, his eyes round as saucers, his whole body stiff with the shock of what had just happened.

"I've never seen anyone stand up to him like that, Esther!" he hissed.

"Yes, I was brilliant," I agreed, trying to make light of it. "But you must give me your word that you will tell no one at all of the scene back there."

I turned him to face me. He nodded solemn agreement. "You understand the importance?" He nodded again.

"And Peter," I added, before letting him go. "You must let me know if he is particulary cruel to you, or to—" Tillie's name clogged in my throat.

"I know. To Tillie particularly. I promise, Esther." He squeezed my hand and was gone.

I watched after him, a sinking feeling in my middle. *I have made an enemy,* I thought to myself, and the thought was grim. *I must not let him frighten me, or I shall be lost.* I moved to where Phoebe and Georgie were chatting with the minister's wife, feeling a sudden need for company and the sound of voices. *We were already enemies. But now Gerard Whittier knows it, as well as I.*

Georgie's Nathan approached the little group at the same time as I did. He smiled and made way for me. Here, I felt, was a true gentleman. Even his looks were coming to grow on me. A slow smile spread over his smooth, somewhat largely drawn features.

"Our turn next, Georgeanna's and mine."

"Are you counting the days, then?" His smile widened. "Once you belong to Georgie, there will be little left of you," I teased.

"Suits me fine, Esther." His manner was frank, but it had a gentleness to it. "That has been my desire and ultimate goal since the first time I saw her."

"She is a gem, to be sure." I returned his warm smile, and we joined the others. Eugene was nowhere about. I could have used the nearness of him at that moment. *Is the notion of weddings contagious?* I wondered. *Something in the air one can catch?*

After a little while I wandered off in search of Eugene, passing a group of ladies among whom my mother sat, contentedly holding Jonathan, his long legs dangling, upon her lap.

*She is a pretty woman,* I thought, *more than most women her age. But she has cultivated beauty, as I cultivate flowers, as some women cultivate kindness and grace.* I moved on, without any of them noticing me. Eugene was ensconced in a half circle of men, heads bent over an advertisement for new John Deere tractors. I waded right in and gently disengaged him, enduring the good-natured teasing in order to have him alone to myself.

Latisha went off on a grandiose tour of the canal zone, as I call it, her face aglow. The rest of us settled back into the routine of daily life. *Routine.* That word did not aptly apply to our doings for these many months past!

It was in the middle of the night that I was awakened to go to Tillie. A cool September evening, with a wet, fragrant wind. I was nervous, but could not quell a sense of excitement. I urged Peter to drive the team faster. "You know the way," I reminded him.

"I do not like the darkness," he said. And it struck me how timid the boy had become since his brush with the life of the canal. Or was it the circumstances of life in these months since he left?

Doctor Ensworth was with Tillie, and refused to admit me at once. So I paced the floor with Tillie's mother, our eyes meeting awkwardly every now and again. I have never been entirely comfortable in Cornelia Swift's company, nor she in mine. I could intone the small pleasantries, but to what purpose? We paced in silence until we heard the thin wail of a newborn. Every muscle in my body tensed, and I lifted my head.

"All sounds well," Mrs. Swift said hopefully.

I smiled a tight smile. *All must be well!* I thought passionately.

At length the doctor came out. The look I had seen him wear

when he had attended my mother was missing. I felt my muscles relax.

"A fine healthy son. And Theodora is doing well. Jane is with her. She'll be able to manage things from this point."

Jane Foster, the best midwife in Palmyra. "May I see her, Doctor?"

The tired eyes softened. "She is asking for you," he said under his breath. Then he turned to Mrs. Swift, rubbing his big hands together. "I'll take that cup of coffee you offered me now."

She had no choice but to go with him. I slipped into the darkened room. Tillie's eyes were searching for me. Oh, how sweet with relief and happiness they were! I bent over the bed. She had wanted a daughter; we have an unreasoned preference for girls, we five. But it no longer mattered.

Jane was still cleaning the baby's wrinkled red body. "He has fistfuls of hair," I reported to his mother. "Dark and thick like his father's. But he has your almond-shaped eyes."

I bent over and kissed her wan cheek. "He is quite beautiful, my darling."

"I am so blessed." She sighed in contentment.

"Yes. And you deserve your happiness," I replied.

I stayed the remainder of the day, administering to my friend's needs, securing her comfort, rejoicing with her. So I was there, in the very room, when Gerard arrived mid-afternoon to inspect his son.

He did not even acknowledge my presence, nor more than glance toward Tillie. First he took the child up in his arms. "He has the dark hair and eyes, the look of the Whittiers. Good," he pronounced.

"But not your beak nose. Look how small and delightfully rounded his is." I could not resist. I saw Tillie stifle a smile, but her husband ignored me.

"You look well, Theodora." He bent and pressed his lips to her cheek, the way I had; a perfunctory kiss.

"His name shall be Edward."

I heard Tillie suck in her breath. "I had thought of Joshua or Samuel."

"Edward Lawrence Whittier, after both our fathers." *Ever the politician.* Tillie acquiesced.

"That is a good strong name," I told her, after the lord and master had departed. "But I, for one, shall call him Laurie. It fits him well."

And Laurie he became, to everyone who truly loved him, from that moment on.

September slipped away with an Indian summer splendor; we could not believe autumn was here. Eugene and I officially announced our engagement and set a date for April, then changed it to May.

"Above all else I need flowers for my wedding," I explained to him.

"I need nothing for my wedding," he replied, smiling, "but you."

Georgie and Nathan pulled it together, though not until after the term started. But before the pumpkins were ripened and the last of the corn harvested, they were wed. She left her parents' home and he his cramped quarters, and together they secured a charming little house to rent not far from their school. Georgeanna was certainly the one person of my intimate acquaintance I need not worry myself about. She seemed consistently solid and sunshiny, even more after marriage, which seemed to agree with her. But then, Georgie has the gift of seeming to *make* everything agree with her or be bent to serve her somehow.

The harvest dance marked the highlight of autumn. Held traditionally the weekend before All Hallows' Eve, this is arguably the third largest social affair in the city, after the Christmas Festival and the New Year's Day party. May Day and Fourth of July festivities run closely behind.

Latisha returned in time to show off her new husband. It amused me to watch her—disregarding, because she was obliviously unaware, all social conventions, all snubbing and attempted ostracism by those of her father's friends who felt themselves offended. She was happy, and happily blind. Tillie had her baby. He continued to be the handsomest child in the city, as far as I could surmise. I sensed that the child had softened Gerard's attitude toward his wife, if only a little. After all, look at the heir Theodora produced!

*You are set up fine and saved from your own failings because of Tillie and her family,* I fumed to myself. But, of course, he could not admit that

95

fact to anyone; most of all to himself. Ah, this would never do. For in admission comes humility, and perhaps even change, and his proud Whittier nature would never countenance that. *You have met your match,* I thought on more than one occasion when I saw Gerard and his father-in-law together. The Swift family was admittedly the nobility of the village. But Gerard, despite his fallen state, did not acknowledge that. His name and his family standing went back as far, and was more widely established, and he used that to uphold him, expecting the respect that he felt was his due to be showered upon him, no matter what. How Mr. Swift fumed and burned! But he found himself helpless before a pompous self-possession that withered his.

So Tillie had our little Laurie to hold on her knee and be admired. Josephine came with a new frock, all warm, earthy shades of autumn, her head held so high that I knew it must ache—perhaps more than her heart did. It grieved me to see the dull sorrow in Alexander Hall's eyes.

"I am not interested in *that* again!" Josephine kept repeating flippantly every time the subject of childbirth came up.

"You learned your lesson, eh?" Georgie would tease her.

"Perhaps I have."

At the last minute my mother refused to go to the dance with Father. Jonathan had come down with a cold. It was a nasty cold, true, and he was running a fever. But Maggie Wells, who had fed him from her own breast when he was a squalling infant, had agreed to come and sit with him. Her husband was bedridden himself with a nasty cut on the foot that prevented him from walking, much less dancing.

"I've no hankering to kick up my heels," she had told Mother, "with anyone else but that man."

But now Mother was demurring. I tried my best to persuade her. Even an appeal to her vanity—how slim and attractive she would look in her dancing gown—failed to touch her. What I said I said in jest, with no notion whatever—isn't that how life is!

"Your husband is a good-looking man, you know. If you leave him so much to himself, Mother, other women will start to take notice."

"Just let them try!" she pouted, reminding me awfully of Josephine. "Besides, he knows better than that."

In the end he went without her, and she stayed home to brood, which, for some reason, she wanted to do. As the evening wore on I realized that another person I loved was missing: Phoebe was nowhere to be found.

"I talked with her yesterday," Tillie said when I questioned her. "Did you know she has taken up even more sewing for several of the dress shops in town? She is using that as an excuse.

" 'I've too much work to do,' she told me, 'and no reason to be there, Tillie, no reason at all.'

"I happen to know," Tillie continued, her voice heavy, "that James Sadler, Josie's old beau, has tried to call upon her."

"Tried?"

"She will admit no male admirers."

"I have always said James will make some girl a good husband," I fumed.

Tillie bent her head close, in that endearing way of hers. "She loves Simon, Esther. I am convinced it is yet too painful for her to put those feelings aside."

"But she must! Else what will there be in life for her?"

97

Both of us sighed. Of their own accord my eyes roved the room until they lit on Simon and Emily dancing. He was holding her close, with an adoring look in his eyes that went to my heart. She was happy. I shall always remember how happy Emily was that night. *I cannot begrudge them!* I thought in frustration. *No matter what.*

I was happy myself, because the hourglass was turned over, the quiet sands running through. And each day brought me closer to a state I now desired more than I feared.

Much of the time I was enthralled with Eugene. But I remember one moment when the music stopped and we walked off the floor hand in hand—one simple moment when I saw that my father was sitting beside Widow Foster, Jane Foster, the midwife, and offering her a glass of cold cider punch. Nothing more. A friendly gesture, surely. I had danced with him earlier in the evening, and urged Josie and the others to give him a turn, which I was rather certain they did. But, after all, he was alone, and she had been alone for a long time. I tried to remember how old Jane was—thirty-five . . . surely not forty yet— perhaps ten years younger than he.

Just as I began to wonder, Nathan and Georgie surrounded us with their laughter and goodwill, and we four traipsed off together, and all else was forgotten for the moment, and for a long time afterward.

# Chapter 12

*Palmyra: December 1828*

Who would have imagined mine would be the first name to come to a near-stranger's mind? It was close upon midnight when I heard a brisk rapping at the kitchen door. *Perhaps,* I thought, *someone is in trouble and has noticed the dull glow of a light within burning still.* I regretted then my decision to curl up in the rocker and read until late. But Jonathan was feverish and fussy still; the tasks of the long day, all diverted from Mother to my shoulders, had worn me ragged; and I needed some time to myself. Then, of course, the hours had gotten away from me, and here I sat, the fire settling to embers, when I heard the knocking. I got up from the rocker, and the wooden floorboards were cold to my feet as I pattered across the empty room to take a cautious peek out the window.

"Miss Parke, it's me," a low voice hissed. "Open up."

"Who is 'me'?" I demanded.

"Jonah Sinclair, 'Tisha's husband. I am in need of your help."

I drew the bolt back, wondering what specter would greet me, not expecting to see the burly man sagging beneath the burden he carried—a limp body with legs dangling, head lolling.

"It's young Randolph. He's been hurt in a waterside brawl and I had to take him somewhere."

"Quick," I said, "bring him inside."

He was too long for the settle couch in the corner; he must have grown tall during the past year. But we positioned him there, anyway, and I fetched a basin of water as Mr. Sinclair directed me.

"Knife wound," he said. "Gone deep, I fear."

"We should fetch Doctor Ensworth."

He shook his shaggy head. "The boy don't want him to know."

"I don't care what the boy wants. I can trust Doctor Ensworth, if he can't!"

"I've taken care of many such injuries, miss. Have you got any needle and thread?"

That decided it! "I shall sit with him, sir! You ride to the corner of Fayette and Foster Streets and bring the doctor back here!"

"Chances are he ain't even in, miss."

"Yes. But we are taking that chance."

It was to Jonah Sinclair's credit that he recognized his defeat and admitted it. In less than a minute I heard the sound of his horse in the lane. *How loud night noises are! How loud even the silence when the heart is beating raggedly and fear prickles the skin with cold chills.*

Every few moments I stopped my pacing to stand over Randolph and look into his face. I could see no sign there of the struggle he must have passed through. He lay so still! I began to wonder if he yet breathed! *How long the doctor is taking! Perhaps Jonah Sinclair was right.*

Thus I agonized until at last I heard noises and ran to the door in my eagerness to hurry them in. Doctor Ensworth said little but set right to work. After long minutes he spoke without turning.

"It is good you sent for me, Sinclair. I believe some of the nerves in this arm have been damaged. I shall have a deuce of a time sewing it up."

I must have gasped.

"He will never have full use of it, Esther. But I'll do the best that I can."

"What does this mean?" I said in a low voice to Jonah. "Surely he cannot continue the strenuous work on the canal."

"No," the doctor answered. "Not for a long while yet."

"Season is winding down, anyhow." Jonah shrugged, but his eyes beneath their bushy covering were dull with worry.

"What of his father?" I asked. "And who is to take care of him?"

"These dressings must be changed regularly, so the wound doesn't fester. And he must be kept quiet so the stitches don't tear."

"I'll take him to 'Tisha. We two can manage."

"Would you like me to keep him here?"

"You must for a day or two, leastways," said Doctor Ensworth. "I don't want him moved."

"What was he doing?"

Jonah shrugged again. "I'm not certain, miss. I was called to break a fight up, that's all I know."

"Into gambling, I suspect."

I glanced up sharply, surprised at the doctor's words. His gray head still bent over his patient.

"Surely not!" I protested.

"Could be so. The lot he was with make a business of preying on others and manipulating things to their liking."

Randolph moaned, and a shudder passed along his body.

"He is a good boy! Can you not steer him in some other direction, Jonah, frighten the bullies away from him? Being right there, as you are—having some little authority . . ." I know my voice trembled with the desperation I was feeling.

"He don't work along my stretch. I hardly see the lad, Esther." He spoke with patience, but also with a matter-of-factness, as if to say, *What can I do? Each man to his own fate.*

"Doctor!" I appealed.

"Perhaps this will bring him to his senses, Esther. Beyond that— well, he's awful young still. He has to make up his own mind about such things for himself."

*Bleak! Bleak acceptance. Why are men like that?*

I put on the kettle and cut bread. Anything to keep busy. I half wished, half dreaded that Randolph would wake. "Would you like me to sit the rest of the night with him?" I asked, as the doctor sucked at his hot drink.

"I'll do that." Jonah sat stolid and determined. "I'm used to long hours. And I'll be able to handle him when he wakes. You get some sleep, miss."

Doctor Ensworth nodded in agreement and patted my hand. "Try to do as he says, Esther. Things will work out as they're meant to. They always do."

His words played in my head as I slid between my chilled sheets and tried to make my mind and my body relax. *Things will work out as they're meant to . . . Doctor Ensworth has come to grips with the forces, fair and foul, that determine our mortal lives. He can see some design,* I realized, *that even the most terrible of tragedies fits into, and make some sense of it all.*

I could not. I fell asleep with frustration still gnawing at me like a

101

bad toothache that made me turn restlessly all night in my bed.

Father shook me awake. I knew by the grayness of the sky outside my patch of window that the hour was early.

"What is this business, Esther?" he demanded.

I explained to him briefly as I slipped into my shift and dress.

"And how are we to care for a sick lad with Jonathan underfoot and your mother fussing like a wet hen?"

"I'm sorry, Father. I couldn't turn him away."

"Of course not, daughter. Well, we'll have to find a way to make do."

The way was that we moved Randolph back to my room where we could shut the door upon him and the child could make all the noise he wanted going about his usual play. I saw to the changing of the dressing and administered herbs that were good for healing: bay leaves for his bruises and the aching in his limbs; borage for the fever; comfrey to help heal the wound. Mother punished me for the first day or two by brooding and almost refusing to talk to me. But I knew how to pamper her, and after a while she nearly forgot the presence of our strange, quiet visitor, so slight was the trouble he caused.

Randolph was awake off and on, sinking into a sort of stupor when the need for sleep overtook him. We had not talked much at all. I saw to his needs and murmured a few soothing words, but asked no questions and administered none of the scoldings that burned on my tongue. Every evening Jonah Sinclair came and changed the dressing for me and fed the patient his thin broth, soaked bread, and tea.

"How is Latisha?" I asked the second night. "Is she very upset? Does she think to tell anyone else in the family?"

He glanced at his broad booted feet and kept his uncomfortable gaze there. "I have not told her, Miss Esther."

*"You have not told her!"* I exclaimed. He shifted from foot to foot, muttering under his breath, looking like a shaggy little beast that had been caught in a trap.

"I couldn't, I just couldn't—knew how worried she'd be—sick with worry—meant to a time or two, but couldn't bring myself—that little face of hers . . ."

I touched his shoulder. "It's all right," I said. "But some time they all have to know of this. He can't stay here forever. And if his arm . . ." I hesitated. We looked at each other miserably.

"Randolph won't take to that, won't take to it well, I can tell you."

"I know. Let me think upon it."

The longer I thought, the more I felt impressed to go straight to his father. The idea unnerved me: to confront that icy man with such ill tidings! He would be likely to bite my head off, out of spite. But what course was better—especially for Randolph's sake? I feared if we "hid him away," so to speak, with Eugene's father (I had considered placing him at the blacksmith shop where he might be given odd jobs to do that would help build up his strength) or with Josie and Alexander at the mill (where he might become depressed at the hum of activity around him in which he could not take part)—I was afraid his feelings would fester worse than his wound and the task of facing his father loom greater and greater as the days and weeks passed. However, if I did it for him . . .

He was sitting up now and spending some part of each day walking. He had been beaten up rather badly before the gruesome gash along his arm had been inflicted and then had lost a great deal of blood. He did not seem to object to the confining routine of his days; exhaustion still played with his senses as the need for healing sleep overcame all else. He complied, as he must. But he would not talk! He refused to communicate anything—by word, by question, by hope expressed, by complaint.

Still I postponed the inevitable. In the mornings I looked forward to the boy's smile, the way he attempted to hide his pleasure at seeing me. The longer he was awake and about each day, the more his hours would drag, I told myself. So I began leaving some of my favorite books about, even volumes of poetry, and casually suggested them for his perusal. To my astonishment, he took them up and consumed their pages with a voracious appetite that must have been born at least partly from the desperation of boredom.

Once, as he handed Scott's Waverly novels back to me, he said, "I like both Irving and Cooper better. They may not be as clever as Scott, but their thoughts are more palatable to me."

*Cleverness . . . palatable . . .* I know the Swifts came from a noble

103

line that can justly claim centuries of superiority. But, despite my affection for him, I had judged this boy as concerned only with the most elemental of carnal, self-seeking desires!

Now things were progressing too quickly. *This will get out of hand, I thought, if I wait too much longer.* So early one evening I told Father what I was doing, left a note for Jonah Sinclair, and rode Tansy to the big house that took up the space of three or four lots on Washington Street. The house Lawrence Swift selected for his banker son-in-law was only a block away, at the corner of Gates and Main, but at least Tillie would not be there tonight.

I left Tansy at the post and knocked boldly on the big front door. Mrs. Swift's maid answered and left me in the hall while she took word to the master.

"It is Mr. Swift, and Mr. Swift alone, I wish to see," I stated emphatically. "Please tell him I have come on a matter of great importance to him."

How nervous I was during those moments of waiting! I drew a few deep breaths down into my lungs to calm me. When I was given the nod and allowed to follow the servant back to the master's study, I was sure she could hear the pounding of my heart in my chest.

Tillie's father looked up when I entered and indicated a chair for me to sit in, but he did not rise from his desk—which is the only polite thing to do when a lady enters. Perhaps that small, mean act gave me the edge of spirit and determination I needed.

"Sir," I launched right in, since he was obviously not in a temper to waste time with the little niceties, "I have some important information about your son, Randolph, that I believe you should know."

*Not a sign. Not even a raising of the imperial eyebrow.* I drew myself up a bit. "Mr. Swift, really, must you play the role with me? Your son has been hurt badly, knifed in a street fight—and, for love of him and Tillie, I have been caring for Randolph these several days in my own house."

I had the pleasure of seeing his long face turn white. His hands, spread on the polished surface of the desk, tightened into fists. But still he said nothing.

"Do you wish to know the details, Mr. Swift?"

A long moment's pause. "Yes. Please."

I told him, as succinctly and painlessly as possible.

"I am sorry you have been troubled by this matter, Esther. You should never have been brought into it." Anger was hard in his voice.

"Of course I should have been brought into it!" I cried. "What are friends for but to succor one another in times of need?"

"Mr. Sinclair had no business. I shall see to him later—and make sure you are compensated."

I rose to my feet. "I came here for one reason, sir, and one reason only—to work out the best thing for Randolph, to hope you would bring him home again where he might rest and heal, where he might be renewed by his family's love and attentions."

I was drawing the picture for him on purpose—trying to shame him into it.

"Randolph cannot come here—for a variety of reasons, none of which, my dear girl, you understand."

"He is but a boy—in trouble, in need of guidance, sir."

"*Esther*—" My name. One word, spoken with such a note of imperious warning that it sent shivers along my spine.

"I am not one of your daughters, that you can think to bully or frighten me. But I *am* willing to beseech you, sir, on behalf of your son."

He looked at me very strangely then. "You are young yourself, Esther. You know little of such matters."

"I know much of love, and of fear—and of how important it is that Randolph be forgiven and—"

"The prodigal son, is it?" Mr. Swift opened his fists and placed his hands, palms down, flat on the desk. "That is my decision to make, young lady."

"Aye, yours the power—*and* yours the responsibility."

Perhaps he could see that I was seething. He pushed his chair back and rose. "Ann will see you out now, Esther. Thank you for coming to me. I know you meant well."

I stood, but I did not move. "Will you be sending a carriage for him, then?"

"Esther!"

"Sir! For mercy's sake!"

He sat down again. "Let me think upon it. I will think upon it," he said, as though by way of some great condescension.

He must have pushed some button, for Ann appeared at my elbow and gingerly touched my arm.

"He is a good boy. He needs another chance. He needs care. Please do think upon the matter of your eldest son long and well, sir."

I turned and followed the young woman, wordless and tense with misery, all the way through the long hall and out the front door. I leaned against Tansy, enjoying the solid warmth of her body. I stood there for moments before I gathered the resolution to mount and ride away from that pernicious spirit, that implacable will that had conquered my own.

That very night, while I was absent, a scene took place which, I suppose, Doctor Ensworth would say was the working of fate. I was not there to prevent or amend it. I came too late—I came home to an empty room and an empty bed and the burly figure of Jonah Sinclair pacing my kitchen.

"Told 'im the truth, miss. He asked and I told him. What else was I to do?"

The poor man was distraught, his eyes haunted with worry. "What did Randolph ask?"

"Asked when I thought he might be up and around again. 'My arm feels so stiff,' says he. 'When will I regain the use of it?' "

"I said, 'The doctor thinks you damaged the nerves, and the arm might never be right.' "

"Why?" I breathed, fighting back a strong urge to shout at him. "He needed to come to that point by degrees."

"I don't know what you mean. I thought it better to level with the boy, man to man."

"Level with him?" I *was* raising my voice now. "He isn't ready for that."

"I couldn't lie to him."

*So simple, so straightforward!* "Where has he gone?"

"Back to his room by the canal, I suspect, Miss Esther. I'll look for him there."

"You do that, this very night—this very minute! And bring word back to me!"

Duly chastened, the man scuttled out of my kitchen. I heard his horse on the road. I heard the wind. I thought I heard a child crying in the smothering dark of the night.

Jonah did not return that night, nor the next. It was the following morning he came. His eyes were bleary and bloodshot, and I wondered how much sleep he had denied himself during the past two nights and days.

"Nowhere, miss!" He ran thick, muscled fingers through the curly tangle of his hair. "I swear he's disappeared off the face of the earth."

I sat down, feeling a bit weak at the joints. "Exactly where have you looked?"

His list was impressive. I could not think of one place to add to it.

"He must have caught a boat, I figure, that took him someplace else—Syracuse, Rochester, any of the cities along the canal."

I nodded. "Will you keep looking?"

" 'Course I will! Day 'n night."

"You'd better get some sleep first." He nodded and shuffled toward the doorway. "Will you keep me . . . informed?"

" 'Course I will." The man's eyes were miserable. "I am sorry—I meant no harm."

"I know that." I took his hand and squeezed it. "Give Latisha a kiss for me."

He went out into the day that was suddenly too bright for my eyes. I did not watch after him. I did not let myself think about what might be happening with one young, frightened boy.

Such clever twistings and turnings fate has in its power! The very next day Mr. Swift sent word that he wished to see me, at my convenience, in his office in town. I kept the messenger waiting at my door while I penned a reply, not even curious any longer as to what his decision might be.

*You are too late, sir,* I wrote. *Your son has vanished. Those searching have been unable to locate him anywhere. He was discouraged for fear the use of his injured arm might be denied him. Heaven knows where he has gone!*

"Take this back to Mr. Swift with my regrets," I instructed. But I took a shameful pleasure in the pain that cruel man might suffer when he opened the paper and started to read.

The snow held off for a good long time, but when it came, it came in wagonloads, the heavens opening like broad barn doors to dump their heavy wet burden. And with the snow came freezing night temperatures and ice—lavishly applied by the master painter, coating fence post and lane, and turning every surface where the least bit of moisture lingered into a thin sheet of glaze.

Life, of necessity, had slowed down now, and I liked it that way: days spent working indoors and long nights by the fire. Josie contrived to celebrate her first wedding anniversary with a very nice little party for us girls and our friends; the days of Christmas came to claim our attentions and pleasure us, then passed on their way; and very slowly the last short, brittle days of the year went by.

## Chapter 13

*Palmyra: February 1829*

I t had all been a ruse from the very beginning. I did not recognize that till too late. Josephine nearly four months with child and eating like a bird so as not to show it. Then a nightmare recurring: Alexander's white face on my doorstep, Josie's white face on her bed, Doctor Ensworth grimly shaking his head at me.

"What is the trouble?" I asked him when we were alone.

"I can't tell you that." His tone was more gentle than usual. "If only we knew. I'd guess it has something to do with the individual makeup of each woman's system—how it is able to tolerate the growing fetus." He scratched at his whiskery chin. "Some women carry a child without one day of sickness—some without one day of feeling well. Some deliveries take an hour, some take a day. Only the good Lord knows why."

*Nothing there to take back to Josephine.* I wondered if anything could comfort or placate her now. Alexander was devastated and showed it by burrowing deeper within himself. Josephine covered her anger with the brittle flippancy she handled so brilliantly. And such an attitude had the effect of turning honest sympathy aside. She would have none of our tendernesses and certainly no tears.

"What is done, is done," she kept chirping, "and all for the best, I imagine. I cannot see myself with a child anyway."

That last statement chilled me. For it meant she *had* been picturing the sweet reality they both had hoped for.

Her husband would have comforted her, if she had let him. I think in his mind he accepted the fault for the matter. Certainly this lovely, vivacious creature he had married could be in no way to blame.

If Josie had allowed him to comfort her, would things have been different? I think so. The loss, the failure—as both of them regarded it—drove a dull wedge between them rather than weaving tender bonds that would have united the two as husband and wife. One does what one must, or each does those things of which he or she is cap-able, and that determines the matter for the moment, and often for years yet to come.

I took joy in my godson, for so little Laurie was christened. What winsome ways he had—and as beautiful as any girl-child! I believe my mother was envious when I took to doting upon him. But Jonathan, after all, was nearly two years old, speaking a string of words, running wherever his stout legs would take him or his mother allow. Laurie was an infant yet. I wish my mother could have accepted him for his sep-arate needs and separate merits. But Josephine's disappointments had become, in a way, her own. She *felt* the depressive hopelessness, as if the loss had happened to her. She could see none of the underlying heartaches of Tillie's life; those things that were carefully guarded from the casual eye. She chose, instead, to make comparisons and envy my dear friend for her affluence, her social position, her healthy, pampered child. In my mother's mind I was a bit of a traitor to rejoice with Tillie, who already possessed overmuch and did not need my attentions in the way my poor sister and my own little brother did.

I knew the bitter anguish Tillie's family was suffering at Ran-dolph's disappearance. I had remained true to my trust, albeit reluc-tantly, and told no one of his terrible injury, nor of the time he spent under my roof. *There* I *did* feel like a traitor. After suffering my uneasi-ness for weeks, I took it up with Jonah Sinclair, briefly drawing him away from his young wife during a visit to Theodora's. I never went to the big house now. If Tillie had still been living with her parents, I do not know what would have happened. I had no desire to encounter her father, nor to pursue the unfinished matters that stood like a stone block between us.

Latisha also doted upon her nephew, so it was not unusual for us to come upon one another of an afternoon or an evening at Tillie's house. Neither sister took much notice when Mr. Sinclair and I wan-dered off for a few moments.

"No one in the family has knowledge of Randolph's injury," I began, "and of his time spent in my house, no one save his father. Is that correct?"

"That is still right, far as I know."

"You have not told Latisha." He shook his head. "Hasn't that been difficult?"

"And more—cryin' herself to sleep those first few nights."

I shuddered. "Mrs. Swift suspects nothing?"

"I don't believe so."

"And my poor Tillie."

"Well, miss, the worst of it is Peter. He's near run off half a dozen times in search of his brother. I spent most of one whole night talking him out of it. His father's forbidden him the run of the stables and told him that if he goes off without gaining permission, he may as well not come home."

"So like him!" I was fuming inside. "Can you do nothing for Peter? I cannot bear to think of him suffering, too." I placed my hand on the good fellow's arm and looked into his eyes. "Watch out for the lad, will you? We can do nothing for Randolph—" My voice broke, and I turned aside. "I feel deceitful," I confessed, "knowing these horrid facts and concealing them!"

"What good would they do, Miss Esther?"

111

"Is that the only question?" I mused aloud. "When the truth comes out, as it eventually does, what will they think of our silence?"

Distress clouded the straightforward gaze. "I can't see us tellin', Miss Esther. Isn't that Mr. Swift's place?"

"Indeed, it is," I agreed. "But do we join ranks in his cruelty by keeping our counsel as well?"

The question was too much for him. And just then Latisha's voice came to us from the next room, and the moment was lost. We went in to join the others and exclaim at the baby's antics, but every time my eyes met Tillie's gentle smile I cringed a little inside.

The ice is breaking up on the canal and in the rivers. February thaws can be awe-inspiring things, especially when the temperate air churns suddenly into a cold blustery wind that slices through the jagged ice shards and licks the land like the tongue of a giant dragon with white, frozen breath. Both the living trees and the shaven wood framed and standing in houses moan in protest. The sun is too weak to break through the gray plate of the sky, and the mildness, brief and sighing with promise, wreaks more havoc than good.

I see no one: not Tillie and the others in the village; not Josie, in her own frozen world beneath the tall elms that ring the gristmills and the sawmills; not my dear Eugene, with his troubling sea-green eyes. I play with Jonathan, read my books, and pore over seed catalogs from my corner by the fire, but I am no longer content. Thus I know that it is right for me to marry and begin my own life with this gentle person I love.

Tonight a strange thing has happened. Jane Foster knocked on our door about seven, her fingers stiff, her nose red from the raw wind. Her buggy was stuck in the gully half a mile from our house with a broken wheel. Father has gone with her to help, for she pleaded that she has two or three urgent calls to make and no time to lose. Indeed, I believe he harnessed Tansy to our own light buggy in the interest of time.

I watch Mother covertly as time passes. She reflects nothing of unease or concern. I entertain my own fears in silence. It is not that I *distrust* my father, or even Jane. But something about the two of them when they were alone those few moments at the harvest dance—and I know my father's need, and his loneliness—and why is it that Jane's buggy broke down right here?

When Mother rises to go back to bed, I kiss her cheek and hasten to put coals in the long-handled bed warmer to run between her cold sheets. I nearly say, "Perhaps I shall wait up for Father," but I cannot get the words out, and she does not mention him.

I go back to the kitchen, where the fire is still burning steadily and the room is warm. I put the kettle on and determine to remain for no more than half an hour, deciding that if the calls were routine and easily dispatched with, my father shall have returned by then. If there are any real difficulties for Jane to deal with, well, they might not be back until morning. I pull Mother's rocker a little closer to the fire and curl up, as contented as the kitten that has now grown to a cat and sleeps on the warm stones of the hearth.

Father's voice awakens me. Which means I did not hear horse or buggy, or the opening of the door, or his booted tread. I struggle to swim out of sleep and crane my neck to get a view of the kitchen clock.

"It is late, Esther. I'm sorry you fell asleep here. It's nearly dawn."

Father's voice sounds subdued, even deflated. I peer through bleary eyes at him. "What happened?" I ask. "I can see in your face that something happened."

I rub the cramped muscles in my neck, waiting for him to put the words together. "Esther." The way he says my name chills me, and all sorts of horrors flicker across my mind. "It is Emily Turner. Jane delivered her of a baby daughter, and the child is doing well."

Something within me begins to tighten. He does not have to say the words. "There were complications. Do not tell me—she is dead—Father."

I lean back against the rocker and close my eyes. Perhaps it is the weariness within me that blocks all thought, all feeling. I do not want this to happen! I feel a terrible remorse, and a weight of sorrow that is nearly too heavy to bear.

Father half lifts me and helps me to my cold, empty room and leaves me alone there. I sit on the bed, my aching thoughts tugging of their own accord toward Simon, who has lost his reason for living; toward Eugene, who has lost a sister; toward Emily's mother, who has lost her only daughter. I perch, dull and stunned, on the edge of the bed for long minutes, until my feet begin to get cold and my stays feel as tight as a vise. And I know I must move, and at least get shoes, dress, and stays off before crawling into my bed.

113

Morning *does* possess the power to renew, no matter how deep the suffering. With the pale diffusing light of a new day I felt I could face the horrors the night before had presented. Though, really, the morning was far advanced when I stumbled out of bed. Father was most likely in the toolshed, where he had been repairing machinery the past week. I found Mother in her sewing room, with Jonathan playing at her feet. "Did Father tell you what happened last night?" I asked, remaining on the threshhold of the room, only peeking in.

"Yes. That is why I thought it best not to awaken you. I'm sorry, Esther."

She did not pause in her work, but I felt a real sympathy emanating from her spirit toward mine. I fought an impulse to go to her and wrap my arms round her neck and bury my face in her lap, as I used to when I was a child.

Instead I disciplined myself to run quickly through the morning chores before saddling Tansy and riding into Palmyra. I had filled a basket with a few items I thought might be useful, though I was certain there would be neighbors aplenty there with offerings of assistance and food. I felt compelled, duty-bound, to offer my help along with the others.

When I arrived at the modest dwelling there were already several horses and vehicles tied up there. I found a spot for Tansy, and when I reached the door I pushed it open without knocking. I scanned the quiet, carefully guarded faces and, to my relief, found Georgeanna's there; kind, practical Georgie, with her arm round Mrs. Thorn's bowed shoulders. There were several women milling about the kitchen and parlor. But where were the men?

I nodded to some of the ladies and caught Georgie's eye for a moment as I walked through to the small bedroom at the back of the house. In the doorway I paused. Simon was there, sitting on a low chair beside Emily's body, which was stretched out on the bed where she died. All had been put in order, and the dead girl appeared as sweet and innocent as an angel who had never tasted of the bitter strife of this life. Eugene, standing beside his young brother-in-law, turned. His eyes met mine, making the muscles in his face distort and then crumble. I moved swiftly and drew his head into my arms. His pain seeped through me, as though the garments he wore were soaked, and the wetness shivered over my thin dress as well. We stood thus for a long time, until he was able to raise his head and meet my gaze again. Then he motioned me out of the room.

He led me out back, away from all the others. It was cold here, and the wind found us. But I tried to ignore the wind and concentrate on his face. "How did you find out so soon?" He whispered the words, and I found myself responding in a whisper.

"Father drove Jane Foster on her rounds when she had trouble with her wagon."

"She sent for my mother about midnight," he recounted. "But she did not wake me or Father. After . . . well, she sent Maggie Wells this morning to tell us. We were expecting . . . good news . . . we were . . ."

His voice broke like a young boy's and he wheeled away from me. Tears filled my eyes as I rested my head against his stiff back. "I know, Eugene, I know." *There is something so helpless and pathetic,* I thought to myself, *in a man's suffering.* I was minded of Alexander, and even my father. I was consumed with a yearning tenderness.

"Eugene." I whispered his name. Then, "Eugene" again before he turned to me. Our lips met, and the touch was more a confirmation of spirit—of the life that throbbed through us—than it was of our flesh.

"We must go back inside," I told him. "But I will stay with you for as long as you want, for as long as you have need of me, dear."

He reached for my hand, and we walked together, feeling for the first time like an entity; two halves of a whole which would be incomplete, even meaningless, if divided or separated, in purpose or form.

I was there with Georgie, on a fair May morning when the flowers were lifting their heads and reaching jauntily toward the warm sun that flooded the whole world with its light. It seemed nothing unwholesome could live in such an atmosphere. Yet, when we approached her doorstep, where a bright pot of primroses had been planted, I saw the rock that had aimed true and shattered the pot to pieces, scattering the fragments, dirt, and bits of bruised blossoms all over the porch.

Georgie leaned down with a sigh and with her hands swept a pathway for us through the debris.

"What is this?" I asked. "Who would do such a thing, Georgie? Is it a schoolboy prank?"

"I wish it were." I followed her in to the cool sitting room and began to remove my hat. "You won't believe me when I tell you," she promised, placing her hat and gloves on the table and heading back to the kitchen. I followed, my interest well piqued.

"Since his arrival in Palmyra, Nathan has become good friends with the Smiths," she began. "In fact, he greatly admires their family, and has made no secret of it."

"And that is the problem." Her words had chilled me. "Still, Georgie?"

"Apparently so."

"But what have they done to offend anyone, especially of late? And what is your husband's offense?"

"Being their friends and speaking well of them to others."

"It cannot be as bad as that!"

"You would not think so, would you?" Georgie lit the fire under the kettle and stood on tiptoe to reach her best teacups.

"Have you any chocolate cake left?" I asked. No other cook in the whole village can touch Georgie's chocolate cake.

"I saved a piece for you." She smiled. "Don't worry about this, Esther. It is nothing but petty things, such as you saw."

"You mean this has happened before?"

"Several times. I suppose, if I think about it, we have done more to offend than merely be friendly. Nathan has asked Mr. Smith's advice on several matters and paid him to do some little carpentry jobs for him. Why, we even had them over to share a meal one Saturday evening."

"Stop it," I implored, sticking my fork into the moist cake Georgie had placed before me. "You will truly spoil my appetite."

"I know. Such behavior is disgusting as well as disgraceful." She sat down beside me, her chin propped in her hands. "But I am still the most popular teacher in Palmyra." The mischievous lights were beginning to dance in her eyes now. "And there is not a student, as well as most of their parents, whom Nathan has not won over entirely."

"Nevertheless, you ought to take care."

"Take care?" Georgie's grin widened. "What a dismal prospect that is."

"Georgeanna!"

"Esther, do not fuss and fret so. You'll wear yourself out." Georgie's voice was tender, so I could not refrain from smiling back at her and attempting to do as she said. I knew the wisdom of her words. I finished my cake and talked babies and patterns for new spring frocks, forcing thoughts that were distressing far out of my mind.

"We came to tell you ourselves. We wanted you especially to know."

Latisha and her Jonah stood in my kitchen fairly bubbling with excitement. "You are going to have a child!" *Good news at last!* "I am so happy for you."

I hugged them both and sat to hear all their dreaming and planning.

"We want a girl—even Jonah says he prefers having a daughter first!"

"And 'Tisha has not been sick, not one day." The proud husband beamed at her.

*Would that it had been so with my Tillie!* "When do you expect this happy event to take place?"

"The end of November or early December—sometime before Christmas."

She seemed very young to me, her face lit with anticipation. And this awkward fellow so in love with her!

"There is more news," Latisha chirped, remembering. "Georgie's brother, James, is courting Phoebe's sister, Lena."

"Oh dear," I replied, without thinking. "They are not at all suited for one another." Latisha nodded agreement, as solemn as any old wife.

"Folk say we are not suited," Jonah volunteered, scratching at his whiskers. "But they know less of the matter than they think."

He did not mean it as a rebuke, I knew. Besides, I had come to be quite fond of him. "Yes, you are right," I responded amicably. "And what's more, when young people have their minds set, what can anyone do?"

They caught the implication in those words and Jonah grinned back at me. "But for you two I could not be happier," I said.

They stayed a few minutes longer, before veritably floating off together. *How impossible it is to judge people and situations accurately,* I mused. *Yet we seldom let that little truth get in our way.* I had wanted to ask Jonah if he had heard any news lately of Randolph. Being on the canal, as he was, he had sent the word out for his friends to keep watch for the boy all along the route, east to Albany and west all the way to Buffalo on the shores of Lake Erie. Such a distance, with so many places where a lad alone might disappear! But he knew of my concern; surely if he had heard anything he would have contrived a way to tell me. If not, I had not wanted to dampen or in any way mar the joyous excitement they shared.

I had my own growing excitement to contend with as my wedding day drew near! Everyone shared in my happiness, except, perhaps, my mother, who was frightened at the idea of losing me, of being the only woman in her own quiet house. To do her justice, even Josephine tried to enter into the spirit of celebration. Phoebe came through for me in that sweet, quiet way of hers, creating delicate masterpieces I already cherished and hoped to hand down to my great-grandchildren. We had not spoken of Emily's death, not once, she and I. Even Georgie thought I ought to broach the subject with her. "If she will open up to anyone, it will be you," she said. Yet I could not do it. Something always seemed to stop me, something I could not put my finger on. So I respected her silence, enjoyed her company, and waited.

Through Eugene I knew that Maggie Wells, who had come through for us so splendidly when the twins were born, had found a wet nurse for the baby, and Simon was keeping her with him, though his mother had offered to take over the care of the child.

"What about your mother?" I had asked Eugene.

"She is getting on," he reminded me, "older than Simon's mother by ten years or more. Besides, I do not think she could bear it—a little girl who looks just like Emily."

"I would think that could prove to be of comfort."

"With some women it might."

Mrs. Thorn is not my favorite person; in fact, I find little in her that speaks to me in a comfortable, intimate way. But she *is* Eugene's mother, and my heart went out to her for the loss of her only daughter, the pain of which I could not even imagine.

"What is Simon naming his daughter?"

"I do not believe he can make up his mind about it," Eugene hedged. "For a time he considered calling her Emily, too, after her mother, but he has decided against that."

"And *for* something else?" Eugene was behaving a bit strangely.

"There is the name Emily had chosen for a girl," he replied. "I do not know what you will think of it." He continued to eye me a bit nervously.

"Well, tell me," I urged.

"She claimed it was her favorite name, as well as . . ."

"Eugene!"

"Emily wished to call her child Esther."

I was silent. I could not believe it. Myriad feelings washed over me, leaving me with sensations of sorrow I could not mitigate, so that the following morning I rose early and rode into Palmyra, and climbed the steep hill to the burial ground where Emily lay. I knelt beside the fresh grave, still sweetened with bunches of flowers, and spoke out loud.

"I am sorry, Emily, that you have been separated from your little one and denied the joy of rearing her. I wish . . ." *Oh, how useless wishes*

119

*and regrets are!* "I failed in life to be all to you that I should have been. I will not fail her. You have my word on it."

After a time I rose and moved to the familiar spot where my little Nathaniel was buried. I could still remember with ease the aching tenderness of the tiny, fragrant weightlessness of him cradled in my arms. Without closing my eyes I could still see his eyes, deep as pools of eternity, gazing quietly, patiently into my own. I experienced again that powerful sensation, half anguish, half comfort: *there is so much about life that I do not understand. So much beauty, so much purpose and endurance!*

After a long while I turned and walked away, renewed and reconciled once again.

If there was one thing that stood out about my wedding, it was the abundance of *flowers!* Blossoms in the church, woven round the posts and railings, standing in large, overflowing vases: daisies, daffodils, ladies smock, wild hyacinths—a sweet, abandoned array: campion, buttercup, yellow heartsease, and even long, trailing branches of the flowering crabapple. There were wreaths of blossoms gracing the shining, braided hair of my maids of honor and my own bridal veil. I placed small bouquets of fragrant tussie-mussies in the arms of every woman and girl I could think of; the tables were lined with blossoms and the bower set up in my father's sweet meadow where we sat amid the abundance to welcome loved ones and guests.

I was surprised that I could think of anything outside myself and Eugene, that I could view the beauty and affection of my dear friends with such delight. But somehow I was able to see them with a clarity of love I had never experienced before—see each for her own distinct graces and gifts. How my heart ached with affection for them!

My poor mother. At one point she bent over me and whispered, "What will happen to your gardens, Esther? I cannot bear to think of them running to seed and ruin."

"I will not let them do that!" I leaned up and kissed her cool cheek, still white-skinned and unwrinkled. "I shall keep them myself if I have to, as I've done in the past!"

*Change, constant change.* But for the first time it seemed glorious, desirable to me. I could smile at everyone and see nothing but the best of whatever was before me. I suppose love has the power to do that, if anything has.

Oh, the kind words and well-wishing, the music and dancing, the food and the laughter, the moonlight, spilling silver and soft all around us, and Eugene's hand warm in mine—his green eyes gentled with incredulity . . . and me feeling truly beautiful for perhaps the first time in my life . . .

"Heaven help us, Esther's a prettier bride than the rest of us put together!" Josephine speaking the words out of laughter, but with tears in her eyes.

Tillie squeezing my arm and whispering, "Be happy for both of us, Esther. I will be so glad if you do."

Georgie, smelling of mint and fresh lavender, kissing my cheek and saying, a bit strangely, "You will come into your own now, dear Esther. Just wait and see."

Phoebe gliding close, like some lovely wraith materializing out of the moon's glow, pressing her thin, capable fingers against mine—no words spoken, only that terrible tenderness that no words can convey.

My mother crying, angry at her own vulnerability, holding Jonathan up to be kissed. My father, so solemn-eyed, embracing me gently, saying, "Do not forget to come home, my Esther, every now and again . . ."

Oh, the sweet, poignant pain and bliss of it all!

And at last the flower-draped carriage, Tansy with blossoms woven into her thick mane—my father handing me up. A mist of tears, of voices echoing and re-echoing, like music inside my head. Then silence, gathering sweet as fragrance about us, bearing us out of the common . . . weaving magic, like the night air, in streamers about our heads.

Eugene's family lives near the edge of Palmyra, yet close enough to the bustle of things so that the blacksmithing business can thrive. We chose for our own a small house I looked upon as a compromise; a bit out into the open country, so as to be close to my own home, but still close enough in to be considered a part of the town.

I had already planted my gardens—herbs and vegetables and flowers—and Eugene had outfitted the toolsheds and barns. My father gave me Tansy as part of my dowry, and one of our freshest milk cows. Alexander had presented us with an exquisite rosewood bedroom suite, so that I could leave my old bed at Mother's, where I believed it belonged. Tillie, unbeknownst to me, sent away to the city for exorbitantly rich bed coverings and fancy curtains for my windows. People's generosity overwhelmed me, and I felt as spoiled as a princess in a dream from which I did not wish to wake.

But Eugene was the quiet, living center of this magnificent dream. He was flesh and blood, less than perfect, but the most overwhelming gift I was given that night. A living legacy—this life that desired to merge itself with my life, desired to care for me—was willing to open the core of its being to my seeing eyes. I was overwhelmed by the joy of desire, of selflessness—by the delights of love which I had never imagined—by the wonder of two people merging, in so many ways, into one. Nothing I had hoped for, nothing I had wondered at, could ever come close to this joy.

I awake in the pre-dawn and stand at the gray square of window and watch for the day. *The first day of my life,* I think. *The first day of my new life as woman and wife.* This is more than change; this is a sort of metamorphosis, slow though it may be. This is a glory—putting on a new self. This is a weaving together, a reaching inward, a reaching outward—this is seeing through eyes that are not my eyes. This is *life.* For the first time I know this and am content in the knowing.

Eugene stirs on the bed. He is no longer a stranger to me, but in a sense part of myself. I feel a hunger for this existence we are creating together—an eagerness, a sense of purpose I have never before felt in my life. I want to sing. I want to laugh. I want to open my arms and hold the whole world close to me in an embrace of gratitude and wonder.

I pick up the slender volume where I write notes on the daily occurrences of my life, where I jot down favorite verses and thoughts I have had. I go to the little desk in the corner that I brought with me and search for my pen. I must at least attempt to preserve some of this wonder and beauty before it filters into the ordinary and I forget the intensity of it, the clarity of vision it lends me.

I curl up on my chair like a cat and begin writing. The morning comes in on soft kitten feet, so as not to disturb me. I feel its breath on my neck. Sweet and cool; it is in no hurry. Nor must I be. Each moment is precious, a pearl of beauty that will never repeat itself and, once lost, never be regained.

For a moment I set my pen and paper aside and move, with the same morning feet, to stand beside the bed, lean over my still, sleeping husband, and press my lips, ever so lightly, against his forehead. He does not move, does not stir.

*The first act of the first day. A prayer, a caress.* I smile at my own foolishness, and return to my desk.

# Chapter 15

## Palmyra: September 1829

The summer passed in a long succession of happy days for me, and I am ashamed to admit that I involved myself far less than usual in other people's affairs. My friends understood, I believe, and left me to my honeymoon idyll in peace—a peace disrupted, aptly so, by a quiet revelation so unexpected and so shocking as to at last divert me away from myself.

Would Phoebe have told me if I had not happened upon her at the market and asked, quite boldly, if I could come to her home for tea?

"Eugene is working long hours with his father. You know the demands on a blacksmith during the summer months. I will admit to missing him dreadfully," I sighed. "And I must confess that my little house is in good running order," I explained, "my garden is thriving, and some days I am bored."

Phoebe shook her head. "You do not know what the word means, Esther." She smiled. "Let me guess. You bake good things for Eugene each morning, right after you come in from the weeding you do very early, while the air is yet cool. If you have time on your hands in the hot, quiet hours of the afternoon, you read your loved books or write in that little journal I've seen you scribbling in. Then you freshen up, and perhaps pick fresh flowers for the table, so you are ready to greet your tired husband when he comes into the house."

Before she was through I was shaking with laughter. "What a picture you paint!"

"Yes, it is lovely—mostly because it is so accurate."

I leaned over and gave her a hug. And we scurried like children to pour glasses of tart lemonade and bring out fresh cheese and crackers and little glazed poppy seed cakes. It was only after we were seated companionably together that Phoebe said, "Esther, Simon has asked me to marry him, and I have consented."

I answered nothing at all, but leaned back against her plump soft pillows, quite out of breath.

"Come, dear friend, you must have some opinion on the matter. Surely you must have thought of the—possibility."

I shook my head. "Phoebe, did you?" *That was an inane, silly question!* I quickly added, "I have been most consumingly diverted, you remember. I have not been thinking, really, of much at all."

"I have been thinking of little else." She spoke the words simply, in a low tone, but the emotion behind them thrilled through me.

"My dear—"

"I have never stopped loving Simon, you know."

"I did not think you had," I replied honestly. "I know you too well."

She stood and moved about the room in a somewhat distracted manner. "We have discussed the matter in detail."

"Already?"

"Well, there is much to consider—not least being the soonest we dare set a date to be wed."

"Yes, well, there will always be those who will criticize, no matter how long you wait."

She nodded thoughtfully. "And what is considered 'proper' must be seriously amended, since there is a child in the picture who is in need of a mother's care."

"I hope people will see it that way and be generous."

"Most will, I believe."

We both paused. We both were thinking of the same thing. "Do you know what Simon has named the infant—well, the choice was Emily's, really."

"Eugene told me what he thought it was to be," I said honestly.

"Yes, it is Esther."

"I am deeply moved."

"So am I. It seems fitting, somehow."

"And will perhaps make it a little easier for you to love this child as your own, dear heart."

"I truly pray, Esther, that I will have no difficulty there."

"And the mother's shadow, everywhere about you in the house?" I felt I had to say it.

"Trust you to face the hard issues head on!" Phoebe sighed, and the sound shuddered all through her system. "He loved me, you know he did. But he chose her before me. I cannot forget that. I have had to live with it this past year and more." She drew her breath, as though the very speaking of the words had been painful. "But I never despised Emily for it. She had no more control in the matter than I did."

"I believe that is true."

"So heaven has ordained that her happiness was short lived, but that I should not be cheated out of mine. How can I not be grateful, Esther—and happy?"

*How can you not be—angel that you are!* "Does Simon know what a prize he has?" I cried. "Does he love you sufficiently, Phoebe?"

"He will. He is still mourning, and he turns to me in need. But the love is there, too. If I did not feel this, if I did not know this, I would have refused him."

"Your wisdom is sufficient," I said, reaching for her hand. "It satisfies me." Her face lit with a gentle glow. "And when you are married, I shall sew your dress, as you sewed all of ours, and it shall be the plainest, most ill-fitting gown any bride in Palmyra has ever worn!"

We were giggling again, like girls. And I realized what a long time it had been since I had seen Phoebe truly at ease, and happy—and it made my heart sing.

Eugene's mother was unrelenting. She would not believe it; she would not countenance it! She would give Simon no peace.

"You must do something!" I pleaded with my husband. "You are one of the few people she will listen to."

"She will listen to no one in this matter."

"Will you not at least try?"

He opened his mouth to refuse me, but I think he saw the misery in my countenance. I watched him struggle within himself. At length he said shakily, "Yes, it is right that you ask me, Esther. I will try, for your sake."

*How good a man you are,* I wanted to say. But the words would have embarrassed him, so I merely kissed him instead, and tried to be especially kind over the following days to compensate for the sacrifice he was resolved to make.

It was in vain, however. His mother was intent upon being miserable and could entertain no view of things but her own. Eugene was frustrated; Simon was hurt; I tried not to think about it. But Phoebe was calm and serene.

"You cannot expect more from the woman right now," she defended. "She is terrified to let go of her pain—I know how that feels. If the pain goes, her daughter will go with it, or so she believes."

She soothed us all. Simon wanted the marriage to take place as soon as possible; a quiet ceremony with no one in attendance but the necessary parties and witnesses.

"That is not fair to Phoebe," I protested. "Every girl deserves a wedding of some sort, and Phoebe has certainly earned hers."

"She does not desire it," Simon and Eugene assured me, sitting on my porch one late summer evening. "She feels it would be unseemly."

"It is not unseemly!" I retorted. I had both husband and brother before me! "It is not Phoebe's fault that Emily died. You are the most fortunate of men, Simon, and you will be for the remainder of your life if you have our dear girl. Can you not think of something to do for her?"

I think my words smote through his fog of loneliness and self-pity at last. I could see his mind thinking behind the shy blue eyes.

After that, I left them to make their own decisions, and the date for the marriage was set.

"What of your parents?" I asked Phoebe. "How do they feel about this?"

"They gave up on me long ago." She said the words with one of her kind smiles. "I am not like them, and they cannot understand me. Lena and the boys, happily, do not give them such woes. Whatever is decided, they will agree with. I believe they will be relieved just to see me married and no longer a concern to them, you know."

So there were less than a dozen of us in the nave of the chapel that Friday morning: Phoebe and Simon, his parents (who were relieved and grateful for this propitious turn of events), her parents (a little less enthusiastic), myself and Eugene, Tillie, Josie, and Georgie.

"All the beauty of the village gathered in one place," Eugene teased me. "It is truly a feast for the eyes."

127

But it *was*, in fact. We girls were dressed in a manner that had been customary on May Day mornings through the past ten years or more of our lives—ever since Phoebe discovered how gifted she was with a needle and thread! I had made sure there were flowers in abundance. And Phoebe, in a creamy gown trimmed sparingly with lace and embroidered lilies-of-the-valley in pale yellow and green, was as elegant a bride as I've ever seen. Her plain features, the straight lines of her face, the high forehead—all were softened by the beautifying effects of her happiness, which permeated us all.

And there was a surprise in store, influenced perhaps a little by my counsel to Simon. He had arranged a short boat trip on the canal; just a few stops, two nights away. But *alone together.* Just what they needed. I nearly cried at the happiness that came into her eyes.

We watched them go off together, waving and kissing our hands to them. Arrangements had been made for little Esther; the wet nurse would keep her. But when Phoebe returned they would wean the child onto goat's milk, and she would be in the care of a mother every bit as good and tender as her own would have been.

That night, alone in bed with my husband, I snuggled close to his warmth, wondering what Power ordained this merging of man and woman into something inexplicably good and meaningful—something neither could hope to achieve on their own. It pleased me to think about people making each other happy. It pleased me to think about love—to relax and accept it, with all its limitations, as the most precious thing we possess.

Few men are as patient as Josie's Alexander; perhaps he was too patient with her. During the long summer months, when time dragged on her hands, my sister took to dressing up and sallying forth in search of adventure. None of us could do such a thing; we would not even know how. In the afternoons she would visit the shops and establishments of business, sometimes upon the most flimsy excuse. There were several young men of our age upon whom she practiced mild flirtations—had not Josie always indulged in such ways? The difference was, of course, that she was now a married woman and dared not fly in the face of convention. When I mentioned my concerns to my mother, I was not surprised by her reaction.

"Josephine is bored and unhappy. You know that, Esther."

"Why should she be unhappy? And, for that matter, why should she be bored?"

"Alexander has provided her with help, so she has little to do in the running of her household." My mother glared at me in the old fashion. "She wants a child, Esther! It is so tragic that she cannot keep her babies, that—"

"She must not run away from it, Mother! We both know this is what she is doing."

"What would you do in her place?"

"Appreciate the good husband I had and the many advantages he had given me. At least, I like to think I would."

"You cannot judge." Mother pushed her hair back from her forehead and looked around for Jonathan. "Will you check on the child, Esther? He went out the door while we were talking."

"Mother—"

"Find him first, then we can continue."

So it always went. I let things ride until Eugene came home from his work at the shop late one evening. "There was a hay ride tonight at Turner's farm," he blurted. "For the young folk."

"How nice," I said, turning the chicken I was frying and adjusting the flame beneath the mustard greens.

"Josie was there—alone, Esther."

I dropped the wooden spoon I was stirring with, and it clattered to the floor. He picked it up for me and touched my shoulder gently.

"Did you see her yourself?"

"I did. Father sent me to take back a horse rake Dave Turner had him fit with new teeth. She was sitting beside Rob Sumpsion—and he had his arm around her."

I sat down, feeling a bit sick. "What has gotten into her, Eugene?"

He shrugged. "I suspect she doesn't let herself think about it. I suspect she looks at it only as innocent fun."

He was right. I had not realized he saw through her so clearly.

"We must do something. I'll ride out and talk to her tomorrow."

"I think you should. But don't work yourself up, Esther, and don't go expecting too much."

❧

I *did* go expecting my sister to come to her senses. But she only laughed in my face.

"Heaven preserve us, Esther, you are making a mountain out of a molehill. I meant no harm. Because I am married, does that mean I cannot join in good times?"

"Yes, if you are without your husband and sitting with another man's arm around you."

"Another man? Rob is an old flame, an old friend—that is all."

"Josephine!" I was shaking in my frustration and agitation. "You are jeopardizing all that is dear to you and doing Alexander a great injustice. I do not wish to see you hurt him."

"Alex takes little notice of me, Esther. And you are making too much out of . . . nothing."

I gave up. In the end, with Josephine, I always give up. I wondered—I hoped that her husband was oblivious of his young wife's antics, and that this nonsense would pass.

❧

Near the end of the summer I determined to make Tuesday my day to go calling. It was a splendid idea. For one day I could put all else aside and enjoy the sweet hours, letting them take me wherever they would.

One week Tillie and I decorated old leghorn bonnets together, making them over according to our own tastes, and were quite delighted with the results. I lined the broad inside brim of straw with rose-colored satin, then trimmed it with a feather dipped in rose dye and a little wreath of anemones. Tillie trimmed hers with bunches of dahlias and bright field flowers.

As we worked I learned that Gerard was doing well at the bank and that Peter had been promoted from the lowest rung of "fetch and carry" to an assistant custodian. And, of course, when school was in session he did not work many hours.

"What does Peter wish to do when he becomes a man?" I asked her.

"Anything but banking! He associates it with too many things he finds distasteful."

"I can understand that."

"Yet he is determined to prepare for a profession rather than common, paid labor. His days on the canal taught him that."

Mere mention of the canal made us both choke up, and I ventured to ask if they had any intelligence whatsoever concerning Randolph. But, of course, they had not.

"It is so singular," Theodora confided. "My mother never makes mention of him at all. I would expect that from Father. But even when we are alone together, and it would be quite natural, she will not speak his name."

"Perhaps that is the only way she can bear it."

"Esther, why does life have to be filled with difficulties so heavy they outweigh the joy?"

"Nothing could outweigh this joy," I replied, scooping little Laurie up into my arms and kissing his plump cheek. "You can pour your heart and soul into this bright receptacle, and all your beauty and intelligence will live through him into generations you have not dreamt of."

She had to smile at my rhetoric. "You make it sound easy and lovely," she sighed.

131

"We *must* choose to see it so, else the darkness will get the best of us, and we cannot allow that."

It was tacitly agreed then between us. We would struggle upward together, no matter what cruelties and heartaches combined to hold us back.

I walked to the office of the *Wayne Sentinel* to meet Eugene, kicking the new autumn leaves before me. I was happy for my husband. His father had agreed to try out a young apprentice, and Eugene had been training the boy, who was a quick learner and deft with his hands. Mr. Grandin had hired my husband to work on his newspaper, learning the trade from the bottom up but encouraged to write copy for the pages of the publication as well.

*How much happier people are when they are doing something they love to do,* I mused. A simple formula—yet a luxury afforded so few.

As I reached the handsome building on Main Street I paused, because there was a small knot of men gathered outside the door. The expressions on their faces were dark; their eyes, as they looked up and past me, hardened by anger. I found myself taking a few steps back and pausing, uncertain.

"I thought Grandin turned Jo Smith down." The words were a growl. I could not tell who spoke them.

A few oaths followed; then another said, "We warned him. He's got no business thinking he can publish this gold Bible of his."

"Fool boy! He asked for what's coming to 'im!"

"What's coming to him?" I posed the question boldly, then shivered at my own audacity, for I had not intended to speak at all.

Two of the men tipped their hats to me, the others lowered their eyes and shuffled their feet uncomfortably. "What has Joseph Smith done that it concerns you men? Haven't you something better to do with your time?"

I was annoyed at their anger, at the ugliness I had heard in their voices.

"With respect, ma'am, you don't know what you're talking about. Leave such matters to those that do."

"If you know what's good for you," one of the mutterers added.

My ire was up and flaming! "*You* leave such matters alone! Joseph and his family are honorable people, and what they believe is their own affair."

"Not when they try to shove it down our throats!" The largest man of the group stepped forward and confronted me, his whole stance combative, his face so close to mine that I could see the bloodshot lines in the whites of his eyes, and the tips of dark whiskers peppering his unshaven face.

I felt a hand on my shoulder and jumped.

"Esther, how nice of you to meet me." Eugene began steering me before him. "Gentlemen." He tipped his hat to the glowering assemblage and fairly pushed me before him until we were safe away.

"Eugene!" I fidgeted in his grasp.

"Esther, what were you up to back there?"

"Do you know what was happening?"

He ignored my strident tone. "Yes. We've had protestors in and out of the office all day."

"Why?"

"Mr. Grandin has agreed to print this Bible of Joseph Smith's—he calls it the Book of Mormon." He lowered his voice. "It's the one an angel was supposed to have given him."

"So." My spirits were boiling still. "So, what if he's right, Eugene? What if he's telling the truth?"

"What if he isn't?"

"Yes, what if he isn't? What harm will it do? Bravo for Egbert Grandin and his pluck!"

Eugene laughed out loud. I had a way of constantly amazing him, and he took delight in what he called "Esther's antics" or "Esther on her high horse." He was always saying, "I like a girl with spirit. That's why I asked you to marry me. Life with you will never be dull, Esther! Not for one blink of an eye."

He meant well. It was one of his endearing expressions of love for me. But sometimes it drove me to distraction. For he had few convictions of his own, few things upon which he held passionate views. He did not mean to ridicule mine, but he did take them lightly. This matter of Joseph Smith meant nothing to him at all.

133

I found myself fretting about it, smacking under the injustice as though the barbs had been driven into my own flesh, my own spirit. *Live and let live.* That, too, seemed a simple enough maxim. Why did people find it so nearly impossible to put it into practice in their day-to-day lives?

# Chapter 16

J ack is gone."

I had never seen Georgie look so pale in her life. I pulled her into the house and made her sit down.

"Mother came to the school this morning. It was terrible, Esther. I couldn't get her to stop crying."

"What happened?"

"He didn't come home last night. His bed hasn't been slept in."

"That's unusual for Jack, isn't it?" Georgeanna's youngest brother is one of my favorites. High-spirited and fun-loving to a fault, nevertheless he has a good head on his shoulders, and there is no guile, no meanness in him. "How old is Jack now?"

"Fifteen. Esther—no one saw him yesterday; I mean, he wasn't in any of the places he should have been. That is just not like him."

"No . . ." My head was whirling, trying to hit upon some clue, some slender thread of light to lead us out of the darkness.

We worried at the matter for nearly half an hour, until we were startled by the throaty chime of the town clock and Georgie jumped up. "Lunch is over. I must get back to school now."

"I will come by later," I promised. "Send someone if you need me."

After she was gone the house seemed so quiet, and her misery hung in the atmosphere like a bad odor. "I'll go visit Tillie and the baby for a few minutes," I determined, "and be back in time to finish my ironing and get dinner started before Eugene gets home."

When I arrived at Theodora's, the girl her father had engaged to help her answered the door and leaned forward on her toes to whisper, "The mistress is lying down with a headache, and I should hate to disturb her."

I hesitated. Tillie, I knew, was with child again, and I disliked the thought of disturbing her, too. As I tried to make up my mind, I felt, rather than heard, a presence behind me and detected the strong scent of a man's cologne as a figure brushed past me.

"Where is your mistress?" The speaker's tone was harsh as well as imperative.

"She is resting in her room, sir."

Gerard Whittier had failed to even notice me, or at least to acknowledge my presence there on his doorstep. Ruth's cheeks colored and she threw me a helpless glance. "Is it necessary to disturb her at this moment, sir?"

"It is necessary to disturb her, Ruth. Go bid her come to me, and be quick about it."

I slipped in behind him and shut the door quietly. Perhaps I would be of assistance . . . if it were not too private a matter.

I heard loud cries from the direction of the nursery; the fretful, somewhat annoying sounds young children make when their comforts and desires have been ignored. I took a few steps down the hallway. Ruth came out of Tillie's room and paused, uncertain how best to proceed.

"Let me take care of Laurie," I suggested. "Tell Tillie I am here and will bring the child in to her after I have settled him."

Ruth nodded gratefully and ducked back into Tillie's room, while I entered the nursery and picked up the little one, whose sobs stopped as soon as I held him and he heard the sound of my voice.

"You can feel the ugly vibrations when Papa talks that way, as well as any adult can," I crooned. "Shame on him for behaving so." I hummed as I took off his wet nappie and dressed him in dry clothes. By the time we reached the sitting room the conversation there was well under way.

"You cannot fault me! I held my peace all morning—just to be certain I waited until the lunch hour had passed. I am trying to be fair, Theodora—"

"It is not like Peter to—simply disappear," Tillie faltered.

My heart gave a painful jump. I entered the room uninvited, feeling the tension like the heavy folds of a curtain I had to push my way through. "Pardon me," I began pleasantly, as though detecting none of the confusion and vexation at my presumption. "Perhaps I can shed some light on the subject."

135

I repeated what Georgie had told me earlier. "Well, that settles the question, doesn't it?" Gerard rubbed his long, dry hands together in satisfaction. "The two boys have gone off on a lark together." He chuckled under his breath, but the sound was not a pleasant one. "I hope what adventures they have are well worth it—for they shall certainly answer for their insolence when we get them back home."

Tillie's face was white already. I saw her tighten her lips against speaking the hasty word. *I* labored under no such restrictions!

"Peter is not your son, sir. Nor are you, in point of fact, his employer. It is not for you to revel in the contemplation of what ill fate will befall the boy."

"Ill fate!" Gerard's distaste for me, for my presence in his home, was as evident as if he had just been forced to swallow a pint of vinegar. I had to work to keep myself from smiling at his discomfort. "Discipline, just discipline to quell a boy's pranks, Mrs. Thorn. Surely you can understand that."

"Not as you understand it or would administer it; no, sir. With your harshness you would quell his spirit, not his naughtiness, and there is more harm in that than good. Besides"—I drew myself up a little as I dandled his son on my knee—"I do not agree with your judgment of the matter, not in the least, sir."

"Oh?" A slash of black eyebrow was raised against me. "Pray tell, then, what do you think?"

"I believe these boys, both good boys with sterling reputations, have—" How could I say this? I had little more than a vague feeling to go by. "Have gone off on some business of their own, that they consider important."

"Secret business of their own?" Gerard's disdain dripped like syrup. He held his hands out, palms up, mockingly conceding the point to me. "I must get back to the bank, dear."

He rose. He was chuckling softly under his breath; a dry sound, like the scratchings of birds beneath autumn bushes. He planted a kiss on Tillie's head and walked out of the room. I did not warrant a farewell; I did not warrant his common courtesy. But, what of his son? He had paid him not the least attention, not for one moment had he even glanced at him since we had entered. He passed by our chair in leaving, so that his leg brushed the child's leg, and Laurie held his arms up. But his father took no notice. Anger, which usually sustains me, did not come to my defense now. I felt only sadness, which swept over me like a great weariness.

When Tillie heard the front door shut she turned to me. "You are right," she said. "I can feel that you are right. And we must have faith in them."

*How nicely put.* "How true. We must have faith in them, sweetness. They will prove worthy of it, I am sure."

Her gaze met mine. There was resolve in her look, a strength I was not accustomed to seeing there. *She is growing,* I thought. *She will be more for that man to reckon with than he believes.*

"Come," she said, rising and putting her arms out to her baby. "Ruth has brewed some gingerroot tea for me. Come and visit for just a few minutes before you have to go back home."

I followed her gladly. Our determination had lifted the burden that had pressed on my heart. *Oh, the sweetness of such felicitous comrades,* I thought happily, realizing at that moment how blessed my life was.

"If the both of you together have come to such a conclusion, I shall abide by it." Georgie's black eyes had a luster, like glossy-skinned chestnuts when the sun polishes and enhances their sheen. "It is difficult, though, is it not, to wait and wonder, and hope no harm will befall them?"

"It is indeed."

"The lot of women—fools that we are, to bear children, and wrap the tendrils of our hearts around them, so that any harm that comes to them tears at our beings as well."

I looked at her closely. "Are you trying to tell me something, Georgie?"

She flushed back. "Perhaps."

"Oh, Georgie—"

"I am not certain yet—"

"You will make the best of mothers," I cried.

"I hope your confidence is contagious when the time comes," she replied. "James has been asking my father what he must do to earn his place as a partner in the dry goods store."

I put my hand to my mouth. "He is that determined?"

"That is what opposition will do. Mr. Hathaway has forbidden him to call upon Lena—chased him out with a pitchfork last Saturday."

I could not help smiling at the image.

" 'You don't come mooning round here until you have something to offer my daughter'—that's what he said. And I don't believe James will cross him."

"Wise decision. They're just children, Georgie." We sighed together, and she went on her way.

I could not get to sleep that night, because a noisy wind was whining in the chimney and causing the beams of the house to creak and rumble. Everywhere there were muffled night noises speaking of darkness and loneliness, and a cold that would chill to the bone.

*Let them be safe!* I prayed, closing my eyes and snuggling closer to Eugene. *Whatever could they be up to?* I had no idea. But the lonely wind vexed me in fitful swells and whispers, and would not be still.

I meant only to check in on Latisha, for her baby was due any time. Goodness, but her figure was trim still for a woman about to deliver! And she was not discouraged, as I believe I would have been.

It was not until Jonah walked in from work that a sudden light flooded over me. "What have you heard of the boys?" I asked. He hedged, effecting a bland expression. "*What?*" I demanded.

"Miss Esther, 'tis none of my business."

"Yes, it is!" I guessed. "Where have they gone?"

He scratched at his chin whiskers and shifted his weight from foot to foot uneasily.

"Latisha . . ." I appealed. But I could see she knew none of this.

"They came down to the boats yesterday morning early. Asked my advice."

My insides were churning. "Concerning . . ."

"Someone had to decide it—matter o' fact, I nearly sent for you. But I b'lieve you'd have encouraged them, too."

"Whatever are you talking about?"

"Seems Randolph sent a letter to his brother via Jack. He's holed up in a jail in Schenectady." He glanced uneasily at his wife. " 'Tisha . . ."

"I'm all right."

"He asked the boys to get the money together to bail him out."

"The nerve of him!" Latisha shook her head in alarm and displeasure. I shared, at least in part, her sentiments.

"You *should* have come to me, you know." The nervous shuffling again. "Did you three confide in no one? How did you come up with the money?"

"Peter had a little savings put aside, and so did I. He sold his pony for the rest of it."

I felt my temperature rising. "Your money is needed for the baby," I complained. "I shall make sure it is returned to you. Is the pony Peter's possession outright? What will his father say?"

Jonah shrugged. "Can't answer either of those questions, Miss Esther. But I thought it the right thing to do."

"Of course. How long will it take—when do you expect them to be returning?"

"No more than a couple more days if things go well. Less than a week anyways."

"And if they bring Randolph back—what then?"

"I suspect he's havin' trouble with that arm, the way you and I expected. I suspect he's run himself into the ground some."

"I'll have to think upon it. I shall come up with something, I promise."

I brought out the sweater and matching booties I had knit for the baby and turned the conversation to happier things, kissing them both good-bye as I left. "Keep in touch, for mercy's sake," I admonished Jonah, "if you hear anything at all!"

I went directly to Tillie and told her everything; I knew she could keep the secret. She dug into her pocketbook at once and pulled out some bills.

"I shall send this money to Mr. Sinclair by way of Ruth; she can be trusted."

"Have you enough?"

"And to spare." She set her jaw in a determined expression, which was not unbecoming. "That is one area in which Gerard dares not oppose me. He knows who butters his bread, and that my father would not want me treated stingily—" She grimaced a little. "Even if Father's motives be foremost those of pride."

139

I went next to Georgie. Her relief was evident. "I have something for you in return for your troubles," she said with an impish grin. And she proceeded to lift from a basket behind a chair—*I should have guessed it!*—a kitten, a kitten as white as new-driven snow, as fluffy as dandelions at seed time.

"My old cat is still home with Mother, you know."

"But kittens so late," I marveled.

"Iris believes her ordained task in life is to produce a litter every six months, no matter the time or season!" When she saw me hesitate she dropped the treasure in my lap. "Come, Esther, your house is not really a home, and you'll admit it, until you have a cat on the hearth."

I cannot resist the winsome creatures, and she knows it! Of course, in the end I gave in. "Dandelion," I said, "be it male or female, that is what I shall call it."

"No, that is a name for yellow cats and tabbies."

"Dandelion," I persisted. "It shall mean to me the frothy white softness of the seeds we blew and scattered and wished on as girls."

"Very well," Georgie agreed.

"Have you an extra you could take over to Phoebe?" I asked, as I was leaving.

"Yes. I did not think of that."

"Can I come along when you do?"

"Let us do it right now. Plop Dandelion back in the basket, and we shall let Phoebe choose her own from the three remaining."

Creatures sensed Georgie's calm and behaved themselves admirably for her. The kittens curled into balls and rode in the basket that rocked on her arm, causing no disturbance at all. We found Phoebe in the kitchen, her bread turned out warm on the board, a stew bubbling on the back of the black stove. She was sitting beside the fire with Emily's child on her lap. It was a sweet picture, and I sensed true contentment behind it.

She was delighted at the idea of the kitten, and let the baby's hands touch and feel before she made her selection, placing the tiny creature against the infant's soft cheek. Little Esther was nearly ten months old now and made the loveliest noises. Phoebe placed her on the floor with the kitten, and she scooted about, chasing and calling out to the frolicsome bundle of fur.

"I could not love her more if she were my own." Phoebe's wonder was in her voice, lending it an almost musical quality. "I did not expect this—a love so fierce and tender."

"I am glad of it," I said, kissing her.

"You certainly keep a spotless house," Georgie observed, looking around.

I wanted to ask about Simon, but did not dare. Phoebe, reading my mind, as she does, gave me one of her gentle smiles. "Things with Simon are improving. In some ways it is slow going with him. At first—at first I believe he was afraid to love me, afraid to even touch me, as if his love would hurt me, as he felt it had somehow hurt her."

*How complicated human beings are!* I thought, with a touch of dismay. I rose and kissed both Esther and her mother good-bye. Walking back I asked Georgie, "What will you do with the last two kittens?"

"Keep them, of course."

"It will get out of hand," I warned her, "and you'll have more cats than you have dishes in which to feed them! What will Nathan say?"

"He likes them, thank goodness. In fact, that is one of the conditions I set down when he asked me to marry him." It is so wonderful to laugh with Georgie when she is in one of her moods!

When I took my own white kitten home Eugene was waiting. "That is where you've been!" he said. But he took the delicate thing into his arms, and found a small box and old blankets we could use to make a bed for him.

"Dandelion is better than Fluffy or Snowball," he decided, when I told him the name. "Cats are women's substitutes for children. You know that, don't you?"

I was taken aback by his unexpected comment. "I never thought of it that way before."

"Babies are the answer," he said, with a wink.

"But they are ever so much more trouble," I bantered back, tying my apron and getting out matches to light the stove. "You can't stick them in a basket and forget them, or push them out to play when they get underfoot."

"I suppose you are right." He came up beside me, parted my hair with his fingers, and kissed the back of my neck. "Babies are still to be preferred," he said. And I wondered where in the world that came from, and what was going on in his mind.

# Chapter 17

## Palmyra: December 1829

Latisha's baby came before Jack and Peter returned with Randolph. Her daughter was born on Josephine's wedding anniversary. I went with Tillie because both girls wanted me there. If Tillie and I were a bit envious of this delicate, curly-haired creature who went to her mother's breast so easily, we did not say so out loud. Nor did I tell my own sister the date of the baby's birth, though she heard from another source.

"Heaven help us!" she exclaimed, when we met at Mother's for Sunday dinner. "I'm glad it was her and not me. To be tied to an infant and a schedule of nursing—with the holidays coming."

The emptiness behind her words was appalling. I wanted to take her into my arms. I glanced toward Alexander, who was carefully dishing potatoes from the platter. His arm had frozen mid-air.

"They have named her Sarah," I said, because I could think of nothing else in my panic.

"A nice enough name, but rather common," was Josephine's comment.

"You have become more adept at cooking since we left," I teased my mother, and for once she had the sense to respond. We talked then of crops, and the dam some of the men were building upriver, and of the alterations Alexander was making in the rebuilding of his mill trace, and the tense moment relaxed and passed.

Later, as Eugene and I were leaving, Josie asked if we were going to the Christmas dance.

"I shan't miss a chance to wrap my arms round this beautiful girl," Eugene said, surprising me again.

A brief flicker of disappointment touched my sister's features. It was gone in a heartbeat, but I fancied I saw the gray film it had left behind on her flesh.

❧

Jack and Peter brought Randolph to my place as I had instructed Jonah they do. All three boys looked like tramps who had been begging from town to town. It was a bitter cold day, clear and biting. I ushered them in and poured hot water for them to bathe in, and gave them old clothes of Eugene's to wear, even before I would feed them or let them speak to me at all.

"It was a grand and foolish thing you did," I began, fixing my eye upon Jack, who had the least emotional involvement in the matter. "You could have trusted someone as confidant, if only to ease the anguish your parents have been suffering."

I explained how I had stumbled upon their secret and that no one knew but Tillie, Georgie, and myself, besides Jonah and Latisha.

"You will have to explain to your fathers," I said. Jack, who was not afraid, nodded, but I saw Peter wince.

"I'm not going back to my father's house," Randolph declared vigorously. I had not yet dared meet his eyes. How dim and faded was the spark of light within them. I looked at him steadily. "No one is saying you must."

All three appeared relieved. "But you have to do something, and I mean it—something useful, to justify the sacrifice these lads have made for you." I thought he looked terribly pale, and his lips were drawn in a tight line, but he nodded.

"Do you have something in mind?" Peter asked. "Not the bank, surely."

"Not the bank." We all chuckled a bit, to help ease the tension.

"There isn't much I can do." Randolph spoke the words stoutly enough. I had noticed already how he favored his arm, let it hang limp, or rest in his lap, using the other almost exclusively.

"I suppose not," I replied evenly. "You've not even managed to destroy yourself yet, though I suspect you've given it a rollicking good effort."

I felt the others draw in their breaths and the room went silent.

"I'll not sit back and baby you," I continued. "I care for you too much for that. What's more, I've seen what self-pity can do to people—even in the case of my own sister. I do not want that for you."

To my astonishment he nodded again, whereas I had expected him to curse me roundly, perhaps to even stomp out of the room.

"Heaven willing, I've worked the poison out of my system," he said. "But I do not know where to go now."

I resisted a strong urge to weep and draw him into my arms to comfort him. I drew a ragged breath. "Josephine's husband, Alexander Hall, runs the grist and saw mills on the edge of town. You know them?"

He knit his brow, but he nodded.

"I've spoken to him. There is work you can do for—"

"I do not want charity from anyone."

"He will not be offering you charity, Randolph. But if you reject others' help and even their compassion, you will find yourself back where you were—only worse."

He saw the truth of what I spoke and fell silent. I continued with care. "Alexander understands your limitations; I have explained already. There are several processes at either site to which he could train you. For instance, you could be taught to grade the lumber—"

"But not sort it."

"In some cases, even that. The flour mill might lend itself better. You could oversee the cleaning and tempering of the wheat kernels before the milling process begins. I do not understand all of it, but there is the care of the millstones themselves, and organizing the sale and distribution of the flour, once the process is completed."

"Manual labor."

"Not altogether. Good, honest labor to keep you occupied while you decide what it is you want to do with your life."

The bitter look he gave me seared into my marrow. "Do with my life?"

I refused to be led where he was taking me. "There are universities, Randolph, which would welcome a mind as fine as yours. There are a variety of professions you could embrace. Once you put your heart into it—"

That was a mistake. There was no heart left in him; no self-respect, very little hope. He pushed his plate back. "Can we sleep in your barn?" he asked.

"Of course not! I'll fix beds up for you here in the kitchen. Jack, would you like to go to Georgie's?"

His face lit. "I would, if I might."

145

"Yes, and you can return home in the morning, after I've taken Randolph out to the mill site."

"What of me?" Peter asked.

I squinted at him, trying to think. "I do not want to send you back," I said honestly. "Mr. Whittier, as well as your father, is bent on making an example of you. When they learn where you have gone . . ." I glanced in Randolph's direction. "Let's sleep on it, lad, and we'll make our decision in the morning."

Eugene, coming in late with tired shoulders and ink-stained fingers, was pleasant with the boys while he ate a late supper and helped me prepare their beds. They were bone-weary, I realized, and when their heads found a pillow their heavy eyes shut of their own accord. We left them to the lingering warmth of the hearthstones and the banked fire, and the kitten curled at Peter's feet. I sensed there were things Eugene might have wanted to tell me, simple talk of the day, but we were tired as well. I was happy to close my eyes, with my head curled beneath his chin, and let the darkness blot out the entangling perplexities of the day.

It is true I arose later than usual. Eugene had refused to wake me when he went off to his father's shop in the morning. "You need your sleep," he had told me the night before. I was certain both boys would be sleeping out their exhaustion, too; and so it appeared when I first entered the kitchen, with the fire Eugene had built burning merrily and the kitten mewing for his morning milk. I went about my tasks for several moments before hearing Peter groan and turn over, half rising, then falling back to his warm quilts again. I knelt down beside him. Perhaps I would not wake him until later, until I returned from taking Randolph . . .

I shifted my attention to the other pile of blankets, rumpled and— empty. I sat back on my heels and stared. *What in the world has he gone and done?* My heart constricted painfully. *Ought I to go and search for him? And, if so, where to start?*

Perhaps feeling my perplexity, Peter opened his eyes. When he looked into my face, he knew. "Where do you suppose he has gone?" I asked.

The boy gazed back at me, sad and deflated. "Anywhere, Esther. I could not begin to second-guess him."

"Nor could I."

We ate a sad, dispirited breakfast together, and the minutes dragged on our hands. At length Peter offered to bring in some wood Eugene had chopped and left piled in the yard. After that he stood on a ladder armed with my long feather duster and pulled down the cobwebs that had gathered in the corners and crevices of the ceiling. We did not say much. We were waiting. But I think we both believed we were wasting our time.

A little before noon I heard a horse in the yard. I started, then froze. There were definite footsteps making their way up the path.

"You have sharp ears," Peter whispered. The footsteps came closer. We saw a slender shadow, a hand reach and pull open the creaking door.

When Randolph entered I knew something had happened. He walked differently. He even stood with a different stance. And there was something in the depths of his eyes that had not been there before.

"I am sorry, I apologize to both of you," he began, "but I could think of no other way to handle this." He sat down. We stood staring at him. A hint of a smile played on his lips.

"I am sorry," he repeated. "Sit down and I'll tell you where I have been and what has happened."

I sat, expectant—but never guessing what it was I would hear.

"It was my place to go, no one else's. I spoke to Eugene this morning and he let me borrow Tansy. I hope that's all right, Esther."

I nodded.

"I went to my father's office and waited. I know it is his habit to arrive very early, before the business of the day begins."

"You went to your father."

He was pale, but he was calm. "I had to," he said.

Peter leaned forward, his hands clenched on his large, bony knees, looking no more than ten years old. I realized that his memories had flared up to meet his concerns, and he was truly worried.

"Tell us quickly," I said.

"I explained all to him. In the beginning each word stuck in my mouth, Esther. At times I thought I would choke. I could not look at him—" His face contorted a little. "I kept my eyes fixed on a spot of wall where the paint was peeling, a few inches above his head."

Randolph drew a deep breath. "I showed him my arm, limp and useless. I gave no quarter and I asked for none." *How well he knows his father,* I thought. "I told him—the kind of disgusting life I have been involved in. I made no excuses, and I asked for nothing, at least not on my own account."

I glanced toward Peter. Randolph drew himself up a bit as he, too, looked at his brother. "I told him that if anyone undertook to punish Peter on my account they would live to rue it, for I would expose their unjust conduct, as well as my own vivid crimes."

"Did he take your meaning—entirely?"

"I believe so." Randolph spoke slowly. "But just in case, I did mention a name or two specifically, besides his own."

"What did he do?" Peter's voice was thin and uncertain.

"He told me that he will no longer think of me as his son. He wishes me no ill but, as far as he is concerned, I am dead to him. I told him that I expected no more from him, but that I did expect him to honor his word as far as my brother is concerned."

"No, Randolph! Let me come with you. I have no desire to go back there. How can I bear to be near him now?" Peter's plea troubled both of us.

"You must bear it for Mother's sake," Randolph replied. "He will not treat you poorly; I am fairly certain of that. You will be free of Whittier's cruelty, and you must endure and make a place for yourself. You deserve it, Peter. Do you not see? Father would triumph entirely if we both walked away!"

Peter saw. He sunk back against his chair, drained and resigned, but entirely miserable. Randolph rose to his feet. "Will you take me out to the mill now, Esther? Or would you prefer that I ride Tansy myself? You can always send for her later."

"I think that is a good idea. Alexander is more or less expecting you."

*He is all right,* I marveled, weak at the realization. *He has faced the very worst, and he will be all right now.*

At the door Randolph paused and turned back. "I went to see my mother," he said. "I felt I . . . had an obligation to—I have caused her such suffering." He straightened his back, which had seemed to slump at his own words. But he looked at the floor as he added, "Thank you, Esther. I'll never be able to thank you, I'll never—"

I waved him on. "Hush. And hurry now. Be gone with you. I'll ride out later with Tillie to check on you and let you see how your nephew has grown."

The door shut behind him. Peter and I sat in silence for a long time. Finally he rose to his feet. "I'd best go report now," he said. "But I believe I'll stop home first and change into some clothes of my own."

"That is a wise idea," I said. "It will make you feel much better."

I crossed the room with him, knowing I had to say what was in my heart, had to try to make him see things beyond his own years and experience.

"If you had not loved him enough, Peter," I began, "none of this would have happened. I do not think Randolph would have ever come home. And for his own sake he would never have braved his father. You brought him to that." I kissed his cheek where the boyish tears wet it. "Is it not amazing what love can do?"

149

# Chapter 18

## Palmyra: March 1830

Winter had taken hold this year with a vengeance. It was March and we were still tight in the grip of his frosty breath, still imprisoned beneath his layers of ice.

There were, amazingly enough, many tasks for a blacksmith to perform during these fallow months. Chief among these was mending the many things the farmers had let go until after the busy harvest time: buggies, wagons, sleighs, axes, plowshares, shafts. Then there awaited the tasks occasioned by the constant demand for wood needed for winter fuel, and Eugene and his father were kept busy forging new irons for sled runners, repairing chains, making grab hooks, refacing axes, and sharpening crosscut saws. But, because of the young apprentice, there was time for my husband to follow his own pursuits, for which his passion had grown.

I was the only one besides Nathan who knew that Georgie was expecting a baby. "I want to finish the year out," she told me. "We need the money from teaching, and I cannot bear to think of someone taking over my position when my children are counting on me."

She did well; perhaps because she knew she could not be sick, she wasn't. But then, Georgie has always been healthy as a horse and serene and trusting by nature. Perhaps that made a difference as well.

Despite the harsh weather, Phoebe and I had taken to meeting on my Tuesdays at Tillie's. Tillie needed the encouragement and something to divert her attention from the nausea and weakness that beset her. And I was given opportunity to fuss then over both my godchildren—Laurie and little Esther, my namesake.

"I must confess I am relieved that I am not with child yet," Phoebe told us once. "I want as much time as possible between Esther and the next child—my child—especially if I give birth to a girl."

"Do you believe Simon would play favorites?"

"It is not so much that as—as his fear of pushing Emily and her memory out of his life altogether. He seems almost desperate at times to see her in Esther. Even when I sit of an evening rocking the child to sleep in my arms, he will remark on her likeness to her dead mother—her eyes, her hair, the way her ears are formed, even the way her mouth moves when she speaks."

"That is not fair," I blurted.

Phoebe fixed her eyes upon me as if to say, *Of course it is not fair, Esther. Why can you not be reconciled to that?*

I wondered. I wondered what weakness was in me that caused me to cling to the ideal, to recoil at injustice, to be disappointed when people failed my expectations.

"You read too much." That was the answer my mother, in the days of my youth, always gave. "You fill your head with notions and ideas that have no place in reality. They only mix you up, Esther. Leave those old writings alone."

But I could not! I read, and I scribbled my own thoughts. And, after all, those writers, who lived in bits and snatches of parchment pressed between leather covers, were people, too. They had to grapple with the day-to-day realities, but they found something in them, or beyond them, to give purpose and meaning to life! I thank heaven that Eugene understands this part of my nature. He, too, is excited by the written word, drawn to the power and persuasion and beauty of man's expressions of his thoughts and ideals.

151

And another concern our weekly discussions had engendered in me: Why was I not yet with child? In the deep safety of my own soul I could admit that I was afraid of being a mother; but I would not say so to anyone else—not even to Eugene, whose consistent hints and gentle teasing let me know that he was eager to become a father, that he would be pleased when that miraculous thing happened to us.

I thought of the troubles my mother had had; I thought of Josephine's failures, and I trembled inside. Perhaps I was marked as they were. Perhaps the prize would be denied me, and I would remain the maiden aunt all my life; everyone's confidant, but with my own arms always empty—and Eugene's silent reproach ever before my eyes.

Dismal, dismal! But that was what Josephine had been enduring, and with much less to call on from within herself for assistance. *Josephine.*

Randolph had been living at the mill for a few months; Alexander fitted out a cozy little room for him, and I believe that he liked it there. Fresh air, good food, and good companionship had their effect on the lad. The other workers were kind to him and treated him with the easy respect they were accustomed to dealing out to their fellows. It pleased me to see that Alexander had become quite devoted to his errant boarder. He took the unspoken task he had been given—of reforming and rebuilding the boy's strength, both moral and physical—with the sober attention he gave to every pursuit that fell into his hands. I was concerned as well as pleased; therefore, I had been watching things out of the corner of my eye as carefully as I could.

One way of doing this was to appear unexpectedly on the premises, with any common excuse that would answer; by and large, I brought baked goods or, in season, fresh herbs and fruits. Once I arrived mid-day and discovered Randolph lunching with Josephine. I gave him the books he had requested and prolonged my stay until he had gone back to his work. Josie was fairly sparkling, that way she does when she has a male audience to woo and enthrall. I asked no questions, but she spoke effusively of him and of how well he "fit in."

The next time I came I noted that she had the boy running errands for her, and this brought him more and more into her domain and under her eye. She laughed at the things he said, even when they were not particularly clever, and she touched him overmuch—casual touching, done without thinking: a pat on the shoulder, a hand laid momentarily over his hand or on his arm.

I agonized over whether or not I ought to speak to her; or should I speak to Randolph instead? I rejected that idea; I did not wish to raise doubts or worries in his mind, to sour his progress there, especially with fears that might prove unfounded. I could not discern what his reactions were; I believe he was very careful when I was around. *He is young,* I reasoned, *bruised by life, beset by feelings of inadequacy. He could easily be entranced by Josie's charms, delighted by her attentions, her apparent admiration of him.*

Randolph is a good-looking boy. He has grown tall and is well muscled, despite the limp injured arm. He has a fine mind, an interesting way of expressing himself, and a smile that tugs at one's heart. Even the reticence and self-containment he has developed by way of protection add to his allure, at least in a woman's mind, I would think. I know my sister. I know her tastes, I know her weaknesses.

I watched Alex Hall, too. His feelings were the most difficult of all to discover. He carried his thin, compact body with dignity and directed the order of his business with very little fuss and very few words. The lines of his face were tightly stretched over nose and cheekbone, and his eyes, small and pale of coloring, were as careful of expression as all else about him. Yet, I liked this man still. I had caught glimpses past the barriers, past the tidiness and circumspection, and I liked what I saw.

March was here. Spring would soon be upon us, then summer; and with summer, picnics and hayrides and dances in the sweet meadow, out under the moon. Something must be resolved before then! I continued my visits, I continued my watchfulness, which was all I could do.

It was the middle of the night, and I was awakened for no apparent reason. I reached over to touch Eugene; he was not there in the bed beside me. I lifted up my head. Moonlight splattered across the floor, like pools of spilt milk. My husband was not in the room. I sat up and called out to him. Nothing but silence answered me. My feet wiggled across the cold floorboards in search of my slippers. An unreasoning fear began to take hold of me. I lit the candle that sat close by on the table and pattered out to the kitchen, still calling his name.

Nothing. The emptiness seemed to have stretched, because he was not in it—because he was supposed to be here! Dandelion opened one eye, saw that it was only me disturbing his rest, and closed it again. He did not move a hair or a whisker. All about me was in order. All about me was mute.

His clothes. I returned to our bedroom. His pants and shirt were no longer draped over the chair back; his shoes and the long woolen stockings I knit for him last autumn were nowhere to be found.

*He has gone some place he does not want me to know about.* There was nothing else I could surmise. *A sick animal*—the thought crossed my mind. But we had only Tansy, the cow, and a few chickens sharing our barn. And how would he have known, have thought to rise up in the midnight hour and trudge out back to see if all there was well?

I sensed something else, something altogether different. But because I trusted him, I thought, *He does not want me to worry. He knows if he wakes me up and I know where he has gone, I will worry.* I felt somehow certain of that.

I wrapped my warmest shawl about my shoulders and sat in my rocker in the kitchen, with only the one candle lit and drafts of air chilling my ankles, and wondered what I should do. Every impulse urged me to dress and go after him. But I can be rash. What if I could not find him? What if my appearance embarrassed him—or complicated whatever was happening? For long minutes I agonized, my mind going back and forth, back and forth, unable to determine the proper course.

He did not come. The silence was too much for me. I drew on shift and dress with trembling fingers, pulled the shawl over head and shoulders, extinguished the candle, and slipped out into the night.

The light from the moon, high and diffused, was enough to direct me; I have come to know my way about the streets of Palmyra, and I had decided already where I would look first.

The murmur of voices, a number of voices, growing louder as I drew nearer, told me I had reasoned aright. But *what?* a cluster of men outside Grandin's printing establishment in the middle of night? Had there been a fire? some mishap with horse and carriage?

Then the answer came to me, clear and direct beyond question, and I instinctively slowed my stride. *Mr. Grandin is printing Joseph Smith's gold Bible. Eugene sets type for it some days. He says that Hyrum brings in the pages, often under cover of night, in small batches. He or another sits at the railing that separates the presses and printing apparatus from the public during the tedious daylight hours. Sits and waits. Sits and watches, for mistakes, for problems—for trouble.*

With a sensation of dread I moved forward, cautiously now. I shrink from the ugliness in men's voices when they become merciless and hardened. I feel at such times that no power could reach them, no power on heaven or earth. I heard vile things now, hurled against Joseph Smith and his brothers. But the doors to the printing house were locked, tightly secured, and in their frustration several of the group suggested riding out to the Smith farm together, to drag the "imposter" from his bed and show him what decent folk thought of his kind.

*Decent folk!* Eugene must have noticed me, standing apart and alone on the dark street. He suddenly disengaged himself from the others and moved like a tall shadow toward me. A few others began to wander off in various directions, and the group as a whole broke up into fragments.

Eugene did not speak until he had led me some distance from the others. "I did not think I had awakened you." There was distress in his voice. "Esther, why did you come?"

I explained what had happened. "Why did *you* come?" I asked. "Such men as these, Eugene!"

He understood my concern and was quick to explain. "I heard murmurings over the past few days and Grandin asked me if I would check the situation out for him, make sure no harm was done."

"No harm done! What would have happened if Joseph had been in the hands of those men this night?"

He felt my trembling and put his arm round my shoulders. "He is no fool, Esther. I believe he is able to take care of himself." He spoke the words softly, as though he were contemplating their meaning, their implication. "You may as well know," he continued, "that a meeting is set for this Thursday evening. Many of the leading men of the village are demanding it. They are determined to stop this publication from coming to light."

"I do not understand why people are so against it!"

"They are afraid of it; that's what I sense. They don't understand what Joseph Smith's up to. And because they don't understand, they're afraid."

I knew he spoke truly. But my ire was stirring as I walked home on his arm. "Cannot this mass meeting be avoided?"

"No. There is not a chance of it."

"Will things be mean and ugly?"

"They may very well be."

We continued in silence. Neither of us had any answers. We felt a depressive weight on our spirits occasioned by the scene we had passed through. A sudden thought came to me. "Heavens, Eugene, will Gerard Whittier and Theodora's father be there?"

"Most assuredly they will," he answered. "They are among the men most opposed."

I wondered for the first time what Tillie thought of such things. I knew Georgie's views on the matter, but really no one else's—except, perhaps, those of my father, who had always treated the Smith boys with compassion; who, indeed, liked and respected them, and was not the type to be party to mischief, jealousy, and deceit.

I made it a point to visit each of my friends before Thursday and bring up the subject with them.

"Gerard has said nothing to me," Tillie responded. "I generally know almost nothing, Esther, of his affairs. He considers me—beneath them." She spoke the words with no malice and less distress than she would have a year before. "Besides, I have been ill, and that keeps me even more isolated from him."

*Isolated from.* A terrible term to use about one's husband. "Remember how we felt when we were girls, when Joseph had his vision?"

"Supposedly had his vision," she amended. "Surely you do not believe such things could really happen."

"I do not know what I believe. Except that people ought to be left alone and not hounded—and that I know very little as far as the knowledge of the world is concerned. How can I say what things might be?"

Our conversation left me dissatisfied, so I approached Phoebe with some caution. She was more prosaic, more open to suggestion than Tillie had been.

"I do remember liking Joseph and his brothers and sisters. I remember that he was one of the few boys I felt I could trust not to tease or plague me. He came to my aid once, do you know, when I was about seven years old. I fell in the mud. I looked up and saw him standing there, but he was not laughing at me, as the other boys were. He picked up my books—I remember he wiped the mud off my slate with his own hands. Then he helped me out and insisted on taking my shoes and cleaning them in the tall grasses. I have never forgotten that."

"It is how I remember him, too," I said. But my mind jumped suddenly forward to our meeting in the cemetery shortly after my brother, Nathaniel, had died. There was a dignity in his presence, and a kindness that reached out to one—

"I shall not go to the meeting," Phoebe was saying, "for nothing will be accomplished there; nothing of value, that is. Safety in numbers. They mean to state their purposes and garner support."

"I believe you are right. Would I be a fool to attempt to oppose them?"

"Oh, Esther, you would!"

I had to smile at her earnestness. "Do you know what Simon thinks of the matter?"

"We have never discussed it. Between running the feed store and farming both his fields and his father's, he seldom has a minute to spare."

We visited a few more moments about this and that. When I left her I still felt a determination to attend this meeting and see what took place for myself.

Phoebe was right. I had not been aware of a portion of what was going on around me. I did not even know that Abner Cole had pilfered some of the pages of Joseph's book and offered them to subscribers in his newspaper, the *Reflector,* attempting to discredit the work. There were many in the crowd who were angry that the ex-justice of the peace had been exposed and forced to abandon his endeavor because it was both unethical and illegal; they cared not a farthing for that!

"They are out for blood," Eugene whispered. The expression chilled me. The town fathers, perched on the raised platform above us, called for a resolution—that the good citizens of Palmyra pledge themselves not to purchase a copy of the Book of Mormon.

"If it comes off the presses we must ban it! It is our duty to stop this imposter, to protect our friends and our neighbors, to do our part in this worthy endeavor. It is our duty to keep others from touching this pack of lies, this devil's work. We will work tirelessly against him—we will expose him and destroy him!" Wilder and wilder the words grew, wilder and wilder the mood of the crowd.

"I care not to listen to any more of this," I said to Eugene, tugging at his arm.

"I will take you home, then."

We walked out into the cool, starry night. I drew the clean air into my lungs, wishing I could expunge the poison that had been breathed all around me, wishing I could erase the words that were ringing in my ears still and making my head start to ache.

" 'Tis an ugly business, Esther, but it will blow over."

"And will Joseph Smith's book be printed?"

"I cannot tell you that. Mr. Grandin is a man of integrity. If Joseph and his friends give him security that the printing will be honestly paid for—we shall just have to see."

We were nearly home before I worked up the courage to say, "I am glad you're not one of them, Eugene. I'm glad you are not that kind of a man."

If those words were difficult for me to say, it was that much more impossible for him to form a reply to them. Instead he took me into his arms. Right there on the front steps. If there had been eyes to watch us, they would have seen him bend down to kiss me. But they would not have known how delicious was the tenderness of him, the touch of him.

My father has always said that the March winds are rascals. They mean no harm, but their ebullient spirits spill over into mischief they cannot control. After weeks of buffeting us about, they have stopped to catch their breaths, and I think the spring has snuck in.

"At least they have blown winter out," Eugene says. He is eager for fine weather to come, and so am I. I have some fine plans for my gardens, both the new ones where we now live and the old ones at home. School will be dismissed soon, so the children can help their parents with the planting, and we shall have Georgie to ourselves again.

"Once summer comes, I can grow as fat as I like," she teases, "and not one person dare criticize."

I am ready for sunshine. I am ready for slower days when the light in the sky lingers into long, gentle hours and the darkness is short.

Today is the 27th of March. Eugene came home from the printing office last evening and told me that the completed Book of Mormon, comprised of six hundred pages, is now off the presses and for sale, wholesale and retail, at the Palmyra Book Store by Howard and Grandin.

So Joseph Smith has won. At least this round. I am happy for him. I wonder what this strange book contains. I believe I shall ask Eugene to bring home a copy so that I can find out for myself.

## Chapter 19

*Palmyra: April 1830*

It happened the same night as the town meeting, though I do not believe Eugene wanted me to know that. They were courting trouble, as the saying goes, those men who rode the Canandaigua road out of town, rode hard into the darkness bent upon an errand of malice, with hate in their hearts. Georgie's father was one of them. He sat a big bay who was fast and spooked easily; surely he should not have chosen to ride him that night. There was a wind to stir the shadows, to raise lonely sounds from the old Indian grounds the horsemen rode through. They rode too fast, they rode too carelessly. And at one point Warren Sexton's tall bay reared and shied, and plunged away from the shadows, out over the uneven ground. When his foot turned and plunged his body hard forward, Sexton hit the ground with an impact that jarred his whole body. The leg twisted and, pinned beneath his body, took the full force of the fall. When the men found him and picked him up from the cold ground he cried out loud. He cried like a child all the way to Doctor Ensworth's, where half a bottle of whiskey quieted him some.

Once begun, Eugene spared me no details. It was a gruesome affair. The doctor feared the bones would not set properly and, as with Randolph's arm, there had been damage to nerve and ligament. "He will always walk with a limp," Eugene concluded. "That is, if he walks at all."

"He and the others, I suppose, accepted the accident as a sign of God's punishment." I made my voice sound light, but the question was in dead earnest.

"Quite the opposite. Some claim the horse was bewitched. Some were determined upon returning before daylight and burning the Smith family out."

I shuddered. "Have we no law and order in these parts?"

Susan Evans McCloud

"I believe at the last that's what stopped them. But Sexton is terribly bitter and black against Joseph Smith now."

If I tried to see things from his view I could understand, I supposed; but there was no way to do that. It disturbed me to think that Georgie had not told me herself. Things must be bad indeed if she hadn't. I knew I must respect her silence and not mention the matter, though my curiosity burned.

Spring brings out the playfulness in Nature, and I felt myself respond to it. Because the weather was fine I used it as an excuse to ride out to Josephine's. I found conditions much altered there.

Randolph, it appeared, had fallen out of grace with his fair young mistress. She pouted or outright ignored him whenever he came into our ken. I noticed a difference in him as well. He continued to be respectful to her, but he was no longer under her power. Unable to help herself, she began to complain.

"Alex fairly dotes on the boy, Esther. It is disgraceful."

"I would think it would be good for Randolph. He needs encouragement, even a little praise."

"Well, he gets it in excess; you can be certain of that."

"Are you not glad the two get along so well, Josie? I thought you were fond of the lad."

How she winced at my words, so innocently spoken that she could not bring herself to attack the implications that were couched beneath them. She could merely sit and bristle ineffectually.

"You do not have to live with it," she whined. "Why, you would think the boy were *his son*. In fact, he has been mistaken for just that a time or two."

Ah, here was the rub! "That is only natural," I replied in a calm, even manner. "Being older than you, as he is."

"Heaven preserve us, Esther! Will you never show me a shred of sympathy?"

*When you sincerely deserve it,* I thought. Then I was immediately pricked in my conscience. *How smug I am,* I lamented, *to think I might pick and choose whom to bestow my favors upon!*

One danger was diverted, but there were others lurking like rats in the woodpile, or in the shadowy entanglements of Josephine's mind.

I made it a point to contrive some errand for Randolph to

perform for me, and he promised to come out the following day. When I had him alone it was not as easy as I had thought it would be to broach the subject with him. At length I began by expressing my pleasure at the sympathy that had grown between himself and my brother-in-law. When I saw him hesitate and appear a little uncomfortable I took the risk and said, "Josephine nearly destroyed any chance of that, didn't she?"

"She nearly put my head on the block!"

It was out. I sighed and added, "I am sorry she is like that. I should have warned you, but I did not think—" I nearly said, "I did not think she would turn her attentions on you." But he might have taken that wrongly, seeing it as proof of his inferiority. Fortunately he finished the thought for me in a slightly different direction.

"She is not easy to resist, you know."

"Oh, I believe you, for I have watched men fall prey to her machinations for years." That made us grin at each other, and the tension was broken, but Randolph became thoughtful again.

"From the beginning I prized Mr. Hall's opinion. He is a good man, Esther, and I wanted him to know he could trust me."

"What a dilemma she put you in!"

"Turned out all right." He shook his head, as if dislodging the memories there. "Of course, she is angry as a hornet now—as though her husband was not mindful of the cause of it all."

"Does he suffer terribly, Randolph?" I winced; I had not meant to ask it.

"She tries him sorely. But he loves her enough that he chooses to endure it."

"Precisely as I feared. Can he do nothing with her?"

"You know the answer to that!"

How good it was to talk about it, though! To bring it all out in the open, like hanging wash on the line for the sun to bleach. I felt I could bear the unchangeable a little more easily now. And how I enjoyed being in Randolph's company! I wanted to say, "You are a changed man." But I think he knew it already. As he left he hugged me, the way he used to when he was a little boy, when he and Peter were to me the brothers I'd never had. I was glad I had sent for him, grateful he had resisted Josie and chosen a higher path.

*If only his mother could see him, how proud she would be,* I thought, savoring the warmth of his affection. It is a constant sorrow to me that one man's narrowness of spirit can imprison and starve an entire family. I look upon it as one of the most tragic injustices of life.

Babies, babies! But nothing stirring with me or Phoebe yet. Tillie's second was due to arrive now in a matter of weeks. She had pulled out of the worst of it, and spring itself would no doubt ease her sufferings. Georgie puckered her impish face in mock consternation whenever the subject came up.

"What ill judgment I have! I must wait out the hot, unbearable months before this child within me will ripen and become something tangible, while you shall have your little one to coo over the whole summer through."

She seemed her old self, as far as I could judge. But she surprised me entirely when she pulled me aside and whispered, "I have something to tell you. Arrange to walk home with me."

Once we were alone, I prodded her eagerly. But there was no lightness in her when she turned and said, "On April sixth there is to be a special meeting."

"Whatever are you talking about, Georgie?"

"Listen carefully, Esther, and promise you will not speak of the matter to anyone, for I am telling this to no one but you."

This was unlike Georgie. "All right."

"Joseph Smith and some of his friends are gathering to form a new church, and Nathan and I intend to be there."

"Is Nathan seriously interested?" I remembered suddenly their friendliness with the Smith family. She mentioned it only now and again. Was there much that I did not know? "How is he so different, Georgie? What kind of things does he teach?"

She waved her hand as if dismissing a silly question from a schoolchild. "I cannot answer such a question in ten minutes on the street corner."

"Is he as strange as people say he is?"

"There is nothing 'strange' about Joseph or his teachings at all."

"You are going for certain?"

"Yes. We are decided."

"What if your father finds out?"

I may as well have struck her as to have asked that question. For the first time I could remember she snapped back at me. "It is none of his business! Nor do I intend to suffer for my father's ignorance, not any more than I already have."

I hoped she was right. I hoped with all my heart that she would not regret the step she was planning to take.

"Absolutely not, Esther. You are going too far with this. I will not condone it—I will not allow it."

"Eugene, you make too much of it!"

"I know more of the matter than you do. And I wish you to leave it alone, dear." I had never seen him like this! "You are my wife; therefore you represent both of us. I cannot afford to be . . ." He searched for words. "To be labeled as a Joseph Smith sympathizer."

"Would such sympathy hurt you—really?"

"Indeed it would."

"I am curious; that is all. I want to—"

"Esther, please. For once can you not simply see a thing and do it my way?"

*Was I that bad?* I scooped the cat up and began to smooth his fur with a vengeance. He meowed in protest and wriggled out of my arms.

I am not accustomed to people opposing me. I am not used to others curtailing me when there is something I really want to do. I walked out of the house, but Eugene did not follow me. I led Tansy out of the barn and rode her, with nothing but a bridle, to my parents' house. I found my father clearing ditches along his south field. I told him my dilemma and he listened with his usual patience.

"Am I being unreasonable?" I ventured at last.

"You are forgetting what it was like to live with your mother." I thought that a strange reply! "Because you had to, you adjusted many of your ways to her . . . peculiarities."

"To keep the peace, to keep things running smoothly. You are right, Father, I have forgot. Is it much worse now, with both of us gone?"

He took a long time in answering. "You could say that." He thought on the matter a few more minutes. He was never one to be hurried. I helped him drag a few of the larger branches over to the pile that had been raked together for burning.

"Fear has a terrible grinding power, like water," he said. "Can wear a body down to the stump." I nodded, pushed the hair out of my eyes, and continued to look at him. "That's what it is with your mother. She won't let go. Too busy protecting herself to enjoy what the moment brings her."

I put my hand over his. "Thank you, Pa. I didn't mean to be so foolish." I gave his cheek a quick peck, then scrambled onto Tansy's broad back. "You don't need to tell Mother I've been here. I'll stop by to visit her Tuesday."

He nodded and went back to his work. As I rode the short distance to my own house—why could I not think of it as home yet?— I felt fairly chastened, even eager to apologize. I called out to Eugene the moment I came through the door.

But he was not there. All the rooms were empty, and the remains of his cold supper sat on the drain board. Swallowing my pride I went out to the barn. There was no sign of his having been there. *He went back to his father's to finish a piece of work, or he is writing in the quiet of the* Sentinel *office,* I reasoned. But I would not go after him this time. Even when things were fine between us, he did not like it that I followed him everywhere.

165

I cut myself a piece of bread and a thick slice of cheese, and read my book while I ate. I did up the few dishes. I darned the last two stockings in my work basket. Then I pulled out my journal and wrote until the flame chewed my candle down to a stump and my eyes began to burn with the strain of trying to see the letters as I formed them.

I would not start a new candle. I got ready for bed in the dark. *Perhaps he will wait until he sees the light extinguished,* I thought, *before he comes home.* I did not care. I would not allow him to hurt me like this over something so inconsequential! I closed my eyes. I knew it was *not* inconsequential, this matter of whose will would be adhered to. It became more than a difference of opinion when it came down to essentials. But I did not wish to think about it at all right now.

❦

Mid-day on Tuesday, April 6th, over fifty people gathered in and around Peter Whitmer's house. Many of them were friends of young Joseph's or members of his family: his father, mother, brothers and sisters, the Whitmer family, Oliver Cowdery and Martin Harris—the latter a man of some means in these parts who has financed the publishing of Joseph Smith's book. A new church was indeed organized, and several were baptized into it right then, as Georgie reported to me. She said there was such a sweet spirit present that she felt as though heaven were very thinly veiled from her eyes.

"They call themselves Saints of the Church of Christ," she said.

"You like that term?"

"I do. I like everything I learn about Joseph Smith's teachings, Esther."

"Georgie—have you thought what this might lead to?"

"Nathan and I have discussed it."

I did not wish to ask the final question—*might you associate yourselves with them?*—because I did not want to know.

❦

Five days later, on the Sabbath, this little band of Mormonites met in the home of Peter Whitmer. I know, because Georgie was there. Oliver Cowdery preached to them, and afterward several were baptized. Georgie's face glowed when she told of it.

"Read the Book of Mormon for yourself," she said, for she knew just what I was thinking. "Then you will know it is neither frightening nor strange."

But I could not yet bring myself to it. As far as Eugene was concerned, we never spoke of the subject again between us. Joseph Smith and all his followers could have fallen off the edge of the earth. But it remained a sore spot to me, a little bruise marring the white surface of our happiness. I did not like having it there. I did not like knowing there was anything, however small, that my husband and I could not be at peace upon, even though we did not agree.

# Chapter 20

## Palmyra: June 1830

*After the trial comes the blessing.* We saw one beautiful example of that when Theodora gave birth to a daughter during the last week of May. Gerard's enthusiasm was much tempered, but ours was not. We celebrated with all the finery we could muster: our best dresses; flowers in our hair, on mantel, and on tables; blackberry cordial; the most delicate of cakes and cookies; and gifts for little May in profusion. Tillie splendidly ignored every suggestion Gerard put forward—"One must expect to suffer disappointments now and again; we cannot always have what we want")—and named her daughter Cornelia, after her mother, and May, to mark the joyous time when she was born.

May and Laurie and little Esther . . . perfect little human beings to carry our lives into the future where we could not go! "What will *you* produce?" Tillie asked Georgie lightly.

"Perhaps one of each, to conserve both time and effort!" Georgie always had a clever answer ready!

Josephine joined with us, but she was unusually subdued and silent. And a little piqued, I thought. She could not pretend to truly rejoice, as the rest of us were doing. But she bit back any remarks that would have been either silly or hurting.

Phoebe seemed content in the daughter she had elected to mother, and we had for a long time forgotten to remember that Esther was not really her child.

Because this was Tillie's house, and not her father's, we had planned a party for "the family," which meant, in this case, Randolph and Peter. There were a few awkward moments, such as the time Tillie started to hand the baby to Randolph and then remembered his arm. The boys were uncomfortable in an element quite foreign to them: that of women and babies, whose secret activities they knew almost nothing about. But the few minutes spent together, as in the old days, felt good to us all.

I noticed that Josie and Randolph did not speak to one another and made every effort to avoid being brought too close together. So much the better, though it was a sad thing to see. So much excitement, but none of it centering around me and mine. Indeed, my own life had grown a little subdued of late. I was cautious with Eugene—*cautious with one's husband*. Surely that is not a good thing to be.

Joseph Smith has sent his brother Samuel and others out to preach the Book of Mormon. They are actually scouring the countryside and the villages trying to stir people's interest. The whole village is talking about it; the entire population appears to be insulted and incensed.

Except perhaps Georgie, who simply laughs at it. "I'll lend you my copy to read, if you'd like, Esther."

But I decline. When I do, if I do, I shall read it in my own way, not with her breathing down my neck.

I wonder how many, if any, invite young Samuel into their homes, feed him a meal, and let him explain his message. I wonder how many will actually pay money to purchase this book. Samuel is an admirable youth; softly-spoken, gentle, and respectful . . . *It all makes no sense to me!*

I suppose it was all right for Mrs. Thorn to criticize Phoebe to friends of her own age and circumstances. But it was particularly bad taste for her to criticize my best friend to me.

It happened too often. Every time occasion brought her to our house, every time we took turns and ate Sunday dinner with them. Her husband, Eugene's father, is a worthy fellow. His hair grows in little finger curls around his forehead and neck, the way Eugene's does. He wears a long mustache, such as Eugene is growing. But he does not have my husband's cat eyes, or his passion and sense of romance. He is an honest, hardworking man. His wife is a hard worker, too; Eugene inherited his slight build from her. But she . . . leaves much to be desired, as far as I am concerned. I had been making sincere attempts to be warm to her, though that which took place on this particular occasion when we were together undid for the remainder of her lifetime any good foundation I may have started to lay.

I truly could not help myself. She was going on and on about Phoebe: "The girl is thin and plain, with a lackadaisical way about her that gets under my skin." . . . "Mark you, the child has Emily's brightness and vitality, though I should hate to guess how long that will last." . . . "Dull, I tell you. I cannot get a word from her." . . . "Do you not wonder what Simon sees in her? Pity he had to marry again at all."

On and on! Until I thought my head would burst! If I had thought, I would have said it was only proper for someone to defend her. But I did not think, I just plunged ahead.

"Phoebe is one of the most tender, guileless women I know, ma'am. She may be timid and slow in her manner, but she keeps a spotless house and takes good care of your grandchild—and she is an excellent cook! Every time I show up she is singing sweet songs to the child or entertaining her with pleasant chatter. Her skills with a needle are unsurpassed in all of Palmyra. Think of it—the other girls will always be envious of the frocks Esther will wear."

169

"What a recommendation you give her, my dear! But then, you have always been partial to her."

The words were not spoken kindly; not even with impatient indulgence, but with a sharp edge that lashed at me cruelly.

"Phoebe *wins* friends," I replied. "She does not need me as an advocate."

"You forget yourself, Esther. And, after all, the child is not hers."

"But she is—Phoebe's marriage to Simon, and his acceptance of her as wife and as mother to his daughter, has made it so." Mrs. Thorn gasped and put her hand to her throat, but I pretended to pay this no mind. "*Love* has made the child hers, Mrs. Thorn. Phoebe loves her truly—and for that you ought to be both grateful and glad."

Silence followed my words, as though some great chasm had swallowed them. The four of us in the room stared at one another, tongue-tied. I arose, my heart thumping in my chest. "I did not mean to offend you," I said, "and am truly sorry if I did so." The silence snapped back again, like the jaws of a trap.

"I shall walk home, Eugene," I said, shaking my head when he made a weak protest. "The exercise will do me good, and it will be better that way."

No one stopped me. I walked with long strides, putting the house behind me, my feet veering of their own accord toward the quiet wooded countryside which I seldom entered now that I lived in the town. I was much in need of the restoration that only Nature, in her lack of pretense and solitude, can provide.

*Strange,* I pondered, *how less than a mile's distance can make such a difference. On one end are houses crammed together along city streets, where vehicles pass noisily all through the day. On the other are cultivated fields and open pastures, blackbirds and blue jays, and little rivulets that sing a tune to the sky. On one end there is the constant bustle of commerce, the constant press of social expectations. On the other is peace, and the flagrant, generous displays of beauty to enchant the heart and relax the mind. No wonder I sometimes feel ill at ease, with nerves jangled.*

I stayed longer than I should have; but how difficult it was for me to turn away and go home. Eugene was there when I arrived. He looked up as I entered, but his gaze did not seek mine. I took off my hat and shawl and hung them on the peg behind the door.

"Eugene." I perched on the edge of the chair that was nearest him. "I should like very much to—"

"Let us not talk of it, Esther. We will only quarrel—since we do not agree on the matter—"

"I do not wish to quarrel with you."

"Then let us leave it alone." He turned back to his newspaper, circling certain items and making notes in the margins.

"Why is there so much of late upon which we do not agree, Eugene? It did not used to be so."

He made no reply. After a few moments I rose and walked out of the parlor and into my own silent room.

Sooner or later, Josephine always goes too far and brings a crisis of one sort or another to pass.

The first picnic of June is always an occasion of sorts. Josie asked Alexander to take her; and, the truth is, he should have said yes. But he told her he had too much work at the mill waiting for him.

"All you ever do is work," she flew back at him. "Work has made you an old man before your time."

He may have winced at her words, but he made no reply to them; and nothing incenses Josie more than being ignored. "Why did you take a wife at all, much less a young and pretty one, if you had no intention to give her any pleasure?"

"My intention was to give her a good name and a good home, to give her my love and protection."

Pretty words that incensed her yet further. "You used to spoil me and treat me a little," she complained. "In the beginning you were not like this!"

"In the beginning you were not a disobedient wife who made of me a laughingstock—a wife who could not be trusted."

He had never spoken to her that way before. "I will go by myself," she declared.

"You will do no such thing. I have put up with enough, and more. I forbid it, Josephine."

She flounced out of the room; always a pretty woman's last defense. When the day for the picnic arrived she dressed up in all her finery. I know—for I drove out to the mill to collect some of the wild roots that grow by the stream. She came out all smiles and looking dazzlingly beautiful. But Alexander was waiting for her.

"This time you will do as I have told you, Josephine. Go back to your room."

She stomped her foot. She was not ready to give up yet. "I am not a child, that you can order me about so!"

"You are worse than a child. Do as I say, or I will see to the matter myself."

She did not look at me, but I saw her brown eyes cloud with tears. She took one step forward, then another. Alexander swooped her up in his arms, draped her across his shoulder like a fifty-pound sack of flour, and carried her into the house.

I did not wait to see what happened. My plants forgotten, I turned the light wagon around and headed back to Palmyra. I spoke of the matter to no one, not one single soul. I felt ashamed. The cloud of their misery hung over me for the rest of the day and lay down with me that night.

Two days later I returned to complete my errand. I saw no one about the place, so I headed down past the mill trace to where the water pools out and the tall ferns and reeds and water weeds grow. When I had my basket nearly full of dripping specimens I heard footsteps come up behind me.

"I'll heft that onto the wagon bed for you, Esther."

I turned round slowly. Alexander stood meekly awaiting my pleasure, but I felt suddenly red-hot and unable to make my mouth work to give him reply. After a moment he lifted the tall basket and set it on the cushion of papers I had laid out for it.

"Thank you," I managed.

He nodded and helped me up to the wagon seat. "Will you stop at the house for a few moments?"

"Where is Josephine?"

"Oh, she is inside. She will remain there long enough to learn her lesson, heaven willing."

A terrible image of her thrust in a little cramped room, without light or food, sprang up before me. I shuddered. "I don't believe I have time for a visit today. Give her my love, will you? I'll return on Tuesday, my visiting day, with a treat for her—will you tell her?"

He nodded, slapped the horse on the rump, and sent us along our way. I fancied I saw Josephine's face staring out of every window as I drove, without stopping, past the big, quiet house.

"Joseph Smith has been arrested." It was Eugene who told me; and I sensed that he did so with a certain quiet satisfaction to which he would never admit.

"Who told you that?"

"It's common knowledge, Esther. I'm surprised you've not heard it already. It seems he and his followers have been disturbing the peace with their meetings—with holding baptisms at all hours."

"You know that is not true!"

"No matter. He was finally arrested outside Colesville for disorderly conduct—*and* for setting the country in an uproar by preaching the Book of Mormon."

"That is ridiculous, and you know it."

"Some people do not think so. Can you see now, Esther, why I have asked you to be careful?"

"No! I cannot see why. You ought to be able to put it away from you and ignore it—there was a time you would have defended him, Eugene!"

"Perhaps there was." His narrow, sensitive face was so somber, his very muscles sagging, his expression distressed and confused.

"Why not now?" I pressed—and I shouldn't have. "Anyone whose good opinion is worth having would respect you for standing against such men and such underhanded measures."

He looked back at me sadly. "You do not understand, Esther—*you will not understand.*"

"I would if I could!" I cried.

But he was shaking his head at me. "Leave it alone, dear little firebrand of mine, leave it alone."

I know he meant to be tender, but my ire was up. "Why is there becoming a list of things we must 'leave alone'—things that divide us, Eugene? One is too many—but the list keeps growing."

"I suppose life is like that," he said.

173

"That is no answer!"

"I have no other answer for you." He turned away from me. "I am going to bed."

He picked up the candle, expecting me to follow him. But I stood in the darkness a while. *There was a time,* I realized, with a recognition that was painful, *that I wanted nothing more than to be part of this man— to immerse myself in him, to do anything necessary to build a unity with him—to achieve the fabled oneness of man and wife. Now . . . now!* It frightened me to realize that my inner self was still lonely, still solitary, still incapable—perhaps even unwilling—to make certain kinds of concessions, to relinquish something *essential* which I could not begin to define.

Perhaps his mocking response was, indeed, the only answer. *Life is like that.* Perhaps there are some things one cannot even hope to explain.

"It was not at all the way people are telling it." Georgie sat in my kitchen with her feet to the fire, her black eyes snapping with the indignation she felt. "It was the troublemakers themselves who did those things of which they accuse him."

I sighed inwardly. "What do you mean?"

"Near the home of Mr. Knight, Joseph and the others had dammed up the stream in order to form a pool where they could perform baptisms. But during the night a party of men tore it out, and then gathered the following day with hopes to lay their hands upon the Prophet, but his friends prevented them."

"Is that what people call him—*the Prophet?*"

"He is a prophet, Esther." Those dark eyes bore into mine with incredible fervor.

"Go on."

"They returned during a meeting and arrested him—they did not care on what charge! Why, even the constable admitted that their design was to get him away from his friends!"

"Did they succeed?"

"No. For the constable saw what manner of man Joseph is. When the constable's wagon was surrounded on the road by McMaster's men, he whipped up the horse and drove out of their reach. Joseph was acquitted at the trial the following day—twice acquitted, for his enemies kept trumping up new charges against him."

"It sounds like a farce, Georgie. Really. Why should grown men behave so?"

"Indeed! It is hard to conceive of, isn't it? A Mr. Reid, one of the men acquired to defend him, said that not one blemish or spot was found against Joseph's character. But the men were so angry in their defeat they threatened to tar and feather him. He had to be protected and then helped to escape—can you even imagine it, Esther?"

I could not. It made me ill to so much as think of it. My own impressions of Joseph came back to me: his gentle nature, his kindness, his concern for others.

That night when we were alone together I asked Eugene if he would bring home a copy of this Book of Mormon for me. "I should like to see for myself what it says," I explained.

"That is not the best of ideas, Esther."

"Best of ideas? It is nothing to make a fuss about—I want to see what it is, Eugene, that is causing people to make such a fuss."

"We haven't the money to purchase a copy."

"Very well. Ask Mr. Grandin to lend you one. Just overnight—I'll make certain you have it to return in the morning."

"I would rather not do that."

I counted to ten. I would not give him the satisfaction of knowing he had upset me! "Never mind, then. I shall just ask Georgie to lend me hers, as she has offered to do."

Eugene put down his newspaper. "Esther, come here," he said. I went to stand by his chair. "What is it about this Mormonite issue that you keep getting caught up in it?"

"Really, my dear. I am far from 'caught up in it.' I am curious, even interested—"

"Because of Georgie."

"Partly. But not altogether."

"I do not want you to get mixed up in it. After a time the whole thing will blow over, and we shall be better off if we keep our distance."

"Those are fine words, but I do not know why you are speaking them. What difference would it make for me to read a little bit in this book—to show a little sympathy toward people who are friends of mine and have been misjudged and misused?"

"What difference would it make if you did not?"

There was a vehemence to Eugene's tone that wounded me. I did up the supper dishes in silence—thinking of half a dozen different things I might have said to him, every one brilliant and convincing. But I kept them all to myself. Nor did I attempt to discourse with him upon any other subject that night.

It was late when the knock came, a rat-a-tat eager pattern. Eugene was already in bed. Reluctantly I rose from my cozy spot beside the fire and opened the door just a crack.

"It is I," came a whispered hiss. "Randolph. Please open up."

*What kind of trouble has he gotten himself into?* I am afraid that was my first thought. But his features did not confirm it. "Sorry to disturb you at this hour," he said, "but I wished to come under cover of darkness, and, more important, return the same way."

175

I stood waiting, wondering to what his strange sentence referred. "Is someone in trouble?" I ventured.

"You might say so." He sat down at the table, and I automatically put a glass of buttermilk and my last slice of pie before him. "I do not wish to upset you—"

"Well, you are certainly failing at that!"

"You are right. I must out with it at once. It concerns your sister— but she is all right now," he hastened to add.

"All right now? Randolph—why must I prod you?"

"Because I am ill at ease in the telling. She has suffered a miscarriage again—the second I know of since I have been staying there." He saw the expression on my face and put his strong hand over mine by way of comfort. "She does not wish anyone to know of it, Esther. I believe she is—humiliated that she cannot produce a child."

"Dear heaven. I had no idea." I sat down beside him and rested my head in my hands.

"She pretends indifference—"

"Indeed she does! Perhaps I should have guessed, but . . ."

"She has worked most diligently to conceal it, especially from your eyes. She wants no pity. Pity is very hard for your sister to bear."

*How strange,* I thought, *that he should understand her.*

"I have come for some of your herbs. I think she is in desperate need of them. But she would never have allowed me to come to you."

"Will she let you administer to her?"

"I believe she will allow Alexander, if he is forceful."

"But she will guess that he got them from somewhere! Ought I not to come along with you, or come first thing in the morning, and—"

"No. She would throw both you and the herbs out! And you can imagine how incensed she would be. Instruct me how to use them, and I'll instruct Alexander—and together we'll think of some excuse."

I went into the cold little pantry off my kitchen where I had hung a variety of herbs in small bags from a string stretched along the low ceiling beams. I selected those that would be most beneficial from among the more common varieties that perhaps many people would have access to. I explained this to Randolph. "Jane Foster and half a dozen other women I know of understand the use of these. Perhaps you can tell her you obtained them from Jane."

176

That appeared as good an idea as any. It seemed no time before he stood ready to go out into the night again. But there was one more question I was determined to make myself ask.

"Will you tell me—can you tell me, in light of the kindnesses I have done you—has Alexander been cruel to Josie these past weeks, locking her indoors, like some sort of a prisoner?"

"Not a bit of it." Randolph spoke gently. "He has forbidden her to leave the premises without his permission or someone to accompany her; that is all. And he attempts to make up for it—I've told you before, Esther, it is almost pathetic how much that man loves her! He cooks little dainties for her many an evening, or brings her a pretty present from town. He will even read aloud to her of a night, although he is so tired from working that he can scarce keep his eyes propped open."

"I had—no idea."

"You made up gruesome pictures, knowing that imagination of yours, Esther!" He was teasing me a little, as in old days. "Come now, admit I am right!"

"She is fine, then?"

"She is fine—except for this other, except for the ways that she plagues herself. But do not worry overmuch, these will help." He patted his broad pocket where the little packets of herbs were stashed.

"Take care, Randolph, it is a dark night," I warned him, for I had thought suddenly and uncomfortably of small bands of riders—angry, perhaps inebriated—looking for trouble, mistaking solitary riders—

"I know my way around these parts, and I have a fast mount," he assured me, then patted my hand again, and I had not time to thank him once more before he had slipped away from the wedge of light that the open door cast, and was swallowed up by the night.

I stood a long time, too long, gazing out into the blackness after him. That is why I saw what I wished I had not seen: a familiar light buggy with two headlamps placed in a distinctive pattern, driving slowly and carefully along the street my house fronts on.

What folk are out at night? I asked myself, *save outlaws and thieves—or doctors and midwives.* I knew already; I knew it was Jane Foster's carriage that had come so many times to our door. As it drew closer I could distinctly make out the forms of two people sitting on

177

the high bench seat together: the taller one, the man, was driving the horse. Jane, appearing slight beside him, was hunched over the large bag she carries, which was now cradled against her lap. Her head and arms rested upon it, and she appeared to be sleeping. So I was bold enough to step out of the shadows and speak to the driver myself.

"Jonah Parke!" I spoke the name quietly, but the head of the driver jerked round at the sound of it and the buggy slowed to a stop.

"Esther, in heaven's name, what are you doing here?" My father's concern was real. "Is someone hurt?"

"No, Father. I—I'll explain later. I just happened to be up, and to see you—and to wonder the same thing." He met my gaze directly. "Is this something you do regularly now? Has Jane hired you on as her assistant?"

"Do not be fresh with me, daughter!"

The lack of motion, perhaps the sound of our voices, made Jane stir in her sleep. My father tucked the carriage blanket around her knees and jumped down quite agilely. "Walk off a distance with me, Esther, and let her rest."

"Does Mother know that you—"

"Hush a moment more, Esther! I had forgotten what a firebrand you are."

*My husband has called me that on more than one occasion!* We walked to my door, and he stepped inside my lighted room before he would speak. "There is a reason, which I suppose I must tell you—"

"I suppose! Does the rest of Palmyra know it? Am I the only one in the dark?"

"Not the only one, daughter. And I suppose very soon now the whole village will know." He looked at me with his clear eyes, and there was no shame or fear in them. "Jane Foster is dying of a heart condition Doc Ensworth says medicine can do nothing about." I caught my breath and put my hand to my mouth. "She grows weaker every day, but she won't give up her practice. 'Women need something better than a doctor when they're giving birth,' she's always saying, 'and I mean to be there, long as I'm able to stand and hand out encouragement.' "

I was silent, but my father did not seem to notice my discomfort. "I *offered* to help her, Esther. She would never have asked."

"Mother knows, then."

"I would not have done it without her approval."

I was overwhelmed. I had never thought of my mother as in any way *noble*.

"Someone had to help her. I believe most everyone we go to knows, or guesses."

"You admire her, don't you? You're—fond of her?"

"Yes, Esther. I will not pretend I am not. But what you fear in that teeming little brain of yours would never happen. I always believed you trusted me more than that."

I could say nothing. The tears ran down my cheeks, and I could say nothing at all. After a while he gathered me into his arms and kissed me. "I can't leave her too long out in the chill air," he said. "I've got to move on."

I nodded and swallowed, and reached for him with the blind need of a child, and he drew me close again.

"Do not fret yourself, Esther. I hate to see you do that. I know—I know you worry for love of me."

I watched him walk out of the light, as Randolph had done. I heard him cluck to the horse and listened as the carriage whirred softly away.

*What a meddler I am!* I thought savagely. *What a mess I make of things—despite good intentions!* At that moment I did not like myself much, nor did I relish the prospect of being alone with my conscience and my ridiculous, wayward thoughts!

# Chapter 21

## Palmyra: October 1830

T he new school term started, but Georgie's baby had not arrived. Nathan went back to the classroom; but, of course, Georgie could no longer teach.

"They will not allow it," she fumed. "I feel fine, and I am as capable as ever. What do men think pregnant mothers do about teaching their children when they find themselves in this state?"

Little Emmeline must have heard and taken pity upon her mother, for she arrived the next day—pink and dewy, with a head of light hair that curled at the ears, and eyes as black as small stones washed in the streambed.

We were *all* thrilled. "Laurie shall keep order," I announced, "over this gaggle of girls we are raising up to step into *our shoes!* Already we have May, Phoebe's Esther, now sweet Emmeline."

I wished I had not said it. I felt instantly miserable. Which ones were lacking in this assemblage? Josie and I! It frightened me a little. Both my sister and I *must* have daughters to replace ourselves, as the others had done. The next generation must not be allowed to flower and bloom without our being represented, having some part in it all!

Josephine was changing, but not necessarily for the better. She seemed at loose ends, like a ship cut from its moorings, with no energy, no impetus, nowhere to go. Far be it from me to have dreamed that I would ever prefer her tempestuous, ofttimes unthoughtful selfishness over this growing state. But I did, and I worried about her more and more every day.

I was not the only one, though I did not know it. There came one particularly nasty day when Josie felt so sorry for herself that no one could rouse her. She stalked about the house, shouting exaggerated complaints, blaming everything from her husband and the weather to fate and God. She refused to eat the evening meal with Alexander and Randolph.

"Neither of you would miss me," she whined, "if I were not here. You have provided Randolph here with a home, and he has provided you with someone to care for and train up to be just like you!"

As Randolph told it, he took one look at Alexander's face and something within him took over, something he could not control. He pushed his chair back and grabbed Josie by the wrist. "You are coming with me," he said. "I want you to see what I came from—what you would be sending me back to!"

Alexander made no move to stop him. Randolph took the light buggy Josephine used to go calling and drove it through the streets of Palmyra like a madman, Josie clinging to the seat, her unkempt hair streaming.

He drove down past the locks to where the land settled, sunless and rank. Here some of the canal boys had cleared a section in the mud flats and erected temporary shelters, little more than shacks, colorless and sagging. Some sat outside now, in the sick glow of twilight, cooking scraps over low fires, shivering in the thin shirts through which their bony shoulder blades poked.

"These are hovels!" Josie shrieked. "Disease-ridden hovels! Why are you bringing me here?"

"Disease-ridden, true. Disease and despair, madam. That is what you find here. The creatures you see before you are orphans, picked up at the docks by the canal bosses and hired out like slaves. They own no property, possess no rights, are shown little kindness. If their bodies are drenched by the cold rain that seeps through their poor clothing, they still must work on. They catch a few hours' sleep between shifts, cook their food only after the horses and mules for which they are responsible have been cared for and fed. Many have died of consumption or pneumonia, or—"

"Why do they stay? Why do they endure it?"

"What choice have they, Josie? A few bold ones run off. But there is nowhere for them to go to, so they end up begging on the streets of the city—or worse."

181

"I do not wish to hear more, or see more. Cannot something be done for them?"

Randolph ignored her and stooped down beside one boy who looked no older than eleven or twelve. "What's your name, lad?"

"Daniel, sir."

"I'm not a 'sir,' Danny. I used to work here myself."

"Ah, but you've got somewhere to go, don't you—somewhere besides this. Look at you now." The boy's eyes traveled to the pretty young lady. Randolph chuckled under his breath.

"This feisty creature has nothing to do with me." He glanced at Josie and winked slyly. "And if she did—I'd have no notion in the world what to do with her!"

Danny laughed with him, surprised to see the young lady join with them.

"You are too clever for your own good, Randolph," Josie said. "What is your last name, boy?"

"I haven't got one, far as I know, ma'am. It's just Daniel to the bosses and Dan to the lads."

"How should I find you again—if I'd a mind to?"

Daniel raised large questioning eyes to the young gentleman, dressed in the rough, honest clothes of a workingman. "I be always here on my off shifts, never anywhere else."

Randolph stood, removed his warm jacket, and draped it across the thin shoulders, glancing toward Josie again for his cue. But for the moment she had forgotten both of them and was looking all round. When he reached for her hand to lead her back over the morass, there were tears in her eyes. She brushed them away with an impatient hand. When they reached the carriage he lifted her up, then took his seat beside her.

"I lived like that, not much better, for longer than I want to remember."

"*Why?*" She was angry. "Like the boy said, you had a choice."

"Less than you would suppose. It became a matter of pride with me. My father is a cold man, and as hard a taskmaster as any here. I convinced myself that this was freedom—that the hardening I got was good for me. I wanted to be any way but the way my father was."

"Out of one trap into another," Josie mused. "Weren't you ever afraid?"

"Most of the time. I would not want to tell you how many times I cried myself to sleep on my hard bed of a night."

They fell into silence and rode the remainder of the distance home that way. When they entered the house Alexander asked no questions, Randolph excused himself to go to his own quarters, and Josie paced the floor, back and forth, back and forth, long into the night.

The following morning Randolph told Alexander all that had happened. A fortunate decision. For that evening, over dinner, Josie announced her plan.

"How many can we take," she asked her husband, "and provide work for? We can train them for something other than that terrible slavery." She leaned forward, excitement glazing her eyes and adding a hue to the chalky white of her cheeks. "There are nooks and crannies here and there in the mill house and barns. They do not need much space, Alex, to call their own."

"But they will need clothing and good hot food."

"Surely, we can provide them. Surely the work they return us will compensate us for that."

"What of education, Josephine? These boys are ignorant and unschooled, with no manners whatsoever—little savages, in some ways, Josie."

"Oh, Alexander, I've already thought of that! I shall set up a school after hours. I know Georgie would help me instruct them, for she is no longer allowed to teach in the city schools. Think how good she would be."

Josie was biting her nails now and fidgeting in her excitement. "We could offer incentives—extra pay for attendance at classes—a bonus of some sort for those who do well."

I wish I would have been there. I suppose the relief in the room was palpable. The relief and the amazement. With an apologetic glance in Randolph's direction, Josie said softly, "Until we have children of our own, it is a way of helping someone's child, of doing some little good."

Alexander would have agreed without half the persuasion she exerted, but this brought him nearly to tears. For a blissful hour the three sat round the table planning; bandying ideas and hopes back and forth.

183

"How many to start with, Alex?" Josie asked.

"Three," Alexander replied thoughtfully. "We can always go for more—but I should hate to ever have to take even one back."

"Will you go, Randolph?" she asked. "Pick out three of the best for us. I'm sure you'll be able to judge." She laid her fingers against his arm, as if to detain him. "Make certain that one of them is Danny. That is all I ask."

Near the end of September the Mormons held another conference session in Fayette. It was reported that there had been some thirty-five new converts since their meeting two months before. Nathan and Georgie were in attendance. Afterward they arranged a place and time a few days later for them to be baptized.

"Will you come?" Georgie asked me.

I stared back at her stupidly. "I do not know if I dare."

She kissed me quickly. "You are right. It is of no great matter." But the "no great matter" weighed heavily on my mind. I found a little present I could give her to mark the occasion, and Phoebe did the same. Tillie seemed unable to understand or join in with us.

"You *celebrate* what she is doing? I am afraid for her. I see more than you see."

And to our woe, to our everlasting horror, Tillie proved right.

Who discovered, and how, that the couple had decided to join Joseph Smith's new religion? As soon as the school board found out, Nathan was informed that his services in the community were no longer considered desirable.

"We have a certain standard to maintain," it was soberly explained to him. "You are no longer considered fit, Mr. Hopkins, to influence the young people of this community. We must ask you forthwith to resign."

Georgie took the announcement sanguinely. "There are other villages, other positions—even other kinds of work we can do."

*We have each other,* was their attitude, *and now this adorable baby. What more could we ask?*

Three days following Nathan's peremptory dismissal he and Georgie joined the other Saints, as they call themselves, at a special service along the banks of the Susquehanna River and were baptized into Joseph Smith's Church of Christ. I was not there to see, or to feel, what Georgie tried to describe for me. I do know the sense of cleanliness and wholeness she emanated; an expression in her eyes that was not excitement, or even pleasure, but what the scriptures call *joy*. For a moment, for a brief moment, I envied her, and wondered if I might be missing something terribly important that she understood and had grasped.

Two nights later, in the dark hours approaching midnight, men rode up to their house—rode in quiet and dead earnest. Two carried firebrands, which they threw in the window. One tossed a rock to which was attached the following message:

> Leave for your own good. Heathens. Betrayers.
> You no longer have place here.

185

The words were handwritten. Georgie recognized the cramped, closely curled handwriting she had seen so often on the bills and invoices of her father's dry goods store. She sat down in the middle of the wreckage and wept like a child.

She was lucky to be able to do so. How long would it have taken the two to awaken—if they'd have awakened at all? It happened, oddly enough, that Tillie's Peter was spending time with a sick friend at a house nearby and thought he saw smoke from one of the windows—stuck his head out and smelled it!—and ran, with his companion, to put out the flames. *Did Providence provide him? Was their deliverance due to fate, or to the hand of God?* I know what Georgie believed, with no doubt in her mind whatsoever. But I was not able to be so sure.

As far as the fire was concerned, the damage did not go beyond the front room, but smoke filled and blackened the house. When I thought of the baby! Poor Peter took them to Tillie's house when it was over, for she had room in plenty. But her husband heard the commotion and turned them away.

"It may as well be said now," he announced grandly, in the presence of all of them, "that I desire this friendship to end. Georgeanna's involvement with the Mormonites has severed all decent relationships."

Georgie, still in tears over her own father's cruelty, could be crushed no further. They were brought to my house and slept in my kitchen that first night. They were all for cleaning the house out the following morning, but we advised against that.

"Do not play into their hands, do not incite them further," we kept urging.

"Let us try Alexander's," I suggested. Peter, Georgie's brother Jack, the little family, and myself all rode out together. When Josephine heard the news she took over at once.

"I need Georgie for my school," she reminded her husband. "We must figure out something. I never dreamed it would come to this!"

At length it was agreed by all that Georgie and Emmeline should take up quarters in the main house, where they could be easily accommodated, while Nathan would scour the adjoining communities in hopes of finding some sort of work. How she hated being parted from him! I had never seen Georgie morose, really miserable, before in her life. It distressed me. Her misery seemed to sap my energy. I felt deflated and weak. Though I had another reason—a reason I had not yet told anyone, even Eugene: *I was with child.*

I had waited long enough to have absolutely no doubt of it before even allowing myself to believe it could be true! Now I hung back. It would seem cruel to chirp out good news when all about me were struggling. And Josie! I would do anything to avoid diverting Josephine now! She had thrown herself heart and soul into the reclamation of her orphans—even spending part of each day, for two weeks, at Phoebe's house learning the fine points of seamstressing. *Her boys* would dress properly and be able to hold their own around town. Once Georgie was installed she lost no time clearing a room for a schoolhouse, fitting it out with old desks, old McGuffey readers she bullied the school board into giving her, slates, inkwells and lined tablets for the boys to fill in practicing their letters.

This was a boon for poor Georgie as well. Action. Nothing works better against lethargy and heartache. Under her tutelage the three young boys bloomed. Fresh air and physical labor that was demanding but not grueling; good food; hours of careful recreation; and sleep in decent beds with blankets to cover them. They almost believed they had died and gone to heaven; I think they would have walked to the ends of the earth for Josephine!

"We can take more," Josie kept urging Alexander. But he refused to allow her to hurry him. Randolph, as gently as he could, sided with her husband. "All in good time," he encouraged her. "All in good time."

I did tell Eugene about the baby. I could no longer contain myself. I nearly laughed trying to get the words out; it seemed silly, like a fairy tale I was making up for both our sakes. He did not think it a fairy tale, but a miracle. He knelt on the braided rug beside me and put his head in my lap.

"At last," he murmured. "It has been a long wait, Esther, long for both of us. Are you as happy as I am?"

"Oh yes!" I twisted his fine curls around the tip of my little finger and kissed the nape of his neck.

"Even though you are discontent with me?"

My heart skipped a beat. What had he said to me? "I am not 'discontent' with you."

"Yes you are, Esther. And perhaps with good reason." He lifted his head and sat up on his knees, so his face was nearly level with mine. "I have not meant to be harsh, I have not . . . intended . . ." He sighed. "It is so hard to put my feelings into words."

"I understand. It's all right."

We sat together for a long time, and although nothing further was spoken, I felt the distance between us had closed somehow. He seemed once again my husband, and I his wife. I felt a tenderness toward him, a tenderness I remembered from a long time ago, and was amazed how something so precious could become tarnished, pushed into a dark corner and forgotten, as if of no great significance at all.

Strange, strange things happen that keep life full of interest and wonder!

One day a gale blew in from the north, such a tempest as October

187

had not seen during my lifetime. When the storm struck, my little brother was playing with his toy horses and wagons—small wooden figures Father carved for him—in one of the ditches that line some of our wheat fields. Here he had constructed elaborate twisting roads, with hills and valleys, with little stick bridges crossing make-believe rivers. Father was working nearby, but he had just taken the mule over to the adjoining field, which was still in pasture, to let him graze for an hour while he and Jonathan sat in the shade of the plane trees and ate their noon meal together.

The sky emptied rain and wind and lightning all together. By the time he reached Jonathan the ditches were flowing with water, mud, and debris. The first impact must have knocked the boy over, or at least made him lose his footing. He had struck his forehead on some sharp object and, as he fell, his foot had caught in the twistings of an old root, and held fast. Father extricated him at once and carried him to the house, but they could not shake him into consciousness. The bump on his head was swelling; one whole side of his face had turned black and blue.

My mother screamed and lunged for the child when she saw him. Father had to hold her back forcibly, bully her into coming to fetch me and the doctor, while he cleaned the mud and blood from his son, and watched over him.

I am amazed she did as he bid her. Perhaps she was, indeed, afraid to be left alone with him, horrified and helpless. I agreed to go in search of Doctor Ensworth, while she turned back at once to the farm. When we arrived, there had been no change. Jonathan's head had swollen considerably, so that the discolored portion looked frightening, even grotesque. Mother sat slumped by the side of the bed, weeping piteously. The three of us together were not sufficient to drag her away.

"You'll do him no good with that sound," the old doctor told her harshly. "If you love him truly, Rachel, then for pity's sake grieve in silence! He may very well be able to hear you, though he cannot respond. And you will terrify his senses, I tell you."

She put her hand to her mouth and pressed hard, willing her terror to turn inward. I turned away from the sight.

"Will you stay with her, Esther?"

"You know I won't leave her."

"Don't overdo, though. I do not want that." The doctor patted my head, as though I were a child still. The gesture brought tears to my eyes. He was the only person, besides Eugene, who knew of my secret, this lovely secret I carried inside.

He walked to the farthest reaches of the kitchen with me and my father. He was not hopeful about the boy. "His fever is high. There is most likely swelling on the brain, as well as this contusion on the outside. If I knew more—if I could see inside that little head."

It was then I realized my brother might die! I realized it, but like some far, distant fact that cannot possibly have relevance for us. My mind thought, in the same cool, detached manner: *If Jonathan dies, my mother will die with him. Or else go mad.*

The doctor gave us instructions. I let my father do the listening. I could not pull my mind back from this fog.

It is a long night. Father brings in the rocker and places it as close to the bed as possible. Mother sits, her eyes fixed on the distorted face. She eats nothing. She says nothing. She sits with her hands in her lap and stares.

A little past midnight I get her to take a few sips of the tea I have brewed for her. I do not know what she sees, what she is aware of. *I* see the feeble flame of my brother's spirit flicker and wane. I see something gentle and other-worldly flit across his features—and am reminded of that other night, in this very room, years ago, when the same things happened with another child, fighting desperately for his chance at life. When the strange colorless light remains, when it settles over his frozen features, then he will die.

I doze. I slip in and out of a troubled slumber, starting at noises, aware that my feet are cold and my neck is cramped. Almost imperceptibly dawn has poured her glow into the darkness; these first gray filterings of light assure me that morning is on her way.

*He may not make it through the night. I must tell you*—Had Doctor Ensworth said that?

I think my mother is sleeping, staring straight ahead, with her eyes open. I cannot sit still another minute. I rise and slip out into the chilly duskiness of daybreak, so that the fresh air might clear my head. A few stars, faint and lusterless, cling to the pearly curtain that stretches over the earth. I am so weary! I am so frightened! In my heart, for the first time in a long time, I start to pray.

I do not see him at first, this man who is walking toward me, cutting through fields, with his trousers soaked halfway to his knees. I look up because I *sense him*—something about his presence. He pauses. He has come quite near. His eyes are more gentle than the dawn that is breaking, and as flooded with light.

"What is the matter, Esther? How can I help you?" *Why does his voice, offering assistance, give me a sensation of hope, and of peace?*

"What are you doing here, Joseph—at this hour?"

A sad smile, a smile as old as the earth, touches his face for a moment. "I am eluding those who would seek me, who would take pleasure in harming me."

*Yes. And not only you,* I think.

"Your friends suffer for the truth's sake, and they suffer gladly," he says. *How does he know what I am thinking?* "They will fare well, Esther. Do not worry about them. They will raise a good family, in a home far finer than they have ever hoped for." He is smiling still. "But I am here to help you and your little brother."

"You have heard, then." A shudder passes through my body. "My brother is dying," I say.

"Would you like me to go in to him, to administer a blessing to heal him?"

"My mother would never permit it."

"Then let us pray together out here."

He kneels beside me in the rough grass. He calls upon God as I have never imagined. He calls upon Him in power, yet speaks to Him as a child speaks to a tender, loving parent whom he adores. His words are more than my mind can contain and remember. They pass into my spirit like light. I have no doubt of their power to lift and to heal.

"Your brother will live. He will recover and live a long, useful life, Esther."

Joseph rises and brushes the pieces of grass and loose dirt from his knees. "Good-bye, Esther. God bless you." He begins to walk away from me. I have not even thanked him—*thanked him!*

I hurry back inside. Fear and pain settle over me like a fog as soon as I enter the house. As I approach the sickroom I hear a sound. It is my father weeping. "Your brother is gone, Esther!" he chokes, groping for my hand.

"No, he is alive, Father," I hear myself saying. "He is alive."

*How can he believe me?* He bends over the small, limp body. Jonathan stirs. His fingers move across the surface of the coverlet. He opens his eyes.

My mother moans. Thank heaven she does not scream at him! I turn to her—I have never looked upon anything so beautiful as the expression I see in her eyes.

Morning trembles against the cold glass of the little window above our heads. I stand and pull back the curtains to let the warm light come in. In the distance I see a tall solitary figure walking across the fields. The sun plays about his head like a benediction as the sunrise, in all her glory, floods over the earth.

191

# Chapter 22

*Palmyra: March 1831*

J ane Foster held out through Christmas, but hers was the last death the old year claimed. It was hard to place in the ground one whose efforts and skills had saved the lives of so many. I was not surprised at the number who braved the bitter day to stand before her grave and pay tribute to the life she had led.

My father was sorely hit. I had no idea what his feelings were for her or how deep they went. But he had helped her, and when a man serves a woman he develops a tenderness for her, as Randolph for Josephine; that is just how it is.

My mother did not go to the cemetery. These past months she had redoubled her vigilance over her son. It took more than a week for the swelling on Jonathan's face to subside, several more for the terrible bruising to noticeably fade. Doctor Ensworth would shake his head and say, "He shouldn't have made it. I don't understand, Esther, he shouldn't have lived." If it were not for that, I would still wonder if I dreamed my encounter in the morning stillness with the young man whom Georgie and so many others call a prophet of God.

What a Christmas we kept, though! With Jonathan well, and Josephine's orphans to fuss over, as well as our crop of babies—and now everyone knowing my good news and sharing my excitement with me.

Nathan found work to do in Fayette, not very far from here. Another converted "Mormonite" hired him to do building and carpentry work. It was not teaching, but it was money in their pockets. Josephine begged, beguiled, and bullied them into extending their stay at the mill house so that Georgie could keep on teaching. That meant no expenses for housing or food, so how could they refuse her? And, as a holiday bonus, Alexander agreed to the addition of two more orphan boys to their brood.

"He is a clever man," Josie informed me one frosty morning as we walked the streets of Palmyra in search of Christmas surprises. "He has found places for two of the older boys as apprentices in the village. No one else could have talked these haughty merchants into taking orphan boys—certainly I never could!"

"It is because Alexander has a reputation for being conservative and trustworthy. They respect his opinion and his judgment. They know they can count on whatever he tells them as being true."

Josie beamed. "You put it very nicely," she said.

"Give your sister another year and she'll have the entire canal company down upon her, mad as hornets," Randolph teased. "She will rob them of all their cheap labor. They shall wake up one morning and find the dock sides deserted, and no one to drive the animals or tend to them—"

"For she will have stolen every one of their orphans away!" I laughed with him. It was good to laugh with Randolph. It was even better to see Josephine with a purpose in life.

So, by and large, the year 1830 ended well for us. We were both grateful and hopeful as we looked to the new days ahead.

The "Mormonites"—the whole lot of them, under Joseph Smith's direction—are moving to a place in Ohio called Kirtland. Georgie came over especially to give us the news.

"How long have you known?" I demanded, without thinking.

"This cannot be happening to us," Josephine wailed.

Georgeanna explained patiently, over and over again, because each time we heard the words aloud we liked them less!

"There are many converts in that area," she told us.

"That is the reason for going?"

"Not exactly." She hesitated, playing for time by securing a toy kitten little Emmeline was reaching for. "It is a commandment of the Lord, through revelation. Ohio is where he wants his people to be."

"I have never heard of anything so unreasonable," Tillie fumed. "Really, Georgie, do you think God cares where a person lives? Do you believe He tells Joseph Smith—not the rest of us, but Joseph Smith—every move he should make, every thing he should do?"

"I believe many things you do not understand, Tillie," Georgie answered in a low voice; humble, unirritated.

"Well, I wish that you didn't. And you are right; I do not understand it one bit."

We were all vexed, devastated at the prospect of Georgie going—of the five of us being separated for the first time in our lives.

"You will not even be here to see Esther's baby," Tillie continued.

"And how will my poor motherless boys get along without you?" Josie chimed in.

"Stop it," I said, for Georgie had put her hands over her ears to shut out their voices, and the tears ran down her cheeks. Then we all flocked round her, cooing and murmuring and petting, and begging her forgiveness.

"It is Georgie, after all, who has the hardest to shoulder," I reminded. "We will all be together still."

It was really too much to bear. We could not pretend we were not devastated and irreconcilable in the face of our unthinkable loss.

"Jack and Peter are going with us. I wanted to tell you first, Esther—before I try to break the news to Tillie."

How many more surprises would we be expected to handle? "Going with you—you do not mean to Ohio!"

"Yes, to Ohio."

"Why? Oh, Georgie, what is going on here?"

"They have both been baptized. They have both accepted the Prophet's teachings."

"They are only boys yet, for mercy's sake!"

"Old enough to know their own minds. Old enough to choose the direction their lives will take."

"Lawrence Swift will never allow it. You know this."

"Peter will go, with or without his father's consent."

"Georgie, do you think that is wise?"

"I think it is terrible! I think a boy should have a father he can
turn to. Do you believe Gerard has kept the word Randolph forced
him to? Peter has been patient and long-suffering; more than you will
ever know. But he has no freedom here. In his way he, too, must step
away from his father and make his own path through life."

I knew she was right. But—*this path! This kind of a parting!*
"Then . . ." The wheels of my mind began turning. "All this time
he has been . . . you have known . . . I detest the way this new religion has come between us!" I cried.

"I do not blame you. If I could only change things, soften things,
Esther."

I wrapped my arms around Georgie's slight body. I thought my
heart would break.

I offered to go with Georgie, as I knew she hoped I would, to face
Tillie. She was very quiet when we told her, but her features hardened
like stone. "It is wicked," she said. "Anything that parts friends and
families is wicked."

"Don't say that, Tillie. You do not know whereof you speak."

"I shall forget you, Georgie. And I shall forget Peter."

"Tillie!"

"That is the only way, isn't it? Oh, I shall keep you both fresh in
my memory, all the grand years together. But you will be dead to me
in the future, won't you, after you walk out of here."

Her words chilled me. She did not relent; not then, and not a week
later when we gathered with the wayfarers to say our last farewells.

"You do not need me there," she explained, "to throw a wet blanket over everything. I have already made my peace with the past and
accepted the future."

"You have not accepted the future, my dearest."

"In my own way, I have."

Peter would be eighteen in three months—I had no idea he had
reached such a great age!

"It would not be worth my father making efforts to stop him,"
Tillie explained. "But he will not anyway. His pride prevents him."

"Yes, I would guess that," I replied. "What of your mother?"

Tillie's face went gray, but the lines of it twitched and hardened as they had been doing of late. "My mother has taken to her bed; she is powerless to deal with things any other way. Whenever Peter tries to talk to her she says only, 'I cannot bear to listen to you. How can I ever forgive you for breaking my heart?' "

"She has learned well, from years of living with your father," I replied unthinkingly.

Tillie grabbed my arm hard and shook me. "As you think I am doing from living so long with Gerard, Esther? Do not demure—I can read it in your eyes!"

"I can swear to heaven it was not in my thoughts," I replied evenly. "It is a thing *you* are worried about, is it not, Tillie?"

I wanted her to dissolve into my arms in a fit of good, healthy crying. Instead, she turned away from me. "I do not wish to talk of that now," she said.

❧

The first part of the journey to Ohio is to be made by flatboat along the Erie to Buffalo. There has been much to-do about this migration of Joseph Smith's Mormon people out of the state of New York. Many of the newspapers are giving it front-page coverage, though I noted that Eugene did not elect to become involved in the matter, or to personally pen one word concerning it, either way.

I had wondered if Randolph would be envious of this adventure upon which his brother was embarking. But he was indeed content with his place at the mill and the work he was doing with Josie's orphans right now. The old sense of intimacy between the brothers was back again, and it wrung my heart to observe them throw their arms about one another in a last tearful embrace.

I have done all my hugging, all my crying, ten times over. But here by the boats, with the taste of the water in my lungs and the far horizon stretching away to the unknown, the reality of it strikes me with renewed force. It is all I can do to not break down like a baby.

"Be careful." . . . "How many cats are you dragging with you, Georgie? Looks like half a dozen." . . . "Write as soon as you are settled." . . . . "We will pray for you." . . . . "Kiss Emmeline every day for me." . . . The last minutes are agonizing!

Alexander is there with Josephine, whose sobbing has a good seasoning of the old self-pity in it, but Eugene has refused to come. Phoebe, too, is alone, with little Esther, like a doll, standing quietly beside her and holding tight to her hand. In the end, when I feel myself going faint and the faces on the crowded boat begin blurring, it is Randolph's one good arm that holds me up and leads me back to the buggy and sees me safely deposited at home.

There I *do* weep, until my sobs become dry, painful gulps and all my hot tears are spent.

197

# Chapter 23

## Palmyra: March 1832

My baby arrived as regular as clockwork. And although everyone kept telling me what an easy time I was having, I was quite overwhelmed by how painful childbirth can be. No wonder women are laid low for such a long time afterward. No wonder it is something spoken of in hushed whispers of respect, even awe. For, in giving birth, one has touched the far reaches of existence, the chasms of the Infinite, and the deepest recesses of the small, vulnerable human heart.

A daughter! How generously God in his heaven has blessed me. Her hair is as auburn as mine, and it curls at her neck and ears like her father's. She has his delicate bone structure, and I swear that already her eyes are green. I wish to call her Lavinia, and Eugene has agreed to it. *If only Georgie could see her! If only*—I will not torment myself with "if onlys," not now.

My mother cannot help herself. She feels it is weak and wrong for her to rejoice in this birth when her favorite daughter is still deprived of this blessing. But—a girl child. She holds the baby in her arms so gently. Jonathan is old enough to hold his tiny niece, and when my mother allows him the privilege he is quite overcome.

"You must come and help me with her," I tell him, "sing to her, if you'd like, and read her your favorite stories."

"The way you did with me. And, oh, she will love it, as I used to!" He smiles at me. His smile has grown quite angelic since his brush with death. My mother is convinced it has set him apart in some way, and perhaps she is right.

The struggles Eugene's mother faces are deeper, more painful. My mother felt guilty at rejoicing; this unhappy woman is incapable of it. I feel sorry for her. I would like to bring her pleasure. I would like this innocent child, so new from heaven, to serve as a source of healing and comfort. But she will not have it so. I try to put away from me the pain her pain causes, and immerse myself in my child.

Surely Eugene makes this an easy, delightful enterprise, for his daughter has altogether enchanted him. He will scarcely let her out of his sight. I remember now his earlier hunger for children and wonder at it and what the source of this longing might be. I, too, have allowed the floodgates of my heart to swing open and pour all my love, my aching tenderness, out on this child.

"You are not disappointed? You do not wish I had produced a son instead?"

"A son to be as pig-headed and cross as his father? No son could compare with this little vixen, who is nearly as beautiful as you."

I revel in his happiness and in the effusion of kindness it seems to produce. I am happy, too; much like those first months of marriage when the world, suddenly of no consequence, had melted into no more than a backdrop against which our lives—precious and won-drous—were daily played out. If possible, this time is even better. Our daughter's pure spirit hallows the very air she breathes and keeps us in a constant state of amazement and joy.

199

This, as well as many other things, took place before we heard a word from Georgie. But I thought of her often, especially on one par-ticular day in early summer when Josie showed up on my doorstep, distraught and weepy.

"I cannot do it!" she wailed, refusing to sit, but pacing the kitchen floor, her long skirts trailing. "I try, Esther, but they do not take me seriously, and they are learning nothing at all."

"The school, you mean?"

"Yes. And Alexander has refused to allow me one more boy until I get things organized and in order again."

"I think that is wise."

"You would! You do not *care* about them as I do."

"We will put our heads together and think of something."

Just as I spoke the words I heard a knock at the door. Some would say Providence, some happenstance; Georgie would have said, "The Lord provides, in one way or another. He is mindful of us."

Be that as it may, my little friends, Latisha and Jonah Sinclair, happily entered and were drawn into Josephine's dilemma, for such is her way. To our surprise, they offered assistance; they were eager at the idea of helping.

"I've enough education to at least get those lads started," Jonah rumbled. "And 'Tisha here can read stories to them. Even poetry, eh, love—the way she does to me."

Of course! I should have remembered that Tillie and her brothers and sisters had received the very best in education: tutors to offset the limitations of the village school, and their father's library to draw upon. I had always looked down on Latisha, just a bit, because she was a little sister and tended to be foolish by nature. I realized she had grown up and had proven herself in many ways, while I still regarded her as little more than a child.

Josephine was interested. We sat down right then and there and drew up a tentative schedule. Latisha would come in the mid-afternoon, when the boys' workday was finished. Jonah would fulfill his portion of instruction in the evenings. Between the two of them . . .

"What about Randolph?" Latisha suggested. "He took to schooling better than any of the rest of us. He can make history come alive, as though he were telling a story."

I could believe that, after what I had experienced with him. I looked at my sister to see what she might be thinking. I had never seen Josephine so excited! She was on fire and could not be patient. We all piled into her carriage and rode back to the mill to discuss the matter with her husband, and to try to persuade Randolph to take a part.

Alexander was amenable to the idea and behaved most graciously to the young, enthusiastic couple. Randolph was, as I had expected, a bit more difficult to convince.

"I've my work, and I like it," he maintained. "Why upset the apple barrel now?"

"Because you are needed!" Josie cried.

I thought he looked at her oddly. "I do not perceive it," he answered her. "I am too close to the age of these fellows. They would accept no instruction from me."

"As though I am an old lady," Latisha rebuked gently.

"You are a female—a pretty, young female; that makes all the difference, you know."

I worked my way close to him and said into his ear, "You have a fine, perceptive mind and much hard-won experience upon which to draw. You could do these boys more good than Latisha and Jonah put together, and you know it."

He turned his mouth to my ear. "I am afraid."

"I know it. Nothing in this world worth doing comes easily."

"What are you two whispering about?" Josephine demanded and, for an instant, I saw a gleam of real jealousy in her eyes. No—it was not jealousy. I believe it was something more akin to remorse and pain.

"Miss Esther here has just convinced me to take a go at it."

There were general cries of pleasure and affirmation. I stepped aside and let the current take a turn around me while I prepared to nurse Lavinia. But I believe, in my own way, I was as happy about what was happening as Josephine was.

A letter from Georgeanna finally reached us near mid-summer. "Arrived safely," it read. "This is the frontier in many ways, Esther. There is not enough housing, not enough employment. More and more Saints pour in daily, and places need to be found for them."

I could not picture the chaos to which she was alluding, nor the sense of confusion and upheaval suffered by those who had left homes and an ordered way of life behind them—for what?

"We are short on food and short on room. The only thing we enjoy in abundance is love—such an outpouring of love one to another, such an outpouring of the Spirit, that no one feels to complain."

If it were anyone but Georgie writing, I would have suspected her rhetoric at once. But Georgie was practical, straightforward, and she had never embroidered the truth, not to my knowledge. I simply *did not want to hear these things!* I suppose in my heart I did not want her to be happy there. I wanted her to try, fail, admit defeat in her usual cheerful manner, and return to the fold. She was so far away! And all her thoughts, her attentions—*her affections*—were fixed upon things I did not understand and could not share.

When I told Phoebe I had received a letter from Georgie she

smiled a bit wistfully. "I also," she said. Though she did not offer to share it with me, I assumed the two correspondences to be very similar. There may have been mention to Phoebe of things personal in nature, concerning Simon and her marriage perhaps. But we were together, and we indulged in a lovely long chat, a nostalgic stroll through the past where things have not changed. And the memories somehow served to strengthen and compensate for the inefficiencies of the present.

When I told Tillie I had received a letter from Georgie she looked past me as though I had not spoken, and replied nothing at all. Her behavior distressed me, and vexed me more than a little, especially since the closeness between us had deepened during the past many weeks.

"Have you no room in your heart for Georgie?" I asked.

"She left us; we did not leave her," was Tillie's inane reply.

"You sound like a child; more petty than we ever were when we were girls together."

"I do not wish to speak of it, Esther—you know that!"

Her sharpness closed my mouth, but it also threw a terrible gray shadow over my heart, which was difficult for me to forgive—as Georgie's leaving was, and always would be, for her.

As the summer progressed into an unhurried autumn, Tillie and I were in one another's company more and more often; it was a natural thing: we both had daughters now, something very wonderful and tangible in common. What grand times we shared! Some of the lightheartedness we had known as girls seemed to return to us, and we spent many long, lazy hours doing nothing at all but enjoying the children, the sunshine, and the flowers—and in that order, I will admit!

It was a relief to put conflict, troubles, and heartache behind us. I could not help noting how calm Palmyra had grown since Joseph and his "Mormonites" abandoned us. People settled back into a common routine and seemed to be content to mind their own business again. *Odd that religion can stir such hatred and cruelty in people.* Even Gerard appeared to have toned down a bit, and reconciled himself to the largess allowing bygones to be bygones, at least as far as his wife's old friendships were concerned.

"Gerard and his friends feel they have won," Tillie said once. "They drove the Smiths out of here. It proves their superiority, and it maintains their power intact."

*Power!* I thought. *What an empty word in the minds and mouths of little men who cannot live without it.*

But, except for that once, we never spoke of the matter. And we never spoke about Georgie. Tillie may be wondering as much as I how she was faring; but she had set her own perimeters, and she would not pass. *This much she has learned from Gerard,* I thought, *this determination to follow one's own prejudices without any glancing to left or right.* Such a quality can be admirable; but I was quite certain it was not working for the good in this case. However, I would not be the one to test or question something I had no power of changing; I had gained enough wisdom through the last months to at least realize that.

So the year ended on an even note, with many of our affairs looking hopefully upward. My mother spent many hours in my company and began to develop an affection for her granddaughter, which is good, since Jonathan will soon be spending part of his days in school. Eugene has been taken on as an editor at the *Wayne Sentinel,* and his work is noticed and praised because of its quality. He is happier; and, therefore, Lavinia and I are happier, too.

203

Our Christmas festivities this year included nearly a dozen of Josephine's orphans, some of whom are apprenticed out to various establishments in the village and making their way quite nicely.

I was grateful for the calm, restoring months as they passed; I am even more grateful now. This season did not come for naught; it was given for no frivolous reason: without the renewal it worked in me I would not have had the courage, nor even the strength, to do what I am asked—no, entreated—to do.

It has been nearly a year since Georgeanna and Nathan left. It has been close on a year since my baby was born. When the letter arrived with Georgie's return address and someone else's handwriting, I knew at once that something was terribly wrong. I sensed it, as one senses the tension in the air and the subtle changes in light as a summer storm approaches.

"Forgive me," Nathan wrote, "but I must beseech you to come, Esther, if it is at all possible. Georgie is ill unto death and needs proper tending. She is in need of family, too. Our little Emmeline was killed in an accident a month ago, and it has gone hard with Georgie. Money for your fare is enclosed, if you can see your way to do this. Forgive me for asking so much. But I shall be eternally grateful if you find it possible to come to us in our great need."

I must have sat with that letter clutched in my hand for an hour. When at length I arose, I had my course laid out before me, and my mind was at rest.

"You cannot, Esther. It is madness, and I forbid it."

"You cannot forbid it; it would be wrong for you to do so. Georgie is a part of me—in a way so real and interwoven with my own being that, if she died, some of myself would die, too." My husband waved my protests aside with an impatient movement of his hand. "If positions were reversed—if it was I dangerously ill, dangerously in need—would you not want Georgie to come?"

He was angry that I had trapped him with this comparison. "You cannot go," he repeated.

"It is all arranged," I said patiently. "Tillie will take Lavinia. She—"

"You cannot leave your baby!"

"I cannot take her and risk her safety! I would be of no good to Georgie like that."

"She is not even weaned yet, Esther—she has not even reached her first birthday."

"Tillie is still nursing May. She will take care of Lavinia. And she has a nurse to assist her."

"And what of me?" It was a boyish cry, laced more with fear than with selfishness. I put my hand upon his head; I began to weave my fingers into the curls at his neck.

"You can take care of yourself, and use the solitude for writing, and for finishing the settle you have been working on. You can take meals at your folks or mine, and you can have Lavinia any time you have need of her; Tillie understands that."

He sat very quiet beneath my touch. He knew I was going. He knew he could not stop me. I wondered what was running through his head until he buried it against me and said, "If anything should happen to you, Esther! I could not conceive of life without you—I could not—"

"Eugene!" I kissed him. I longed to comfort and reassure; I longed to pour some of my strength and resolve into him. It was not until later, lying sleepless beside him in bed, that the quiet conviction came: *This parting will strengthen his love for me. It will strengthen the cords that bind us to one another, and remind us how precious love really is.*

## Chapter 24

*Kirtland: June 1832*

T he journey was a nightmare; I could not have survived the journey with a baby. The insects would have eaten her alive in the first place, not to speak of the filth, with the only washing on board being done with dippers of murky canal water, and with men spitting whenever and wherever it pleased them best!

There *was* beauty, breathtaking beauty, and wildlife to observe along the waterway and an abundance of birds, hovering above us, tiny bright-colored escorts that never seemed to tire. And the food was not bad—just excessive, with too many meats, cakes, and pies. Fresh hot bread was served every morning, accompanied by mounds of butter, and pitchers of honey and syrup, which many of the passengers poured, with liberal indiscretion, over everything on their plates!

Nights were by far the worst, trying to sleep in a crowded, ill-smelling roomful of strangers, on bunks so narrow they were little more than shelves, set so close together that I could not turn over without falling off nor raise my head without cracking it on the shelf directly above. We ladies removed our bonnets and shoes and loosened our corsets, and that was the extent of our preparation for bed. I was cold and cramped all night long, every night, and my head rang with the sounds of night noises from the boat and from the men's quarters adjacent to ours, separated only by a flimsy curtain drawn between the two.

The cook beat on a pan to alert us that breakfast was ready, and we ate in the saloon where we had been sleeping just hours before. Stuffy and unhealthy it was, and I tried to spend as much time on deck as I could, enjoying the brisk spring air, even when it happened to chill me. At such times I would wrap in one, or even two, of the thin blankets and situate myself on a chair, where I could write observances in my little journal. That was the part of the trip I liked best: the lazy daytime hours that I could while away as I saw fit, reading, writing, daydreaming, or merely sitting, my mind as smooth and blank as the surface of the water stretching ahead and behind.

I had two occasions during those days to make use of some of the medicinal herbs I had brought along with me. And each time my thoughts leapt unwillingly forward to the scene I could not picture, of my dear friend in an unknown place, locked in the darkness of dying. Would she wait for me? Would she hold on until I could get there—and would my coming make enough difference?

These were the agonizing questions that haunted me, especially during the endless hours of night I spent shut up in my narrow cell, surrounded literally on every side by other human beings, but feeling more lonely than I had ever felt in my life.

*Kirtland.* It does have the appearance of a raw frontier village, as I had expected. But there is such a bustle of industry here as to astound the observer who happens upon it. Every available building—house, shop, and barn—is crammed to capacity. There is the constant sound of building and the fragrance of lumber, shaven and sawn, in the air; and the streets are very crowded with wagons and teams. The people are, by and large, patient in their privation, and generous, despite their poverty. Of their own accord they have left behind the comforts of possessions and society in order to—what? Gather to this place with strangers, who at once become friends, with "brothers and sisters," as they call one another. And no sacrifice, to them, seems too heavy to bear. I wonder: *Can religion appear so desirable as to outweigh all else one has valued and worked for, sometimes throughout a lifetime?* These odd people seem to answer that question in the affirmative and throw themselves into "the work" with a will!

I note all this—I am shown it, I hear it talked of, from the very moment I arrive. I have come to *help!* Yet neighbors, anticipating my arrival, pooled their scanty means together and appear on Nathan's humble doorstep with offerings of food: everything from eggs to dainty baked goods to freshly dressed chickens and pickled preserves. One woman even brings over a beautiful long Paisley shawl that had been her mother's, telling me that I must borrow it against the raw spring winds and wear it happily during my sojourn here.

I do not know how to react; I would rather be on the giving end than the receiving. When I first walked into the house, still and darkened as much as possible against the late afternoon glare, I felt like walking on tiptoes; I dreaded what I might see when I entered the bedroom. But, to my astonishment, there was Georgie, sitting up in her bed! True, she appeared pale and emaciated and weak as a kitten—propped up by pillows—but she was sitting there staring at me. Both of us turned open-mouthed to Nathan for an explanation. He hunched his shoulders over and looked back, chagrined.

"What are you doing here, Esther?" Georgie breathed, at the same moment I began to ask, "What are you doing sitting up in bed, Georgie?" We turned again to Nathan and he said miserably, "I have bungled things terribly, I know! But I did not mean to!"

"Sit down," I entreated. "Explain what happened—slowly, if you will."

"The doctor treating Georgie had given up hope when I wrote to you; he said it was only a matter of time. And she kept moaning, day and night, crying for her baby. I thought if you came—with your love and your healing powers—there might be a chance."

I nodded. His words had seemed to take the air out of Georgie. She slumped back against the pillows, and there were tears in her eyes.

"I did not know—I did not realize there were other healing powers as well."

"What do you mean?" A slender thread of memory begins to vibrate within me.

"Some of the Apostles learned of the severity of Georgie's illness and came to administer to her. They laid their hands on her head and rebuked the illness, and from that moment she began to improve and gain strength." He pauses, miserable still. "This happened but two days ago, Esther. There was no way to let you know."

I put my hand on his arm. "I understand," I say gently. "I am not sorry to be here."

"But your family—your own child—it is all for—"

"It is all for a reason. Georgie still has much healing and strengthening to do." I pat the little leather case that sits at my feet. "I have many things here that will help her. And—it will be good for both of us to be together again."

Nathan smiles and begins to relax just a little. I want to ask him what it was like to watch this healing—what it felt like, what he thought about it. I want to tell him about my experience with Joseph Smith on a cold autumn evening. But I dare not, and turn a bit sadly to other concerns.

So I spent spring with my dear friend Georgeanna. For the first week I administered herbs and teas and soothing words, and Georgie slept. During the second week, for a portion of each day I read to her, and she sat in bed and listened, stroking one of her interminable cats. And sometimes we talked briefly about this and that, matters of little account. During the third week I took to bringing my sewing in with me, and she darned one or two of the worst stockings; I had never been very adept at that. During the latter part of the week she said, "You have been here nearly a month, Esther. I will soon be able to manage without you."

"I will soon go home, then," I said.

"You must," she urged. "You have been remarkably brave and kind to linger so long."

I was distressed to feel the tears begin to gather behind my eyes. "You need me," I replied simply. "Isn't this all that matters?"

Without knowing quite how it happened, we were in one another's arms. She cried—for the first time, I was sure, since Emmeline died. I held her tight and let the sobs pour out of her, shudder through her thin body, knowing the necessity of them. "I am here, sweetness, I am here," I kept repeating, as I smoothed back her damp dark hair.

During my last week in Kirtland, Georgie was able to really talk to me, and the days, rich and full, slipped between our fingers like sunbeams that scatter in every direction and cannot be held. I had long ago told her every scrap of news concerning home and the people there. Now, at last, I felt free to ask questions concerning her life.

"I do not know how to answer you," she said in the old forthright manner. "My answers will be almost meaningless to you."

"Well, try it," I said.

"Will we stay in Kirtland forever, now that we are building our own settlement here? I do not think so. Brother Joseph speaks of the land of Zion—"

"Zion?"

"Located in a portion of the state of Missouri, chosen by God as a gathering place for his people."

"Georgie, I thought Kirtland was that!"

"It is, for a season. There is talk of building a sacred place of worship, a house of the Lord in Kirtland."

"This religion is so demanding!" I complained. "What do you do in your lives, because of it, that you did not do without it?"

"What do I do as a member of this church that I did not do previously? I look upon myself and upon God differently. I know He is my Father, that I truly came from Him and that I will return to Him. I know He loves me! I pray to be worthy of that love."

"How—worthy?"

"To be honorable in my doings, to be kind, to be compassionate— to serve and give."

"You have always been that way—and look at Phoebe!" I cried.

A strange soft expression played along her wan face. "I find purpose in what I do," she attempted. "I know why I am doing it. I serve God through serving His children. I have something to work for, something to look forward to."

"Heaven, you mean?"

"Returning to live with my Heavenly Father."

"Because He loves you?"

"Yes, because He loves me. Because I know this."

"Even now . . . even after . . ." I was sorry to say this, but I could not help myself.

Georgie smiled at me, as I might smile at a child of whom I was very fond. "It was bitter at first; I will not try to pretend it wasn't. To see my precious child cry out in fright as the wheels of the wagon passed over her—to hold her limp, unseeing form in my arms—to see her slip away from me without even saying good-bye."

I could feel her pain; it reached out like a flame to sear me.

"It is not fair!" I cried. "If He loves you, if God loves Joseph

Smith's people especially, then He ought to favor you, He ought to at least take care of you."

"He does." She spoke very softly. "Loss can temper and strengthen us. I have seen it happen with many. I know a woman here, Esther, who has buried five children—not as babies scarcely born and unable to survive for some reason, but as children: two years old . . . six years old . . . eight years old . . . all taken from her."

In horror I put my hands up over my ears.

"She is a woman I would do anything to emulate," Georgie continued in the small, quiet voice. "She has been tempered into a spirit so radiant with love, with wisdom—so powerful, so full of life and vitality."

"That makes no sense!" I protested.

"But, Esther, our lives here are but a season, a small part of the whole of our existence—and they are a time of testing. I know, through my faith and because of the promises God has made, that I will be reunited with Emmeline."

"You cannot say that you *know!*"

"I can and I do, my dear. And that is where you cannot understand."

211

I rose and paced the floor, because there was a great churning inside me, a terrible confusion that was as bad as any pain I had felt.

"Esther, Esther, dearest of all of us. I wish I could give to you what I have. I wish I could pour my own joy into you and see it shine back in your eyes."

I smiled through my tears. We had been closer these days—more one in spirit and love—than ever before through the long growing years of our friendship. Yet when I left the next day, I would leave behind a woman who was partly a stranger—a woman who had visited beautiful places and learned beautiful things that were unknown to me.

Georgie and I walked through the city of the Saints, with my friends Peter and Jack trotting like frisky young puppies beside us. Everywhere people lifted their hands in greeting; several stopped to ask after Georgie's health, to engage us in a few words of conversation before moving on. We stopped in the churchyard and knelt beside

Emmeline's grave for one last time together, and my head hurt trying to hold back the tears. *Dear little soul. She and May and my Lavinia were meant to be a new beginning, were meant to go on after us!* I could hardly bear the thought of walking away and leaving her there.

The day was sunny, yet the morning was mild. There was promise in the air here, but also stirrings of hatred and envy, which these people had given up home and friends in order to leave behind. The persecutions were real. In the early spring, before I arrived, Joseph and his friend Sidney Rigdon had been dragged from their homes, roughly treated and reviled, and then tarred and feathered in a frenzy of brutality. The horror of such scenes was nearly beyond bearing! Nathan said that his friends spent the night in scraping the tar from Joseph's bruised body, then washing and cleansing it. And the following morning, what did he do? Go to meeting and preach to the people assembled, with his flesh scarified and defaced. And—Georgie added in her quiet voice—one of Joseph and Emma's adopted twins, an eleven-month-old baby, caught a severe cold that night and died four days later. Her looks said quite clearly, *God does not spare even his elect.* But there was nothing of the fanatic in her expression, nothing of the smug, only the gentle, yearning affection that had bound us together these past weeks. A newspaper with a little pluck reported the tarring and feathering as "a base transaction, an unlawful act, a work of darkness, a diabolical trick."

I wanted to catch sight of Joseph the Prophet. I wanted to set my eyes on him one more time—this man who had stirred malice or adoration in the hearts of men since he was a boy in Palmyra and claimed to have seen a vision in the woods near his house.

Men spoke evil of him freely. But most, if they spent any time at all in his company, found themselves strangely moved and subdued. One man said of him, "He is the most profoundly learned and intelligent man that I have ever met in my life, and I have traveled hundreds of thousands of miles, been on different continents, and mingled among all classes and creeds of people, yet I have never met a man so intelligent as he."

Georgie smiled when I jotted down these sayings as I read them printed here and there, but I did not care. I had my own opinions, my own feelings and memories. I knew for myself of this man's kindness and integrity. I also knew of his light—this power that drew others to him. I experienced it that night when I listened to him pray for my brother. I knew there was nothing strange, nothing self-serving in what I felt, in what happened, in what existed in Joseph Smith's heart. This much I knew. This much I could bear witness to if it ever came down to that.

I was to be taken by wagon the twelve miles from Kirtland to the steamboat landing. I would ride only a few miles on the steamboat before transferring to the canal at Fairport, from Fairport to Buffalo, from Buffalo to Rochester, Syracuse, then *home*.

Although it cost the rather outrageous sum of twenty-five cents to post a letter, Georgeanna and I promised to write often. I believed we would keep that promise.

I was so very eager to go home, but I was not eager to be leaving. My weeks here had been very precious and of great value to me. I kissed Georgie's smooth, fragrant cheek one more time. Nathan gathered me to him in a tenderness that nearly unbalanced my precarious hold on myself. I climbed into the wagon and the driver started up the horses, and in a very few moments we had left Kirtland behind. The sensations remaining were those of the sun warm on my hair, the sounds of meadow birds overhead, and the fragrance of new-mown hay in the fields we passed through. And Georgie's eyes, as shiny and wet as stones in a creek bed, smiling after me.

213

## Chapter 25

### Palmyra: October 1832

The first person I wished to speak to upon my return was Phoebe. As soon as I had immersed myself in Eugene and my baby, feasted my eyes upon the sight and sound and nearness of them, refusing to leave their side for even a moment, I paid her a call. Perhaps I was all the more anxious for a sympathetic, listening ear because of my encounter with Tillie when I had gone to collect my treasure, examining her from the top of her head to the tips of her toes, smothering her with such a profusion of caresses that she began to whimper and hold her arms out for Theodora, both frightened and confused.

"This is what comes of leaving an infant who cannot understand your sudden removal from her existence."

"Eugene said he has spent part of every day with her and taken her home to sleep in his bed with him every night."

"As if that is beneficial for the child! Besides, Eugene is not Lavinia's mother. And Eugene did not leave her."

"Do not torture me with details," I pleaded. "Certainly you know how hard this was for me, Tillie! Every day I was away from her was like a little death."

"Now that you have returned, do you still believe it was necessary?"

"Yes, most certainly. Not only necessary, but good."

She waved her hand at me, a short, imperious gesture. "I do not wish to hear the details, Esther; they will only frustrate and anger me."

"Please, Tillie—*this is Georgie!* Let me share our days with you, let me—"

"I cannot, Esther. Perhaps later. Let us calm the baby and talk of your precious darling right now."

Phoebe, on the other hand, was as eager for every detail as I had thought she would be. Some choice bits I repeated for her, just so we both could savor them and laugh or cry together. When we got to the matter of religion and I told her the things that were happening, the persecutions Joseph Smith suffered, she seemed to be truly distressed.

"What is it, dearie?" I asked. "There is something you are not telling me." It was only a guess. But perhaps she was tired of dissembling. She said, winding the thread she was sewing with round her finger, "I read the Book of Mormon shortly after it was published, Esther."

I tried to conceal my amazement. "Why didn't you tell me?"

"There were many reasons, if you remember. But that is not all. I was baptized shortly before the Saints left for Kirtland."

My hand went up to my mouth. "Oh, dear. Georgie, of course, knows this?" She nodded. "What about Simon?"

"He knows. I have been doing my best to convert him. I have stressed the teachings that are not easy for me, but ought to appeal to him most."

"Which are?"

"Our belief in the eternal nature of families. Not some vague heaven where we all exist like winged angels who play on harps and praise God. Joseph teaches something more literal and far more beautiful."

"And even this has not won him?" I never cease to marvel at the true selflessness in Phoebe's nature. When I am around her I feel humbled by it, by her ability to forget herself in serving others, not worrying about what the consequences might prove to be.

She shook her head sadly. "I think it is religion altogether. He is not drawn to it; at least the depths of his need do not draw him, nor the depths of a burning desire to know!"

My heart trembled for her as for a delicate bird, beautiful as gossamer, swooping too near a flame that may singe its frail wings, or even suck it in to destruction. *Why do we too often love,* I thought almost savagely, *where it is not wise?* The highest within her was lonely, waiting for a soul mate to understand and respond to those precious things that were locked yet within her heart. Always giving. Never questioning, never demanding.

"Esther, there are tears in your eyes."

215

"I'm sorry." I wiped at them clumsily with my handkerchief.

"I love him, you know. It is all right, because I truly love him."

"No, it isn't. It is not right for him to be less than he could be—so much less than *you*, Phoebe!"

"Perhaps you are right. Perhaps it isn't. But I love him, nevertheless. And I understand what it is that frightens and stops him."

I sighed in frustration at her nobility. "What will you do now?"

"Keep trying. Perhaps this child will help things."

"Phoebe!"

"Yes. I have been well thus far. And I pray every day for a son—Esther, it must be a son!"

I put my hands out for hers. "I will pray with you," I promised.

But as I walked back to my house I wondered how effective my weak prayers would be beside hers and Georgie's. I felt both slothful and ungrateful as I contemplated my life. When Eugene returned from work I had an exceptionally nice meal ready and waiting. I was determined to appreciate the good qualities in my husband, which I do not always do.

He *was* receptive. Ever since my return from Kirtland he had been different somehow. More amorous and attentive; that is natural following a long separation. But there was something more, something very elusive, which I could not identify.

After Lavinia was asleep in her bed—kissed dozens of times on rosebud mouth, on ear and eyelid and forehead by an adoring mother—I curled into the soft candlelight, like one of Georgie's cats, with Eugene beside me, content to enjoy the fine evening together. But he sat rather stiffly in his place and said, in a tight, formal voice, "Esther, there is a matter I must discuss with you—something I have been putting off ever since your return."

My stomach gave a nervous flip-flop. "That has been nearly two weeks. Is it a thing so difficult to talk about?"

"Indeed it is."

My mind shrank from all the possibilities that sprang up before it. "Tell me now and be done with it, Eugene," I urged.

"You will scoff at me, and you will be angry," he warned me.

*Whatever in the world?* "Please, Eugene, tell me. It will be better after you do."

Thus he began. And thus I listened to a tale so simple, so amazing, that I would never have guessed at it, never dreamed of it happening, not in a million years.

"While you were gone—shortly after you left, really—a strange little man came into the newspaper office asking about Joseph Smith. He was disappointed when I told him that the prophet of Palmyra is no longer here. 'I have come a long distance,' he said, 'in order to meet this man.'"

" 'You shall have to go a great distance farther yet,' I responded.

" 'I will, and gladly,' he said.

" 'Why?' I asked. He made me more curious, Esther, than some of the others. Though strange in looks and manner, he had a pleasant countenance, and he was well dressed and gave the impression of one to be reckoned with.

" 'There are but few truly extraordinary men born in this world of ours, young man,' he responded. 'Joseph Smith is one of them. His influence will be great, and he will be remembered long after you and I, yes, and even our children and our children's children are dead.'

"He tipped his hat to me, thanked me politely, and went on his way. I asked some of the other editors if they knew who he was, but none had ever seen him before. For some reason I could not get him out of my mind, and when I came home after a day at work, the wind was blowing something terrible and the yard was scattered with odd bits of debris. And there before me, Esther—"

He stole a quick glance at my face, to see how I was receiving this. I nodded encouragingly. "Right there at my feet was a copy of Joseph Smith's Book of Mormon. *How did it blow into my yard?* I thought, *and why?*

"I let it sit, Esther. I did not touch it that night, or the following morning, when it was still there. When I came home from the printing office I had forgotten the book altogether—but there it sat on the door stoop, all brushed off and waiting. I bent over and picked it up and carried it inside with me."

I listened in amazement, and bit my tongue to keep from asking, "Why did you do that—when you forbade me the same opportunity of satiating *my* curiosity?"

"As I sat down to eat my solitary supper I opened the pages. I only meant to thumb through it, but I was lonely, Esther, and I had all this time on my hands."

"Of course," I murmured. By now all my senses were primed and I was listening carefully.

"I read for several hours that night, and the following night, and the night after that—until I finished it." My husband reached over and took my hand. His was trembling and cold as ice. "I read it through from cover to cover, Esther, and I believe what it says to be true."

I could not reply. What reply could I possibly make to him? We looked at each other for a few moments, a bit warily. "I am aware of the unfairness in all this, I am, Esther. I am aware of the irony—most surely of that!" I could feel his agitation through his fingers—but I could also feel his enthusiasm!

"I did not wish to believe it—I never intended to! *You* know that, Esther, better than anyone!"

"Yes," I replied. "But I was gone tending to my old loved friend, who has gone away with the 'Mormonites,' while you—"

"I know, I know, Esther!" He gazed at me with such anguished appeal in his eyes that I leaned close and brushed his cheek with my lips.

"You say you 'believe it.' Believe what exactly, Eugene? I do not know what those words mean."

I could see the struggle play over his features. He wanted so badly to help me understand what he was feeling. "I believe it is what Joseph Smith says it is: a record of ancient people, translated by him. I believe it is scripture, every bit as much as the Bible."

"Scripture—in what way?"

"There are prophets in the book who teach and warn their people. I believe they are—I don't know how to say it, Esther! I believe they taught their people the words of the Savior. And I believe that Jesus himself visited these people, as it is recorded there."

*So this is what the Book of Mormon is!* I marveled. "I want to read it," I said. "Will you wait for me to read it before we talk about this further?"

"By all means," he agreed.

The question burning my tongue was, "If this is your belief, what do you intend to do about it?" But I did not *dare* ask this question, for fear of what his answer might be.

He was gentle and solicitous with me for the remainder of the evening and for days after that. I read the book when I was alone; I could not bear to do so beneath his veiled scrutiny. When I had questions I was too impatient to suppress, I asked him, and he answered me briefly, and then I returned to my reading.

Perhaps I went slowly on purpose, drew out the inevitable, considered all points with care. I was afraid. Yes, I was afraid of my own feelings—I will not deny that. I had been to Kirtland, I had seen into the heart of the life this Book of Mormon required of the people who believed in it, and I was afraid.

And perhaps that fear would have triumphed, if the love in those pages had not been so powerful—that love Georgie had spoken of with such peace and such joy. When the Savior visited the Nephite people following his resurrection, when he took their little ones unto him and blessed them one by one—I *felt* as they did: the awe and wonder, the adoration and love. And these words, these words made the difference to me:

219

He himself also knelt upon the earth; and behold he prayed unto the Father; and the things which he prayed, cannot be written, and the multitude did bear record which heard him. . . . The eye hath never seen, neither hath the ear heard, before, so great and marvellous things as we saw and heard Jesus speak unto the Father; . . . and no one can conceive of the joy which filled our souls at the time we heard him pray for us.

Had I courage and love enough to face the prospect before me? Dared I turn away?

## Chapter 26

### Palmyra: March 1833

I f the word *time* is synonymous with anything, it is synonymous with change. As the old year bustled about, sweeping out the cobwebs that had accumulated in corners, in attics, along the eaves, we mortals shuddered before the relentless, onward press of its breath.

In November, as Eugene and I made our decisions and laid our quiet plans, Alexander lost his balance and fell from a high wagon bed onto which he had been loading lumber. As he slid, trying to catch himself, many of the loosely placed logs slid, too. He hit the solid ground hard, and several heavy lengths of lumber smashed with a punishing weight against him.

Randolph and the boys managed to get him into the house and laid out on the long kitchen table. He was bleeding profusely from several cuts on his arm and head. When Doctor Ensworth arrived his examination was short and terse. "The blow on the head killed him instantly," he told Randolph. "Where is that wife of his?"

Josephine was off in the village with Latisha, purchasing new supplies for the school. "Will you please stay to tell her?" Randolph entreated.

"I haven't time for that, my boy," the doctor replied. "But if I happen upon Esther in town, I'll send her out."

"If you happen upon Josephine?"

"I shall let her pass. I do not want her falling apart in the streets of Palmyra. She has a right to hear such news in the privacy of her own home."

So it happened that the good doctor knocked on my door and told me. "You'd best get out there, Esther. I know you are up to it."

"Thank you, Doctor," I said.

When I arrived at the mill all work had ceased, and the very air about the place hung and sagged like a pall. The boys all sat stiff-backed and sniffling in the parlor. They had helped Randolph move the body, so that it was laid stretched out on the large four-poster bed, the bed Alexander had bought his young wife as a wedding present not so many years before.

The relief that flooded Randolph's face when he saw me compensated for any suffering, any burden I might lift from his young shoulders. I gathered the lads together and we spoke a prayer over the body; then I sent them back to their work. I put the pot on to boil and had herbs waiting in a large tea mug: a strong portion of saffron to relieve mind and body, with a little clove to calm her digestion, and rosemary to ease. Then Randolph and I sat down to wait.

In what was less than an hour by the clock we heard her carriage rattle into the yard. Randolph tensed; I felt myself do the same. When she and Latisha sailed into the house, red-cheeked and high-spirited, I felt like a traitor to have to show her my somber face. She knew at once. She took her hat off slowly, placed it with her gloves on the cherry wood table, then arranged herself in the tall wing-backed chair that was her husband's favorite.

"What has happened, Esther?" Her face was white but composed.

I told her what happened. I told her Alex died instantly, probably painlessly. I expected her usual profusion of tears and wild ravings. "Heaven help me," she said under her breath, so softly that I had to guess at the words. "How will I go on without him?"

She rose, in regal slow motion. "Where is he?"

"Upstairs on his bed."

She turned and walked with the same deliberation; she climbed the stairs. I heard the door brush open, then shut with a sound of finality. During those interminable minutes she had never once glanced at either Latisha or Randolph; she had never once met my eyes.

We buried him with much tender ceremony, in the costliest coffin Josephine could find. She did not weep. She hardly mentioned his name or spoke of him. She was like a figure in a dream. My mother did all the abandoned mourning for her, but Josie remained still, staring out at us all with those lovely, shrouded eyes.

I grieved for the life and work of such a good man cut short. But

221

I was comforted by the fact that he had regained his wife's respect and affection during these last remarkable years. She had poured out the profusion of her emotions upon him, at first in gratitude only, I believe. But tenderness, born of true regard, sent up its shy shoots and blossomed and became a blessing to both their lives.

I thought to myself, as I walked with my arm through my husband's: *This is the last time I shall come to this spot for a burial. What will happen when my father grows old, when he dies? What will happen when my mother's strength fails her and she lashes out, in her fear and pain, at all about her? What will happen if I am not here?*

I spent long minutes beside every low spot that was dear to me. Eugene stood back a way, understanding and willing to wait. Dear Jane Foster, whom I had so foolishly mistrusted; my little Nathaniel, long sleeping, who had first awakened the stirrings of motherhood in my heart; Emily—Emily! *Was your dying a blessing for Phoebe,* I wondered, *or only a curse? What would she have done with her life if you were still living today?*

I paused for a moment beside the mound where Alvin Smith was buried. I pulled out a few of my loveliest autumn asters, goldenrod and meadowsweet, wound them into a sort of posy, and placed them upon his grave. I felt as if every pore in my body were silently weeping, silently yearning with pain. I stumbled over to Eugene. My feet felt too heavy to move; all my body felt heavy, as though some weight were pressing it into the ground. He held out his arms to me. With a sob I buried my head against his warm strength, and wept.

During the days that followed, Randolph refused to leave Josie, even for a few hours. He conducted the work at the mills with an air of efficiency and determination that rallied the men who had been accustomed to only one overseer for many contented years of their lives. He sent the boys into Palmyra on whatever errands were required, even entrusting them with deposits of money to be placed in Alexander's account in the bank.

No one questioned his assumed authority; no one questioned his devotion and integrity. Near the beginning of December, before Christmas and the date of her marriage came cruelly to taunt her, he asked Josie to be his wife.

At first she refused to answer him. She locked herself in her own room for two days; heaven knows what went through her mind! When she came out, she went at once in search of the young man who, for some reason she could not fathom, wished to continue to devote his life to her. She placed her small hand in his and gazed up at him with those clear, somewhat provocative, somewhat child-like eyes.

"If you are still resolved that this is what you want, what you truly want, then I will marry you, Randolph."

Thus one lonely soul was granted true happiness; another, more security, devotion, and love than her unplumbed heart had ever imagined before.

Perhaps it was unwise of Eugene and myself to linger—to torment our own feelings with the last apples picked from the trees that line my father's meadow; the last pumpkin and squash from the garden; the last Christmas parties and dinners and quiet home evenings; the last new year in Palmyra ushered in; the last ride in Theodora's sled, the razor-sharp runners cutting over the smooth canal ice. The last Sabbath day dinner shared with Eugene's parents, the last with mine. The last tender rides to visit all the places that were dear to us, that our eyes would never look upon more. The last Tuesdays—oh, the last Tuesdays of farewell visits to those I so dearly love!

As soon as our minds were decided, we wrote at once to Georgie and Nathan to expect us to come on the first boat that is allowed through the canal in the spring. She replied that they will scout out a nice little house for us—"with enough space for a garden. Farm your dear cats out to others," she scribbled. "I shall have a new batch of kittens by the time you arrive."

So we are leaving. Though it does not seem possible; it appears more as a dream—some strange wonder which has caught me up in its net and is carrying me on.

My mother is not reconciled, though my father, at least to some extent, understands. They will have Josephine and her steady young husband to care for them when the time comes, and perhaps a new

223

batch of grandchildren as well. Josie is determined to try again—"just to see if it makes a difference!"—this spoken with the old sparkle back in her eye.

As tenderly as I can I question Phoebe.

"When this baby is born," she says, with that amazing calm. "I cannot even think about other things until I have gotten him here."

We do something quite silly, that harks back to our girlish days, and make a secret determination to "meet in prayer" once daily, at seven-thirty of the clock, or as close to it as we can manage. We are comforted by this arrangement; we are comforted by what each takes with her as we both turn away.

Theodora will not speak to me. Somehow I did not expect this; I thought that I alone could always touch her, could always break through her reserve. I *know* what loneliness and fear her brittle shell is protecting, and it makes my heart break. What of my godson? What of the next generation, and the long years ahead? I return once more to Phoebe and beg, with her slender hands in mine, that we include Tillie in our prayers every morning. With tears in her eyes she agrees. Heaven help us! That is all we can do.

All is done. All is ready. The last specks of time have run through our fingers, and we are ready to leave.

I stand by the window, my shawl wrapped round my shoulders, and watch the dawn come. Lavinia and her father sleep, with the safety and love of our little home enfolding them. Soon we will step through the door out into the wide world, where we have nothing to guide us save our love and our faith.

*My last morning in Palmyra.* I press my face against the window glass. *How can I take it all with me?* I cry. A winter-bright cardinal flashes across my eyes and disappears into the high branches of an elm tree. Life here will go on without me. *What patterns will my own life, my new life, weave?*

Lavinia stirs. Automatically I cross the room and go to her to see if she is well covered, to see if she chokes in her sleep.

For a moment the face of one man comes into my mind—one man, responsible for all this! One man who has taken my life and the lives of so many others into his hands. Taken them and lifted them upward—hoisted them heavenward on the strength of his own shoulders—spending all his love, all his devotion and wisdom on our account.

When I reach Kirtland I shall find him. I shall tell him that his brother Alvin rests peacefully still. I shall tell him that my brother lives and grows strong and is happy. I shall tell him that Phoebe is waiting, and is in need of our prayers.

When I look into his eyes again, I shall tell the Prophet Joseph that I am ready to be baptized. I am ready to give of my strength to the One who gave it to me in the first place—I am ready to say, "Thy will be done."